# ABSOLUTION

D1730892

# ALEŠ ŠTEGER

# ABSOLUTION

Translated from the Slovene by
Urška Charney and Noah Charney

First published in English in 2017 by
**Istros Books** (in collaboration with Beletrina Academic Press)
London, United Kingdom
www.istrosbooks.com

Originally published in Slovene as *Odpusti* by Beletrina Academic Press
in 2014

© Aleš Šteger, 2014

The right of Aleš Šteger to be identified as the author of this work has been
asserted in accordance with the Copyright, Designs and Patents Act, 1988.

Translation © Urška Charney and Noah Charney, 2017

Cover design and typesetting: Davor Pukljak | www.frontispis.hr


ISBN: 978-1-908236-30-2

Printed in England by
CMP (UK), Poole, Dorset | www.cmp-up.com

This Book is part of the EU co-funded project *"Stories that can Change
the World"* in partnership with Beletrina Academic Press | www.beletrina.si

**Co-funded by the
Creative Europe Programme
of the European Union**

The European Commission support for the production of this publication does not constitute an
endorsement of the contents which reflects the views only of the authors, and the Commission
cannot be held responsible for any use which may be made of the information contained therein.

God forgives ordinary people but
severely punishes the high and the mighty.

*– Wisdom of Solomon* 6:6

*Dear Reader*
*This is a work of fiction. Names, characters, places and incidents are*
*the product of the author's imagination or are used fictitiously. Only*
*Maribor is real.*

# Contents

# Dramatis Personæ

*(In order of appearance)*

Adam Bely, a former dramatist and a Scientology leader
Rosa Portero, Bely's ally and a radio journalist
Samo Gram, also known as Mister G., an innkeeper, a former customs
    officer and a secret service collaborator
Peter, a waiter
Tine Butcher, an administrative director of Butch, Inc.
Tine Butcher's secretary
An old beggar with death in her mouth
Ivan Dorfler, manager of Off and dean of Maribor University
Laszlo Farkas, a state prosecutor and a member of the Twin Cult
Pavel Don Kovač, Director of the European Capital of Culture (ECoC)
    and a former theatre director
Miran Voda, mayor of Maribor
The Hungarian, member of the Twin Cult and Rosa's lover and
    abductor
Aleš Šteger, head of the ECoC Terminal 12
Anastasia Green, a theatre director and Bely's former girlfriend
Maister, a renowned Maribor attorney
Lady with the brooch, a typical Maribor citizen
Magda Ornik, a funeral home director
Maus, a police inspector, Miran Voda's former schoolmate and his
    greatest opponent
Gros, an assistant to Maus, the police inspector
Electrician in the Blue Night strip club
Sister Magda, a nun in the Archdiocese of Maribor
Nameless poet, a former broker at the Trieste stock market
Father Metod Kirilov, the chief financial officer of the Maribor
    Archdiocese
Disinfectors and specialists in city pigeon removal
Three drunken clowns
Franci and Lojs, workers at Maribor's public service department

Dolores, secretary to the Director of the Maribor National Theatre
Gubec, an investigative journalist and owner of a news agency
Hostesses in the Maribor Theatre
American and British military attachés
Waiter in the theatre bar
Janez Maher, a Maribor businessman
Nana Numen, a fortune-teller
Chirping black swine

All quotations from the play *War and Peace* originate from its
theatrical adaptation by Darko Lukić.

# The New World of Mister G.

Some people, strangers to us, forgive in order to help others. Most of us forgive in order to help ourselves. Others forgive solely out of a belief that they will save the world by doing so. But what inspires their belief? Who assigns them their unique role? Who whispers those thoughts into their ears? Dangerous thoughts that always strike at a specific place and time? We don't know, but does it matter? Would knowing change anything at all? Isn't it just the thickly woven, brocaded stage curtains, the weight of the fog that falls through the dusk, the moisture, the cold that matters? Silence. Darkness. The stage curtains open, and all we see is a man. He hunches behind the high collar of his winter coat, hands buried in its pockets, black briefcase dangling off his right wrist. He sways a little. The pavement has not been shovelled. The man tries to balance his way along a narrow, already beaten track. He nearly falls. Behind him stretch unkempt art nouveau façades, and in the pallor of the streetlights drizzling rain turns into snow. The few passers-by are quietly spat out by the dusk, only to be swallowed again a moment later, just as quietly. The whole time the silhouette of a woman has been at the man's heels. A figure draws near them, and it looks much like the Devil. And so it is. He staggers a metre in front of the man. The ice, the narrow snowy path and the bottle, emptied of its contents and held in his claw-like hand, did the trick. His feet sail high into the fog. For a moment the wet cuffs of the jeans the Devil is wearing under his costume slip out. A chain jingles against the curb; the bottle rolls away across the dirty snow. The Devil tumbles over. Cursing.

A church bell strikes ten. The man hears the woman, still close behind him, say, '*Der arme Teufel.*' A sign burns faintly through the frozen fog: NEW WORLD. Strange how surprising a small neon sign can be on such a night. It feels like an epochal discovery, even though the restaurant has been tucked into the same street corner for over thirty years. The man turns around and gestures to the woman behind him. They have arrived.

The automatic door closes slowly behind them.

'After all these years nothing has changed,' the man says quietly in German.

The silhouette behind him takes off the hood of her coat. Instantly, the room submits to the sway of her long, black, curly hair.

'*Das ist gut,*' says the woman in coarse voice, looking around the inn.

Wooden pillars, fishing-nets entangled with corals and shells, anchor-shaped chandeliers, dusty wicker fish traps, a wall clock with a mermaid on the pendulum, a pastel-coloured marine sunset on the wall. The restaurant is empty. The sound of frying from the kitchen, the air heavy with fish and oil. Pasted on the wooden bar is a poster of a red cross against a black background from under which the words AND PEACE peak out. It is partly covered by another poster of four happily smiling sailors announcing a Dalmatian *a cappella* musical performance.

'The kitchen is closed!' echoes through the sultry air. The waiter vanishes through the swinging doors. Held out before him, two crystal goblets of ice-cream and sweet cream on two flying plates pull him across the room. The restaurant is empty except for an elderly couple seated in the back corner. The crystal goblets land on the table in front of them. The woman raises her spoon and buries it deep in the cream; the man counts his money and places it on the table.

'We're closing for the night, I'm sorry,' the waiter says again without looking back.

'We're looking for your boss, Mr Gram,' says the man in the winter coat. The waiter points to three shallow wooden stairs leading up to a booth. The black-haired woman looks in that direction and follows the man with his black briefcase. The creaking of stairs.

'Good evening,' says the man.

Samo Gram, also known as Mister G., the owner of the New World restaurant, sits alone behind a big table, hunched over a newspaper. Lush white brows rise over a pair of grey spectacles perched on the tip of his nose. Drops of sweat bead up on his forehead. Gram is evidently the sort of person who is always too warm, and the overhead light hanging low over the table only reinforces this. His presence permeates the surroundings with an unusual obtrusiveness. Despite the years he's spent in a fish restaurant, Mr G. doesn't smell like fish; instead he gives off the unmistakeable odour of pig – and the more he sweats, the more he stinks.

'Good evening,' says Gram, visibly tired, and sizes up the two newcomers. 'May I help you?'

'You probably don't remember me,' replies the man. 'My name is Adam Bely, and this is my colleague Rosa Portero.'

Gram gets up and shakes their hands. They all sit down behind the newspaper-covered table.

I'm from Maribor originally, although I haven't lived here for sixteen years. Back in the day, I used to be one of your regulars. Now I work as a journalist for Austrian national radio. Well, actually I'm just an assistant. My colleague here would like to do a portrait of the city. Austrians are very interested in Maribor now that it's the European Capital of Culture. We figured it would be best to start with a place that is well-known among the locals and can serve as a good departure point for our report. After all, it's the restaurants that keep the history of this city alive, and I'm sure yours must be well-known among our Austrian listeners.'

'Of course, of course,' mumbles Gram. 'Are you hungry? Would you like something to eat or drink? A glass of wine? Peter!' Gram shouts before they can reply.

'That is most kind of you, but we're not hungry. Thank you,' says Bely.

At that moment Peter walks in with a plate of dinner and cutlery for one.

'Please forgive me, I've been on my feet all day long and haven't eaten yet. Please, let me offer you something. It's on the house, of course,' adds Gram.

Peter sweeps his hand across the newspaper-strewn table and places the plate before Gram.

'Thank you very much. We're not hungry, but I'll have a glass of mineral water if you insist,' says Bely.

'You can't be from Maribor if all you drink is water, although your accent sounds like you could be,' replies Gram. 'Don't you know that mineral water isn't good for the teeth? And you, madam?' He lays his eyes softly on Rosa and the dark orchids weaving diagonally up her crimson dress.

'*Ein Viertel Weisswein. Riesling, bitte,*' Rosa places an order, her voice surprisingly coarse, like that of a man.

'You know, Ms Portero doesn't speak Slovenian, only a few words, but she understands a lot,' Bely explains.

'Of course, of course,' replies Gram, noticeably startled by her voice. He tucks a napkin into the cleft of his unbuttoned shirt, into the dense outgrowth of silver hair on his barrel chest.

'Please, don't let us disturb you. *Bon appétit*,' adds Bely, and glances at his companion.

'*Guten appetit*,' adds Rosa in her deep voice.

Gram looks at his grilled octopus, its legs hanging over the edge of the plate. Roasted potatoes surround the cephalopod's body along with half a lemon.

'I love octopus, don't you?' Gram asks and continues eating, as if his question wasn't meant as a question. 'Did you know they have three hearts? Three!' Gram cries theatrically and wields his knife like a knight brandishing a lance before battle. 'And that they're incredibly agile? Even giant ones, like this one, can squeeze through crevices as small as my thumb.'

Gram raises his right hand, gripping the fork and extending his thumb toward Rosa.

'Not to mention how intelligent they are!' he says.

Peter comes in with mineral water and two glasses of wine, white and red.

'Boss, you want anything else? If not …'

'I'm fine. You finish up, and I'll close,' says Gram, relieving the waiter of his duties by waving him off with the knife.

'So, where was I? Right. Octopi and their intelligence. Do you think that intelligence has anything to do with our brains? Think again! We believe that we wouldn't be able to think if we had no brain, but just look at octopi. Their brain is tiny, and yet they're intelligent as hell. Do you know why? Because they have intelligent bodies; their whole damn bodies are intelligent, not only their tiny brains. Now look at us, brainwashed by our blind faith in science, which sells us a skewed view of the way things really are.'

Gram wipes the sweat off his forehead and leans back on his squeaking chair, visibly upset.

'That is a rather interesting line of thought,' says Bely peacefully and takes a sip of his mineral water.

'Look, man created computers,' Gram continues, 'but, instead of taking the computers as a largely simplified approximation of human functionality, we take them as a model for us to look up to. We imagine the brain as some sort of a hard drive. Wrong, it's all wrong!' Gram cries out and lays down the knife and fork, which, just a moment before, he held pressed into one leg of a beautifully grilled octopus. 'The chicken doesn't come before the egg. Do you get me? The truth is, nothing is stored in the brain. Nothing! The brain functions only as a converter, a transformer, a switch, a current that flows, the current that doesn't flow, that's all. You don't believe me? Just look at the octopus. It'll tell you everything.'

All three of them direct their attention to the plate. For a moment, they can hear the ticking of the wall clock next door.

Gram grabs hold of his fork and knife again and picks up where he left off in a whispering, almost conspiratorial voice.

'There's something else for which octopi serve as an example of how things are in reality. Just look at how they die; they don't die of old age, they always die after mating. Either they're killed, or they die on their own because of fucking. Male octopi die a few months after they detach their penis tentacle; while females, *meine liebe Dame* – Portenyo, right? – female octopi starve themselves to death while guarding their eggs.'

Gram finally makes a cut across the centre of the octopus. A big chunk of juicy meat perched on the fork drifts into his mouth. Chewing with delight, Gram nods to himself. The guests say nothing. Shamelessly he eyes Rosa Portero's beautiful hair. Her black curls fall thickly across her right cheek. Seductively he smiles into her dark-brown left eye so that it softly and bashfully closes then immediately opens again, while her right eye remains hidden behind a cascade of thick black curls. Gram winks at her and takes a sip of his wine. Rosa smiles warmly. She is still wearing a pair of thin leather gloves. The left one clings to her glass of Riesling, which she drains in two infinitely long, deep gulps.

Adam Bely pulls a fountain pen out of a buttonhole in his jacket and shifts it around on the newspaper.

Rosa puts down the glass, a red crescent from her lipstick plastered on its rim. She fingers the corners of her mouth and brushes her hair out of her face.

Is it only Gram's imagination, or is there really a green glass eye glaring at him? He feels as if any moment it might strike, like a snake, and devour him. He feels as if he could fall right into the green eye, deeper and deeper, so deep he'll never come back, never surface again. Bely picks up the fountain pen and slowly waves it back and forth; tick-tock goes the clock in the next room, tick-tack goes the pen. The eye, there's the eye, which is also a mouth, a glass voice within it. Mr G. can be as brave a little boy as he wants, running barefoot across the meadow going who knows where away from home – but he can't escape. A sharp stabbing pain in his feet, the soft vertigo of fear and surprise at himself.

Gram chokes. He coughs. Bely leans forward and hits him hard across his back. The chunk of octopus shoots out of his mouth back on to the plate and fuses with both halves of the cut octopus. Its limbs stir and curl up around the edge of the plate. The octopus on the plate suddenly comes back to life. Its tentacles tremble, begin to move, and a moment later it darts under the table. All that remains on the plate are a few potatoes and the damp meandering tracks of the octopus's suckers on the newspaper.

This can't be happening, is Gram's last thought as he tumbles deeper and deeper. That thought is the last crumbling stone he clings to as he falls through the green vitreous haze. The entire landscape falls deeper into greenness, tick-tack, the meadows keep getting brighter, the hayracks and the trees and the peaks of green mountains in the distance seem to be sucked into the vortex. No, now there is no way back, no home any more. Now Gram can no longer gaze at the grass that trembles and sways in the wind. As if it were alive, as if it were growing all around him, enveloping and submerging him deeper and deeper with no possibility of escape.

'Listen to my instructions, and you'll be fine,' says Bely and removes the plate, the glasses and the cutlery from the table.

Rosa stoops and clicks her tongue twice in Gram's face.

'He's in a deep state of hypnosis,' says Bely. 'There's no way he can lie, but I'll still plug him into the E-meter.'

Rosa nods in approval.

Bely pulls a leather case out of his black briefcase. In it is a metal box with a few buttons and a gauge, which he connects to a pair of wires that end in cylindrical metal electrodes. He hands them to Gram.

'Squeeze hard,' orders Bely.

Gram obeys. He gazes absently, clasping the electrodes.

'Start recording,' says Bely.

Rosa retrieves a Dictaphone from her fur coat. She presses the record button.

Bely bows his head and softly asks Gram a question.

'Who are you?'

'Samo Gram,' answers Mr G.

'What do you do for a living?'

'I'm a customs officer.'

'What else?'

'Depending on the situation, I've had a number of names, real and fake.'

'Who do you work for?'

'Myself. Now I work only for myself.'

'Who did you work for in the past?'

'For customs. Also for Yugoslav intelligence, then later for Slovenian.'

During the interrogation, Bely keeps track of the E-meter needle, which floats consistently in the middle of the dial.

'I see you're telling the truth,' says Bely.

Rosa gets up and disappears behind the door.

'Nothing but the truth,' says Gram.

'What comes to mind when you hear the word "lie"?'

'My kitten. One day he went missing. I searched everywhere, all around the farm where we lived. I searched the fields, even the nearby hills. I cried inconsolably, and Mama promised me he would come back. I knew right off that she was lying.'

'What's the first thing that comes to mind when you hear the word "happiness"?' asks Bely.

'I remember. The slaughter at the border.'

'What was that?'

'I was a young customs officer then. It happened in Koroška, at the border between what used to be Yugoslavia and Austria. I walked the woods all day long, I made good money and there was lots of messing around. Today when I look back, I know I was happy then, but back then I didn't know it.'

'Go on.'

'There was a farmer who had a house right on the border. It ran right through his kitchen. Technically he needed to use his passport to get from his kitchen, which was in Yugoslavia, over to the other side of the Iron Curtain to take a dump, since his toilet was in Austria. Anyway, this guy wanted to slaughter a pig. To slaughter a pig in a restricted border zone! He asked us, the customs officers, if we could find him an illegal butcher. First, we brought him a butcher and then, a few hours later, when the pig was already open and chopped to pieces, we showed up with some Austrian customs officers and scared the hell out of him. Not only because he had organized the slaughter under the table but because he could have been accused of attempting to help the butcher cross the border illegally, which at the time was punishable by twenty years behind bars. The farmer begged so hard he fell on his knees out of sheer terror and pissed his pants. Jesus, we laughed like crazy, along with the Austrians. But the farmer, he didn't feel like mucking about.

He was kneeling in his piss and just kept pleading. In the end we split the pork between us in exchange for not denouncing him. All we left him was the swine's head, which lay right on the border. It didn't make much sense to argue over whether it was Austrian or Yugoslav.'

'That's what made you happy?'

'You have no idea. I also became quite rich. Well, I earned enough after ten years of working in customs to be able to buy this restaurant.'

'What's the first thing to cross your mind when you think of something sad?' asks Bely and stretches in order to see what Rosa is doing. The sound of clattering glasses from behind the bar echoes across the empty space of the restaurant.

'Football.'

'I mean, what hurt you on a personal level?'

'My mother used to beat me up because I would bring home bones. Supposedly they were human. They were all over Pobrežje, where I grew up, sticking out from the ground. Us kids, we would pull them out and play hockey with them in the fields. But I wasn't allowed to bring them home. I still remember her taking me over her knee and the crackling sound of the bone she hit me with.'

'That's as sad as it gets?'

'I don't know.'

'You don't know?'

'There's something worse than that. But I don't know if it happened to me, I mean, me in this life.'

'Who else then?'

'It happened to my mother. I can hear her screaming. Everything around me gets tighter, it's smothering me. I feel something fleshy pushing against my little head.'

'Where are you?'

'I'm in my mum. I haven't been born yet.'

'Is it your father?'

'No.'

'What happened to the man later?'

'I don't know. I never found out who he was.'

'Why not?'

'It's a good thing I didn't, otherwise I would've had to kill him.'

'Who are you?'

'Samo, Samo Gram. The kids at school were teasing me. They said I'm nothing but a gram. Who's nothing but a Gram now? I showed them.'

'Who were you before that?'

'I see green light. I'm blinded by the meadows. They'll go up in flames, can't you see?'

'I will ask again. Who were you before you were born as Samo Gram?'

'Many.'

'For instance?'

'I'm a rafter, here on the Drava River. The river, its current, my life. Those were wonderful years, but I didn't know it. I just missed my family too much, my four sons and my wife. We love each other.'

'More,' says Bely.

'I can smell a damp darkness. My bloody cough eats through my lungs and nostrils. I see a small lamp that flickers down the tunnel where I work as a mercury miner. Yesterday three miners were killed when the tunnel next to this one collapsed. While I dig I keep seeing the images of those disfigured bodies that I helped to carry out. They were so cold, even though we dug them out right away.'

'Go on.'

'I was also a nun in a convent. It was before the First World War.'

'In a convent?'

'I healed lepers in Bavaria.' Gram giggles.

Bely looks at the dial. The needle is still floating in the middle. 'Why are you laughing?'

'I was a lesbian, but fortunately nobody ever found out about it, except for Anna.'

'Anna?'

'She was another Benedictine sister, my lover.'

'What are you truly afraid of?'

'Calvary.'

From behind the bar comes the sound of rattling bottles. Rosa flings a bottle on to the floor so it shatters. Then she brings one over and places it on the table before Bely. Jack Daniels. Bely looks sternly at her but continues to interrogate Mr G.

'What Calvary?' Bely continues.

'Calvary.'

'Do you mean Christ's Calvary?'

'You must be kidding me. Not that Calvary. I meant Calvary, the hill above the city of Maribor. I thought you were from around here, but I see you know shit about it. I'm scared of Calvary and the power of the Great Orc.'

'What's the Great Orc?'

'Great Orc, the thirteen guardians of secrets.' Gram giggles again.

'What's so funny this time?' asks Bely.

'Some people don't even know they belong to the Orc,' replies Gram seriously. 'Most of them don't know who the other members are. The thirteen of the Great Orc run this city. They run it, but they're clueless as to the whys and wherefores …'

Rosa tilts back the bottle, takes a swig and places it back on the newspaper. Her cloudy brown eye hangs at half-mast.

'You know a lot,' says Bely.

'That was my job, to know a lot. If I hadn't known a lot I wouldn't be here today.'

'*Namen. Wer sind Sie*?' Rosa cries out.

'I can't, the Great Orc, they'll kill me,' screams Gram, terrified. He begins to tremble, and the oppressive stench of pig emanates from him.

'Don't worry, we'll save you,' says Bely.

'The Great Orc will kill me. No one is powerful enough to escape the Great Orc!'

'Do you believe in absolution?'

'I don't know what absolution is. What do you mean?'

'It doesn't matter,' says Bely. 'Just keep in mind that you'll be leaving here absolved. You'll be alive, and the Great Orc won't be able to harm you.'

'I'm too old to escape abroad. Besides, there's nowhere I would be safe.'

'Don't worry, we know of a place where you'll be perfectly safe. You won't have been so safe since the day you were born. Now, just tell me their names.'

'I don't know all of them. I only know a few.'

Bely watches the needle on his measuring device. Now and then it swings violently to the left.

'*Namen. Wir wollen Namen*!' shouts Rosa. She dips her left glove into the drink stain feeding on the newspaper headlines, text columns and photographs and draws a big circle on the paper.

Gram lists six names. 'Tine Mesarič, Dorfler, Laszlo Farkas, Pavel Don Kovač, Anastasia Grin, Magda Ornik.'

'More. We need all thirteen.'

'That's all I know.'

The needle on the E-meter leans heavily to the left.

'How can he be lying when he's in such a deep trance?' mutters Bely.

Rosa pulls a cork out of a bottle with her teeth, spits it out, then tilts the bottle and smashes it against the table so the whisky splashes all over Gram. Gram remains motionless. Vitreous shards lie scattered across the drenched newspaper. Rosa sweeps them off and points at a photograph.

'Ja. Him, too.'

'What do you know about him?'

'Too much. We used to play together as kids. Later on he was my room-mate at cadet school, which I failed to finish because of him. Somebody stole the director's wallet and slipped it into my locker. We haven't been able to stand each other since. When he was appointed mayor he tried everything to drive me out of the city. But I'm no easy target. I have my own information, which is why he lets me be now. He knows very well I could harm him or even bring him down.'

Rosa looks at Adam.

'Is he telling the truth?' she asks in Slovenian.

Adam examines the needle and nods. 'Any more?'

'That's it. I don't know any other names.'

Bely and Rosa look at each other.

Rosa turns off the Dictaphone and wipes it against the black orchids on her dress.

'We've got something for you, old soul. Take it, and you'll be absolved of all your pasts,' says Bely.

Rosa sets a silver compact on the soaked newspaper. It's full of light-brown oyster crackers.

'For thirty years I've eaten only fish, no crackers,' says Gram.

'What's thirty years compared with eternity?' says Bely and shoves an oyster cracker down his throat.

A few minutes later, the New World neon sign outside turns off. Two pairs of legs, one of them staggering slightly. Trudging through the fresh snow, which comes down as if it were going to consume the city, the whole world, once and for all. The bells strike three times. Posters of red crosses on black backgrounds. A cat dashes across the empty street. Midnight is fast approaching.

# Butcher

'Mr President, the Austrian journalists have arrived.' A secretary announces the appointment to Tine Butcher, director of Butcher Inc. meat products.

In truth, Tine Butcher is not the president of a country, he is president of the board of directors of a meat-processing company. But Tine Butcher is a practical man, so, to facilitate communication with his foreign business partners, he changed his last name. And to facilitate association with the company, which he both directs and owns a majority share in, he changed its name, too. In this way the Agricultural and Food Processing Cooperative of Upper Drava Livestock Farmers and Meat Processors became Butcher, Inc. His employees are expected to address him accordingly with the proper respect, especially at the headquarters of the company over which he presides.

'Please have a seat, gentlemen. May I offer you a cup of coffee, tea, juice?' Butcher asks while signing a few documents on the desk.

A bland, modern office interior: walls painted in somewhat incompatible shades of cream and rose, a tall *Ficus benjamina* in the corner, a gigantic plasma television, a desk with the company flag on it, leather armchairs on the other side of the president's desk, the feeling that we could be anywhere were we not exactly where we are.

'You're local, aren't you? I don't need to tell you about the Maribor Automotive Factory and how they went under, do I? Anyway, it was on the site of that former industrial giant that we started our business sixteen years ago. Hitler himself ordered a factory to be built there, which produced aircraft-engine parts until the end of 1944. After the Second World War the same site boasted the biggest Yugoslav factory for the manufacture of truck and tank engines as well as light weaponry, mostly hunting rifles. But that's all gone. We don't manufacture rifles and aircraft any more, the way Hitler and Tito did. Today all we make are scrumptious local Kranj sausages,' Butcher says confidently, as if he had trotted out the same sentences countless times before.

With a nod of her head Rosa Portero thanks the secretary for the Coca-Cola she has brought her then checks the Dictaphone to make sure it's actually working. Despite the grey winter's day, she wears sunglasses and seems exhausted. Every now and then, during the president's performance, Adam Bely leans over to her and quietly recapitulates his declarations in German.

'You've mentioned Kranj sausage,' Bely cuts in politely. 'We are talking about the crown jewel of your product line, correct?'

'That is correct,' replies Tine Butcher. 'Annually we produce about 16 million hand-skewer-bound sausages, first-class sausages. We export them to over forty countries worldwide. Our sausages travelled into space with the American astronaut Nancy Sing, who has Slovenian roots; and, if we're lucky, it will become the first sausage ever to land on the moon. Negotiations with NASA are well under way.'

'The Kranj sausage travelling into space has been covered by Austrian news media, but what I want to know is, what made it so popular? It doesn't come from the city of Kranj, even though it's named after it. It doesn't even come from the Kranj region, but all the way from Lower Styria, isn't that right?' Bely asks.

Pleased with the question, the president leans back comfortably. His body language indicates he is happy to be asked something in his area of expertise, his terrain, his wheelhouse. This was *his* question. He takes a deep breath.

'The Kranj sausage is a typical European story,' he continues confidently. 'The European Union has approached us with a historical opportunity here. You know what I'm talking about? No, not the free market; we practised that back in the days of Yugoslavia. I'm not talking about Western marketing manoeuvres either. We mastered that under Communism, too. No, what the EU has given us is a once-in-a-lifetime, historical ...' the president struts his stuff, his voice filled with zeal and emotion. 'Are you listening? *Historical* opportunity.'

Adam Bely stops translating into Rosa Portero's ear. They both stop, stunned by the president's half-finished statement, which soars before them like a soap bubble, then trembles, rises, sinks, then rises again and bursts.

'An opportunity?' asks Bely. 'What sort of opportunity, Mr President?'

'The opportunity to register our own trademark, what else?' The president of Butcher, Inc. smiles, thrilled that yet another pair of tiny, ignorant deer are caught in his grandiose rhetorical headlights.

'We successfully registered our Kranj sausage, and there is no one in the entire European Union who can take it away from us. Do you know what that means? There are only eleven registered manufacturers of Kranj sausage in this galaxy, and we're the biggest of them all. We're the best of them all, and we have the best market penetration of any of them. Are you recording?'

A little baffled by his abrupt question, Adam leans over the Dictaphone and nods.

'Of course, it's not true that our sausages aren't made in Kranj,' Butcher continues unperturbed. 'It's not true that the Kranj sausages we manufacture here in Lower Styria aren't authentic Kranj sausages from Upper Carniola. Let's take a closer look. What makes a sausage a Kranj sausage? The recipe is brilliant in its simplicity: the best pork, young elastic pig intestines, a pinch of salt, some pepper and top quality garlic. And beech tree smoke. That's it. So, Kranj sausage is mostly pork. Correct?'

The president leans over to Bely, who hastily nods.

'Now, please tell me what place can claim an animal, a pig in this case, as its own? If you ask me, it's not the place where the swine was born, and it's not the place where it was raised. It's easy these days to feed a Canadian-born swine with Czech grain somewhere in Bangladesh and not even know it. Do you see what I'm getting at? The only thing that determines whether we're dealing with Kranj pork or not is whether the pig was slaughtered in Kranj or somewhere else. Our first-class Kranj sausages are made of top-quality pork, which always comes from pigs slaughtered in one of the certified Kranj slaughterhouses, full stop. All our pork comes from Kranj, but it is here, in Maribor, where this certified meat is processed into sausages. And so it is entirely possible that the best-quality Kranj sausages actually come from Lower Styria.'

'But would you say that Maribor and its inhabitants are aware of the developmental potential that the Kranj sausage holds for them?' Adam Bely pauses before uttering the word 'developmental', as if he had a lump to swallow.

'Maribor is my city. I would never want to live anywhere other than in Maribor. But, let's face it, Maribor is a synonym for fast food. Maribor knows nothing of quality cuisine. Sure, we all sin at McDonald's at times, and there's nothing wrong with that. But if that shit is all you eat, then your ears will fall off, your veins will atrophy, you'll get fat and your body will inevitably deteriorate. That's what happened to this city mentally, too. After they chased out the Germans at the end of the war the city only got intellectual fast food, cheap sugar, fatty steaks. And fifty, seventy years on, that's the new norm.'

'You're being quite critical of your city,' Bely says and crouches behind his black briefcase. Rosa nervously shifts in her chair, takes a sip of her Coke and readjusts her shades with her white-gloved hand.

'Tough criticism is the only thing that may save us. That and building on the potential of this city, that's it. That's why we should look up to others sometimes, so we can learn something. Just look around. There's no creature on the entire planet as durable and flexible as we are, aside from viruses maybe. The dinosaurs didn't adapt. Coral didn't adapt. The Tasmanian tiger didn't adapt. But then you've got us, humans, who can change dramatically even within a single generation. Take the Chinese, for example. A notoriously short nation only thirty years ago, now they're producing NBA stars.'

Satisfied, the president draws closer to the Dictaphone, slurps his chilled coffee out of a plastic cup and continues speaking. 'Our deepest survival instinct is closely tied to what we eat. What do our bodies long for when we eat something really healthy, let's say something home-made, a roasted chicken or a bowl of soup in a macrobiotic restaurant? They want something fatty, sweet, something heavy and forbidden. But why? Because they know that eating filth regularly is a ticket to building up immunity and being adaptable. Look at babies. They lick filthy floors, they stuff themselves with dirt and worms, and we think they're dumb and not yet socialized. The truth is, they know what's right because they listen to their unspoiled instinct. Kranj sausage has been labelled unhealthy and criticized by vegetarians, and it's no secret why. But, let's face it, no one can smell a sizzling Kranj sausage without salivating like Pavlov's dog! We love it because of that, and that's why it's good for us. The person who eats Kranj sausage on a regular basis will be strong and healthy every day of his life. But it's crucial that we eat home-made food, that is to say, Kranj sausages slaughtered and processed in the Kranj region, at home …'

Adam nods, slowly pulls a fountain pen out of his pocket and sways it like a pendulum.

'… it is absolutely crucial for our energy intake that we …'

The president follows the swaying of the pen, his voice growing softer.

'… eat meat butchered locally. Animals slaughtered locally are …'

The president smirks, pouts his lips and clenches his fists between his legs, like a little boy who takes comfort in wetting his pants.

'… special animals, they have …'

The president pauses in the middle of the sentence, mesmerized by Bely's fountain pen.

'What do animals butchered locally have?' asks Bely and puts his fountain pen back into his jacket.

'Our death paradigm,' the president of the board of the meat-processing company Butcher, Inc., says slowly, syllable by syllable.

Adam shoves the E-meter's cylindrical electrodes into his hands, turns on the switch: the needle floats to the centre of the dial and comes to rest.

'Repeat that,' says Bely.

'Our death paradigm.'

'Repeat it again.'

'Our death paradigm.'

'Again,' says Bely.

'Our death paradigm.'

'What is a death paradigm?' asks Bely.

'The moment when bodies are exchanged,' Butcher replies. 'When the paradigm is calm it is reflected in the flavour of the meat. The pigs must be as still as possible when they die. It's best if they have no idea what's about to happen to them. That's the best recipe for Kranj sausages. The secret isn't the garlic and the spices. The secret is in how the pigs die.'

'What kinds of death paradigm do we have?'

'Our death paradigm is different. Slovenian souls are restless by nature, especially people from Kranj. Our animals are under too much stress when they die. Not good for the sausages. That's why we usually mix in 15 per cent finely ground car tyres, just to calm the meat down. But that can be changed. The only important thing is that we eat meat that we killed ourselves. Because in this meat we eat ourselves; we eat the levels of energy that we passed on to the animal during the kill.'

'Who makes the best Kranj sausages?'

'Bosnians. Nobody is as easy-going and calm as they are. But they won't butcher pigs, only chickens.'

'Do you also slaughter chickens?'

'We have the Halal certification. The Nazis built the factory on two levels, the ground floor and basement. The ground level was designed so that it could be lowered underground during an aerial bombing. The orientation is perfect, and with very little renovation we were able to fix up the underground level and turn it into a slaughterhouse for chickens facing Mecca.'

'And upstairs?'

'Off the record, that's where we make our sausages, although officially the space upstairs is registered as a hunting-rifle factory. Our Muslim clients would skewer us if they knew we were stuffing pork intestines right over their chickens.'

Bely observes the E-meter. The needle hasn't left the centre of the dial.

'Aren't you scared?' asks Bely.

'I'm scared that somebody might find out about our moving the hunting-rifle production elsewhere because of the steep increase in orders. The Chinese are huge fans of shooting.'

'Do you export rifles to China?'

'We do, rifles and chicken claws. It's a big business.'

'What do you see when I say blue?'

'I see the sea.'

'What do you see when I say sea?'

'I see my dreams. Black ink spilling in them. Everything is dark. But it's not ink, it's old oil. Hitler was a genius.'

Butcher screws up his face and grins.

'He knew how to construct gigantic complexes,' Butcher continues. 'He would know how to put things in order today. But there's oil covering everything. The old hydraulics are broken,' Butcher grins again. 'There's no one who can lead us through this petroleum night.'

'The hydraulics that raise and lower the platform in your factory?'

Bely now gestures to Rosa Portero, who slowly takes off her sunglasses and retrieves the silver compact from her fur coat.

'My God, can't you see the hydraulics going down?' Butcher grins and emits a strange, animal-like wheezing. 'Hitler's dead. The mechanism is broken. Help, can't you see the platform lowering? The sausages! Kranj sausages,' Butcher wheezes once again, turning pale. 'Down below, there, they'll squash the entire hall with thousands of halal chickens facing Mecca. Help!'

The president lets go of the E-meter cylinders, jumps up and starts wheezing again, as if choking on his own tongue. He's drenched in sweat, disoriented, his eyes wandering the room. Bely jumps up and tries to get him to sit back down again.

A knock on the door. The secretary enters the room.

'You called, Mr President?'

Bely whispers into Butcher's ear, his back to the secretary.

'Repeat after me. Everything's fine, you may leave.'

The president whispers, 'Everything's fine. You may leave'.

'What was that, Mr President?' asks the secretary.

Bely whispers, 'Repeat it, louder'.

'Everything's fine. You may leave. Repeat it, louder!' The president shouts out each word individually, as if slicing the sentence to pieces.

The secretary takes one last glance at her boss and haltingly closes the office door on her way out.

Bely breathes a sigh of relief. 'Sit down, Butcher, sit down and stay calm.'

Tine Butcher takes a seat. Rosa Portero slowly opens up her silver compact with its yellow-tinged oyster crackers.

Tine Butcher stares deliriously into the air in front of him and continues hallucinating. 'At the last minute the catastrophe was averted. Hitler has come back; our Führer is back. What good luck!' Suddenly Butcher's eyes become very clear and wide. He wheezes again. 'The mechanism stopped, and now the platform is rising again, just as he ordered. My Bosnian butchers, my Halal chickens, all my machines in the slaughterhouse down below! Finally, they can breathe again. And the platform is still rising,' Butcher grins. 'The shingles are falling off the roof, and the Kranj sausages are creeping out from under it and through the windows. Nothing can stop them. Only I, Tine Butcher, can stop this river of pork that is heading towards the city, burying the houses. People are suffocating under the oppressive weight of intestines and pork,' Butcher cries out and raises his arms as if to block the river of pork with his bare hands. 'Some people take refuge higher up, in skyscrapers or church belfries. They look down at the river of pork as it inundates the city of Maribor, coming to a halt only at the slopes of Calvary. Only I was chosen to change the direction of this city's fate.' Butcher wheezes, shoots up and with all his might rears up into the air above him.

Bely puts his hands on Butcher's shoulders and sits him down again.

'You,' wheezes Butcher, staring blankly up into the air. 'Do you know what this city needs?'

Bely shrugs his shoulders.

'A scourge of God! Or, even better, what Maribor needs is a chainsaw of God. One with a long, long guide bar; the sort my Bosnian butchers use to cut the biggest Kranj pigs in half in a single pass.'

Butcher stands up again. Bely hurriedly pulls him down into his chair and places the E-meter electrodes back into his hands.

'Sit down, Mr President, sit. Tell me, are you part of the Great Orc?'

'I am the Great Orca, and I will devour all this pork off the streets of Maribor.'

'Tine Butcher, I will ask you one last time, are you part of the Great Orc?'

'We must let Calvary sleep in peace. May the men and women of Maribor sleep in peace. May all Slovenia sleep in peace. I will save you from the pork.'

'Tine, do you know what the Great Orc is?'

The president turns his head and looks past Bely vacantly. His jaw shudders violently and drops open. The E-meter needle begins swinging left to right and back again. Butcher clutches the cylindrical electrodes and bangs them against his forehead until it oozes blood. Rosa lunges at him and prevents him from injuring himself further.

'The hypnosis hasn't kicked in,' hisses Bely, caught among the jostling elbows.

'It's kicked in too much, that's the problem. He's lost his bearings, and I've got no idea how to bring him back,' says Rosa Portero, kneeling on the president's chest. Butcher's entire body is overcome with convulsions.

'Give it to him; let's absolve him,' says Bely and looks at Rosa.

'Now? He's given us nothing.' Rosa grabs hold of Butcher so he won't tumble off the leather sofa.

'You think there's still a chance he might give us something useful?' asks Bely.

The president manages to shout, 'Attack the undulating mass of Kranj sausage!' before Bely is able to cover his mouth. Bely groans with pain and pulls back his hand, now perforated with the president's teeth marks.

'It's seized the entire city in its tentacles and suctioned itself on to Calvary. Can't you see? We need a saviour!' screams Butcher.

Rosa reaches for the silver compact.

A few minutes later the secretary knocks on the door and cautiously enters with a reminder that two business partners from Abu Dhabi have been waiting for over twenty minutes at the reception. As she opens the door, she sees Rosa Portero in a black, unusually shiny fur coat – it must be made of chinchilla or sable or something like that? – and Adam Bely putting a device away into a leather bag. The secretary notices that Bely is holding a bloodstained handkerchief.

'Mr President, your guests from Abu Dhabi are waiting for you.'

'Have them come in,' says the president in a strangely quiet voice, wheezing slightly. He has a plaster on his forehead and stares absently into space.

Bely and Rosa Portero say goodbye. The president doesn't respond to their words, but from the foyer the thick musk of the Arab business partners' perfume creeps in and settles around him.

# I'm Not Cold
# When I'm with You

'Nothing is as it seems. Everything is what it is, yet at the same time it's something entirely different. When I was young I found this city beautiful. The park, summer at the Three Ponds or on the Drava, sitting around in front of the secondary school, growing up in the old city centre, which back then was still alive, full of people and hope. But today I see just what a mess it is. Sixteen years ago, all of a sudden, my city turned into my executioner. But today the roles have changed. All these people, all these destinies, clumped together into a single filthy ball. Sixteen years ago I was endlessly overwhelmed with anxiety; today I'm only endlessly apathetic,' says Bely.

He opens a tiny bottle and shakes it a little. A pair of blue pills land in his palm, then vanish behind his lips. Rosa stands beside him. She is dressed in her black hooded fur coat. She takes Bely's hand in her own and looks at the scar.

'Does it still burn?'

'A little, but it doesn't matter,' says Bely and pulls his hand away.

'With a wound like that it'd be impossible to read your palm. Your lifeline has been interrupted, and it's unclear.'

'So fate has no power over me? You mean I have time to change my future, at least until the wound has healed?' Bely laughs and puts on his grey winter coat.

Mounds of snow lay in front of the Hotel Eagle. Leaking gutters, voices from Castle Square, shoes drowning in slush, a few people hiding out under a rusty canopy. Udarnik Cinema, a poster for *Cinéma Féministe*. High-school students in front of McDonald's. One of them throws a snowball; the girls giggle; an upside-down rubbish bin, a relic of Yugoslavia, dented all over from having been kicked so often. Overhead, plastic wires, small rings, mangled snowflakes hanging in the air, teddy bears, stars that won't light up, not even at night. The New Year's decorations haven't been taken down yet; they still hover over the streets of the old town like a cobweb in the sky, holding captive all who walk beneath it.

'The façades were so hostile I wanted to kill myself.'

'How come you're talking about façades and not people?' asks Rosa.

'You don't get it; façades are people. But, unlike people, façades never lie. Even well-kept façades can be hostile, at times even more so than the dilapidated ones. It's not about how well-kept things are, it's about what the city radiates. See these bricks, the concrete, all that glass? There're souls who live behind them, night and day, who keep them warm with their presence. Sixteen years later I look at this city and I know that, no matter how hostile it is, it can't break me. Back then I felt threatened; I found myself in a life-threatening situation simply because I didn't understand. Today I understand. We're surrounded by possibilities, energetic potentials, dormant reservoirs of history and human fate. In the end it's up to us to decide whether we want to activate these reservoirs and make use of them. But keep in mind that everything around these possibilities is subject to constant reconfiguration. The constellations never cease to change. Today will never come again. That may feel like a huge relief or a huge responsibility. The only thing to do is to persevere and wait for the moment that promises transition. A transition from one state into another. That moment has arrived.'

'You never regretted leaving?' asks Rosa, kicking at an empty can.

'Never. Rationally, we never know for sure what we were chosen for. Why me and not somebody else? This knowledge is greater than us. Just think about it. Sixteen years! Who were you sixteen years ago? How have you changed since then? In the course of sixteen years I've learned about structures I hadn't a clue about before. I'm talking about structures from the distant past that determine our present and future. I was desperate before I discovered this knowledge. Nothing I did, no matter how well-thought-out or well-intentioned, had the desired effect. Just the opposite. Before I left Maribor my life was a mess. Regardless of what it was, I never accomplished what I set out to do. Everything seemed to be against me, and I sank deeper and deeper into the sewer of this city.'

A skating-rink next to Revolution Monument on Freedom Square. Some fifteen children, behind them a large mound of snow. Next to the rink, a stall serving honey schnapps, a pair of drunks, a group of workers in blue workman's overalls and woollen hats; further on, three men in coats and ties. At the back stands a wooden pedestal; above it a huge inflated balloon, embellished with a black circle and a sign: MARIBOR – THE EUROPEAN CAPITAL OF CULTURE. In the brief silences when Radio City stops blaring, the sound of balloons inflating and children shouting can be heard.

'Look at them,' says Bely. 'There's your typical Maribor Mikado. You know that game of pick-up-sticks, right? Where the person who moves first loses? There's a good chance they'll waste their lives like that.'

'I don't know,' replies Rosa. 'They seem completely ordinary to me, the sort of people you meet in every city.'

'I told you, nothing in this city is what it seems. I don't want to moralize; I don't know them. But if they're from Maribor, and if they manage to remove a stick from the pile without anyone noticing, they'll immediately stab the guy next to them in the back with it.'

Rosa looks at Bely. 'Don't you think you're exaggerating?'

Bely shrugs his shoulders and gives her a forced smile. Rosa walks off to buy cigarettes. Bely waits, observing the people around him. It seems like it was only yesterday that he was standing behind this very bar. It was morning, before things got going in the theatre. Talking about performances, making megalomaniacal plans that were clearly unfeasible from the start, street chatter. Isn't that man next to the stall one of the theatre technicians?

Bely slips. For a moment he glimpses the yellow bulge of the sun, a rotten egg in the sky, then tumbles on to the compressed snow. When he looks up again, an old woman is leaning over him, her breath smelling of onions and alcohol. Bely looks around in confusion. No one cares that he fell. Only this old drunk woman holds out her grimy woollen mittens to him, her enormous mouth looming behind them. The black hole of her mouth is missing most of its teeth, with only a few yellow ones remaining on the sides. Bely shudders with fear. Death and putrefaction emanate from the chasm of the old woman's grimy mouth, as if through it he could catch a glimpse of the other side, the dark side, where there is no life. In his confusion Bely takes the old woman's hand. But instead of helping him, she pushes him away, so he falls once again on his back.

'Alms for the poor, for the poor, sir.'

Bely quickly gets to his feet. Realizing she will get nothing, the beggar woman spits at Bely's feet and limps away. As he watches her go it hits him – his black briefcase – but it doesn't seem to be damaged. Relieved,

Bely dusts the snow off his coat. Rosa is back again. She lights a cigarette and loops her arm in his.

On nearby Leon Štukelj Square a cold wind sways the lights that hang, slightly lopsided, overhead. The scaffolding of a concert stage. A woman leads a boy in a ski suit by the hand. The boy has a pair of enormous mouse ears and a mouse nose pasted on. Bored, he drags his feet as he walks. The woman is in a hurry; she is wearing a black hat pierced with an arrow. She drags the boy against his will towards the office building of the local newspaper, *Večer*. The boy resists, sticks out his tongue, but follows her anyway. Bely feels his chest beginning to itch, at first barely noticeably but soon so intensely that he unbuttons his coat and begins vigorously scratching himself between the buttons on his shirt.

City Hotel. At the reception. The receptionist points them to the lift, fifth floor; the hotel smells of fresh paint and plastic.

'You've got a stain here,' says Rosa and cleans a mud stain off Bely's coat with her glove.

'It only seems that way,' replies Bely. 'My soul is clean.'

Rosa looks at Bely in disbelief. 'You know, sometimes you make it really hard. You turn every ordinary conversation into some sort of secret message.'

'Rosa, I know this may sound messianic, but when you experience what I have, when you've seen your own fate with the clarity that I have, then you don't want to waste your time with meaningless phrases any more. When I said that my soul is clean, I meant to say that I can see clearly who I am and who you are, the reason we're here and what task lies ahead of us. Listen, if I weren't clear, cleansed of my past, I'd never be able to grasp the task I've been entrusted with. The here and now is no different from what it was back then in the distant past. One of those ancient souls had a different programme from the rest of them, do you understand? When the souls of our ancestors were destroyed and overwhelmed by darkness, it was the soul that survived. One *thetan* preserved its memory and has waited until now. Look, today seems like any other day, but today offers us a historical opportunity to free ourselves and cleanse ourselves. The filth on my coat is nothing compared with the filth that once darkened our souls, Rosa. Now it's over, once and for all!'

A waiter takes their coats. Rosa keeps her gloves on. They are shown to a table. The restaurant opens on to an outdoor terrace, bar tables and patio heaters. Rosa steps outside and lights up a cigarette, huddling against one of the heaters. The cigarette smoke billows in the direction of the snow-capped mountains behind them.

'They're called the Pohorje Mountains. They say here that everything, good and bad, comes from Pohorje. That's the Pohorje ski resort,' says Bely.

Bely points at an area in the form of the letter Y on a treeless, snow-covered slope.

'If you look down you'll see the old and new bridges over the Drava River, the industrial part of the city is just across the river, and what surrounds us is the old part that stretches out into dormitory towns and nearby villages. Welcome to our capital, the capital of Lower Styria.'

Rosa slowly blows smoke from her lips and stubs out the cigarette with her gloved left hand. Shuddering with cold, she presses against Bely and lays her luxuriant black hair on his chest.

'So this is where you're from,' she says gently.

'This is where I'm from,' replies Bely, standing still. 'Although we all have many places we could call home.'

'Or none for that matter,' replies Rosa and adds, 'The thought of having no home makes me happy. It's horrible to have a home. I like being at home nowhere. I like being a guest, a tourist, a traveller. The idea that I might one day return to where I came from is devastating.'

'I understand,' says Bely. 'When I left sixteen years ago I swore I'd never come back. And now look at me. I'm back. But there's a difference. Sixteen years ago, as I was leaving, I remembered the words of a Yugoslav entertainer. The man had escaped the ravages of war in Sarajevo and took refuge in Maribor. He liked to joke about how, on his way up, he'd prayed to God to take him to Austria because he so wanted to go to Vienna. And just outside of Maribor his tyre blew out. There's something malicious in this city. Sixteen years ago I didn't know what it was. Now I do.'

Bely stares at the swirling currents of the Drava beneath them. Big plates of floating ice move through the grey of the day; a puzzle being solved by a strong current. A handful of trumpeter swans on the banks of the river mingle with pigeons. A big shopping mall across the river, signs with brand names and tired New Year's decorations leading people into temptation. Beside it a construction site, a huge sign on the fence enclosing it: YOU, TOO, ARE ONLY ART.

'What rubbish. "You too, are only art." What's that supposed to mean?' Rosa whispers and presses harder against Bely's chest.

'Self-proclaimed artists, I'm sure,' says Bely catching himself indulging in the warmth emanating through his shirt from Rosa's body, leaving a heat mark on his skin. Bely steps away. 'The sign should say: "You, too, are only past." These days everything is so easily proclaimed as art, but in reality there aren't many people who have fresh ideas.'

Bely puts his hands on Rosa's shoulders. He gazes into the depths of her brown right eye and her glassy-green left one, into her small Cuban face, at her mocha skin and her snowy-white teeth. He gently touches a lock of her hair, moving it to the side.

'Our goal here is for everything to change, for the past to become the future. For as long as I can remember, people here have lived in the past. You see, the past is an infinitely large net that they drag behind them; they get tangled up in it, and it's not long before they fall, swaddled in the past like mummies. Only a few succeed in saving themselves, or they appeared to.'

Bely lets go of Rosa's shoulders and searches the pockets of his jacket.

'What are you looking for? Your pills?'

'I think I left them in my coat. Brrr,' Bely blows on his palms. 'Should we go in?'

'I'm not cold when I'm with you, but if you're cold ...' says Rosa and looks at the ground shyly, like a little girl.

Bely scratches his chest nervously and readjusts his shirt. 'Rosa, since I met you, you've meant a lot to me. Really, a lot. We're on course. We've got the list of eight names; we're still after the other five, but it won't be long, I'm sure. Once the entire Great Orc is absolved, everything will be different. Look, my whole life I thought I had to fight, to resist, take an eye for an eye. It's true that nothing comes from nothing, but it's also true that everything is already here, we just need to ask ourselves what we are, what we see, what we recognize and what we make out of it. The world is infinite, and still we're blind to everything it offers us day after day. And the road to that moment of recognition is a difficult one. Sometimes a person has to relinquish everything and be a kind of hermit just so he can see.'

'I'm not exactly an ascetic, let alone religious,' says Rosa, lighting another cigarette.

'This has got nothing to do with religion, nothing at all. But it does relate to the past, the truth about where we come from and who we are. Mostly it relates to the truth of who we might have been if we hadn't constantly been hypnotized, confined and boxed in within our very own boundaries. Which, by the way, happen to be even more confining, even more airtight in this city than anywhere else in this part of the world. Maribor is a truly unique city in this sense. There's no other city anywhere that is as narrow-minded as this one. And that's not a coincidence, just as it's no coincidence that we're here, you and me, today, in this moment. Coming here means entering the pyramid of mud. Its guards will bury you alive, and you won't even realize it. Instead of burying you in sand like an Egyptian pharaoh, they'll bury you in useless stories and intrigues. The spirits of the past will bury you, and not for the sake of some local folklore. No, you'll be buried for a reason. They've got a damn good reason for putting us out of action, Rosa, a damn good reason!'

'The Great Orc,' repeats Rosa, taking a deep puff.

'That's right. The Great Orc, the guardian of the past, its secrets and energy. We'll incapacitate them in order to give the future of this city a chance. The Great Orc is made up of thirteen people. We've seen two, so there are eleven more to absolve. We've got a lot more oyster crackers left in the compact, but we'll get there. But Rosa, you're shivering all over. See, you're cold, even in my company. That must mean something. We'd better go back in. I'm hungry, and I've heard the food here is excellent.'

# Off-Stage

Deep in thought, Bely paces the hotel room. Squeaking floor and a mild scent of decay. Beyond windows, solid greyness. Rosa sits on the bed, earphones in her ears, rewinding the recordings. She turns off the Dictaphone.

'I don't know. This could be a big mistake.'

'What do you mean, a mistake?' mutters Bely under his breath.

'We didn't get enough information from them. It was impossible to get anything out of Ornik this morning, with her colleagues next door, so we should've been that much more thorough with Gram.'

'Don't go there! Further interrogation would've been a waste of time, trust me. No one in the group knows all thirteen members,' says Bely as he scratches his neck. 'They're linked through small pieces of information, which they don't even know they have. What we're dealing with here is the truth that is of a different mental dimension and is only regenerated directly through the past. We're talking about the truth that's stored elsewhere, not within our brain, not within our physical bodies.' Bely keeps going and then flops into a chair. 'We could've quizzed them for many more hours, but we'd get nothing but little bits from their current and previous lives. To reach deeper we'd have to perform a radical regression, which requires time and numerous sessions, otherwise we'd be at risk of losing their souls forever.'

Bely discovers the little bottle with his pills on a table. Two pills slide down the bottleneck and out into his hand.

'A soul breaks away into this interspace, and nothing can bring it back,' mumbles Bely while swallowing the pills.

'This interspace you mention, is it the same as the space that the souls we absolve go to?' asks Rosa as she readjusts her gloves.

'That's a whole different story,' replies Bely then resumes pacing the creaking carpet of the hotel room. 'Listen. The body of every single person, including yours and mine, is inhabited not by a single soul but a number of souls. Quite insignificant if you consider the number of souls that are trapped in those who comprise the Great Orc.

We're talking thirteen human bodies who are weighed down by the unbearable weight of the past.'

'Are these the souls from our previous lives?' asks Rosa with a quizzical gaze beneath her brow.

Bely stops and looks closely at the abrasions on the hotel room door. 'We have all lived many lives, we all were many in the past, but that's not what's crucial here. That's obvious to all who have ever experienced *déjà vu*. Over many thousands of years you and I met on many occasions, we both know that. We met in different physical shapes, different genders, in different relationships and at different times. And to some degree, with special techniques, we can trace our pasts. But don't forget, our souls are comprised of many souls, which are much older. So when we perform absolution we absolve these ancient souls that were brought here millions of years ago and have roamed aimlessly ever since their bodies were violently murdered. It is these ancient souls that determine who we are here today.'

Bely halts at the other end of the room and looks out the window. The firewall of the adjacent house grows invisible as the grey of the day yields ground to twilight. The shaft in front of Bely's reflection in the window fills with thick, fluffy darkness.

'In Scientology we dedicated a lot of our time to interviews that they call auditing. But that would require time we just don't have. But yesterday, when we entered the New World, we launched a series of processes. At this point the only way forward is to pick up every little piece of information from all the names we have before these processes have the last word. We have six more names on our list. They must give us the names of the other members, all of whom we must find and absolve before it's too late.'

Rosa puts down the Dictaphone and sits on the edge of the bed. 'And that's where you got your E-meter?' she asks, pulling out the cigarette case, which she then places on the desk next to the Dictaphone.

'You mean from the Scientologists?' Bely asks.

Rosa nods.

'Yes, it's the only thing I took from them, which is nothing compared with what I left behind. But that's how it's got to be. I absolved them, too. Generally speaking, the worst thing that we can bring upon ourselves is to drag our past with us. I disagree with many things in Scientology, now that I'm not biased and can look at it from a distance, but they had a breakthrough in one thing: we must get rid of our own baggage, especially that which we're not aware of.'

'Ah, Bely, from your mouth everything sounds so simple. I'll never be able to the forgive people who tried to kill me,' says Rosa, lighting up a fresh cigarette.

'Do you have to smoke in here?' asks Bely.

Rosa steps to a window, opens it slightly and puffs out into the fresh air. 'Listen, these socialist hotels far surpass all that capitalist opulence in one thing – they're so impregnated with tobacco smoke that nothing can make them stink any worse. And this one doesn't even have smoke detectors.'

Bely shrugs. 'Rosa, you say that you'll never be able to forgive. But that's the only way we could have met. We should be grateful to those people who made our paths cross. Without them we wouldn't be sitting here.'

'Bastards,' Rosa hisses and flicks her half-smoked cigarette into the night, white smoke pouring out of her mouth. With her blunt metal grip she grabs hold of the window handle and twists it shut.

'Yesterday I dreamed about the swamp again. I couldn't get back to sleep afterwards. That absent look on Gram's face when you gave him the cracker. He just wouldn't leave me alone, but after a while I finally drifted off. Leeches everywhere, little tadpoles crawling all over me, and I couldn't run because my legs wouldn't move. Horrible.'

Bely looks at the clock. He reaches for the little bottle again, spills two pills into his hand and swallows them.

'You're a pill-popper, you know that? You stuff yourself with this shit way too much.'

'They're not pills, only a dietary supplement,' replies Bely, scratching his abdomen.

'And look what they've done to you, these dietary supplements of yours. They've turned you into a walking skeleton. In the month I've known you, you must have lost at least five, six kilos, in spite of eating normally. It's must be the pills. What else?'

'These pills break down fat cells in your body. I believe that it's much harder to identify souls that inhabit corpulent bodies as opposed to slender ones. Fat acts as their shelter, it's where they become unidentifiable and hide, out of sight. Human fat is the source of their food. It's no coincidence that clarity of thought can only be achieved through fasting. When we starve, we deny these souls their chance to hide, to pollute our minds, to subdue us.'

The moment Bely utters his last word, Rosa nervously grabs the bag on the table. In it are two large bottles of Coke, crisps, a packet of chewing-gum. She pulls open the bag of crisps and digs in. Bely looks at the clock.

'We should leave in twenty minutes. I'll just go to my room quickly. I'll knock when I'm ready. OK?' Bely takes the little bottle and drops it into a pocket in his coat.

Rosa steers her hand full of crisps towards her mouth. The residue of small yellow potato flakes and sparkly crystals of salt are embedded in her glove. Anxious and munching away, she watches him leave.

Once in his room, Bely first takes off his shirt, then his undershirt. He lights up the room and observes his reflection in the cracked bathroom mirror. Lush body hair across his chest, moles, large and small, scattered everywhere. Bely leans closer under the light above the mirror. His fingertips travel carefully across the upper part of his body. He lifts his left arm, feels around the armpit, turns around and examines his neck and back, leaning towards the source of light to ensure that nothing remains unexamined. Nothing, nowhere, nothing.

'Strange,' mumbles Bely, 'really strange.'

Rosa is already in the corridor when Bely steps out of his room. Outside, the sky flickers in the white snow. Hastily, Rosa lights up a cigarette, takes a deep puff and swings her hand under Bely's arm. Together they trudge along Gosposka Street, once one of the city's most élite thoroughfares, but today a harbinger of the old city centre's impending decay. Feeble street lamps, closed stores. Above their heads the web of gloomy New Year's decorative silhouettes dips ominously low from the snow that adheres to the wires. Passers-by are few. On the corner a man with a radio on top of a cardboard box. Dalmatian folk-songs intertwined with static. In his hand, a marionette soldier dangles off long, translucent threads. The marionette promenades, floating above the soiled snow. Glittering in the night. In the middle of a square further on stands a Baroque plague column. Behind it, another balloon featuring the unusual sign, beneath which stands the inscription: EUROPEAN CAPITAL OF CULTURE. Squealing, the snow-stifled sound of the balloon-rotation mechanism, the roar of the puffing air that keeps the balloon aloft.

Slippery bridge. Falling snowflakes, moisture, the banks of the Drava River, cars pulling invisible cloaks of noise and lead, the rustling of the river, the icicles trickling off the cast-iron rail. Bely stops in the middle of the bridge. He leans across the rail, above the drifting darkness. Lamps flicker above Rosa and Bely. Snowflakes now hurriedly plunge into the depths to be swallowed by the river, the hallucinogenic attraction of its current, the feeling of its inescapable power.

'He plunged in somewhere around here,' says Bely.

'Who?' Rosa asks.

'This guy. I knew him pretty well. The same generation. We grew up together. He was a performer and a songwriter, and I was into theatre. Anyway, we both had a huge crisis at about the same time. He lived with his mother, while I was already renting an apartment. He stayed at his mother's, and I ended up fleeing the city, which probably saved me. Had I stayed like he did …'

Bely stares into the depths. The wind picks up his hair and tousles it.

'Who knows …' Bely adds quietly.

'What happened to him?' asks Rosa and swipes the black curls off her cheek.

'He jumped off this bridge. On a wintry day, like today, early in the morning. They tried to save him but couldn't. Since then, he's been coming to see me every now and then. He toys with me, tells me I'm still irreversibly egotistical. I say that's positive egotism, but he pretends that he doesn't understand. Some things never change. Ever the cheapskate, always short of money, but in company he was the big-hearted genius who never had it easy in life. Me, the one who actually made some money, I was always the cheapskate, the geek. We spent a lot of time in Off. It's been nearly twenty years.'

Rosa lights up a new cigarette, inhales and flicks the cigarette over the bridge. They see it fall, a tiny light smothered by the night and consumed by the devouring rustle of the river.

'I don't feel like smoking tonight,' Rosa says and cuddles up to him again.

'Let's go,' he says, 'to Off, that sub-culture club right behind the city hospital. Some time ago I read in the Austrian newspapers that this is the best hospital in Europe, at least in terms of successful resuscitation. An interesting piece of trivia. People who have long been destined to die are more often brought back to life in this city than anywhere else. Although coming back is not up to those who are dying. It's decided on by the souls that inhabit them. The souls of people here aren't interested in leaving; they want to stay in an environment where nothing ever changes, like here in Maribor. Every soul was subject to radical brainwashing. They'd be in pain if they found out who they are and how they got here. Millions of years ago people were not only killed – by which I mean their bodies, that's the easy part – they also found a way to manipulate their souls. You can't kill a soul, but you can dispossess them of their self and reduce them to shadows with no future. Our souls, the way we perceive them, aren't real souls. They're only the remains of the manipulated souls of our ancestors. Our souls are only sad remains, which cling to each other out of fear of being forever lost.

Bely notices Rosa's covert laughter. 'Why are you laughing?'

'I'm not laughing. I believed in souls myself when I was a child. Then, for about two decades, I was convinced that there's no such thing as the soul and that we only get one chance at life. Then something changed my life forever, split it in two, and suddenly I believed in souls again. The question is, do we believe in them because we fear that there's nothing out there? Or because we're helpless? I don't know.'

'But, Rosa, they do visit you, don't they?'

Rosa nods. 'Yes, they're with me the entire time, and that's why I believe in them. Tell me, though, are some souls really scared of being destroyed, even when they're here with us?' Rosa asks doubtfully.

'Not the souls that are self-aware, not them. It's the phantom collage of our souls that's scared. Why else would they be so determined to keep their shells alive? Life in this city can't be so damned wonderful that the fully conscious souls would want to stay at any cost. Of course, there're other things to consider here, but we'll discuss those later. We've arrived.'

The courtyard of the old industrial complex, graffiti, above a door a sign that reads OFF. The round door recalls that of a submarine. A couple of guys, leather, cigarette smoke, each holding a bottle of beer. Out of the night a pack of dogs emerges. They sprint across the white-coloured courtyard and chase the scent of a bitch. The men follow them with their eyes then turn their gaze to Rosa, who walks past them and in through the door.

It's spacious and chilly inside. A roughly chiselled log bar, behind which a girl in a red turtleneck eavesdrops on a conversation that is being held across the room. Some twenty people sit in the corner, involved in a heated debate. One of them rises and tells the rest that he opposes maintaining a gradual increase in pressure on the mayor and that immediate resistance should be employed, and that strategic stalling is no longer an option. The chair of the meeting listens carefully, and while acknowledging these concerns as legitimate he advises that they're in it for the long haul and that they all remain thoughtful and persistent. He puts it to a vote and is backed by the majority.

'The next public protest against the wastewater treatment plant construction at the base of Calvary will be held on Friday next week in front of the town hall. The organizing committee will meet again on Monday to finalize the details of the protest. The public will be kept informed via the usual channels, principally through Facebook. That'll be it for tonight,' says the chair.

Everybody rises, some change tables, others step out into the fresh air. The speakers crackle with death metal.

'I must be dreaming! Adam Bely! Are you still alive? I can't believe it. I'd never expect to see you here!' The chair of the meeting shakes Bely's hand and pats him on the back.

'Meet Ivan Dorfler, the legendary boss of Off. This is Rosa Portero, my colleague from Austria. Rosa's working on a radio piece about Maribor, so I thought I'd show her around Off a bit. I'm guessing that few journalists head straight for this place.'

'You'd be surprised, Adam. We've hosted a bunch actually, especially over the last year. This is a hipster joint, not an old hole-in-the-wall any more. Come, let me show you to my office so we can talk. It's too noisy here.'

Books and CDs everywhere you look, total chaos, dozens of semi-disintegrating binders strewn across the table, portraits of Tito, Mao Zedong and the Virgin Mary with a hammer and sickle piercing her heart. Next to it, a poster of the dove of peace with an olive branch in its beak. The air is warm, stale with cigarette smoke. Empty bottles are scattered across the floor; two worn-out leather sofas, a table and an ashtray, cigarette butts, stains all over the table.

'Adam, I haven't seen you for ten years, maybe more.'

'Sixteen,' says Adam as he takes a glass. Dorfler pours them each three fingers of whisky. They toast. Rosa gapes at Adam as he empties his glass. She can't believe her brown eye. Never since they met has she seen him drink alcohol. Dorfler refills their glasses. He offers them cigarettes. Dorfler and Rosa light up.

'I can't believe my eyes. You're thinner and you've gone grey, but otherwise you look exactly the same. Where've you been hiding, for God's sake?'

Bely reaches for his coat, pulls out his bottle and flushes down his pills with more whisky.

'Well, I moved to Austria. First, I was in Graz, then Leoben. I do visual communication now, ads, marketing and stuff like that.'

'And theatre?' Dorfler provokes. 'Since when have you been able to live without theatre, Adam?'

'I'm better off without it,' responds Bely, draining his glass.

Dorfler tops it up again. 'I can't believe that. Your friend here', says Dorfler in German as he turns to Rosa, 'is the biggest theatre fanatic I've ever met in my life. And, believe me, I've met a few. Back in high school he sold his soul to theatre, the worst of devils. And now he claims that he no longer cares about it. What happened? You wouldn't know anything about it, miss, would you?'

Rosa smiles and lights up a fresh cigarette.

'I'm all right, no worries. What about you? It seems that the revolutionary Eros hasn't left you even after all this time.'

'The people you saw outside, they're a wonderful group. Intellectuals, very erudite, proactive youngsters who are fed up with this neoliberal shit. Have you heard what's going on in the city? Huge deals, that's what's going on. All while people are starving. We must put an end to it. This city is rife with discontent; every other person here is unemployed. And all they do is show scorn for us and steal from right under our noses. Do they think we're stupid, that we're blind? The group you saw is the core of the organizing committee in charge of protests against the corrupt city administration. No politician in the entire country is as corrupt as our Mayor Voda, if you ask me. He cut money for social support to build this art palace down the street from us. Have you been? A useless gallery with an enormous hall at the top, a private elevator, an office and a private Jacuzzi. All for the price of a hospital. Do you know what that means? You know how things are built around here, what public money is spent on. A truck full of bricks, potholes strategically located in front of every politician's house, the truck bounces and hop, one by one, the bricks disappear into their courtyards until finally the truck arrives at its destination empty. They deserve nothing but the gallows. They're crooks. We'll let them have their carnival.'

'I see you haven't changed at all,' Bely smirks at Dorfler's fiery speech.

'Of course I have! Last time we saw each other I was only a teaching assistant, and now, now I'm a dean,' grins Dorfler. 'I'm not kidding. We must put an end to this neoliberal theft. The worst is yet to come. Just today the city council confirmed the "rebalancing" of an investment worth two hundred million euros, which exceeds the annual city budget. And for what? For a wastewater treatment plant in a protected water area, which is right next to the old city centre. According to our calculations, such an undertaking should cost no more than one tenth of their estimate. But no, in order to clean shit they plan to release wastewater into the ground under Calvary. They'll burrow into the hill and, oh-by-the-way, they'll also erect a garage for the mayor at the bottom, near Pyramid Hill, and an apartment building or two for all of his sweethearts. And since the porous ground can make building into a hillside unpredictable, the investment will rise and rise until its value outweighs all the souls that still live in this city. No. We need revolt, we need change, and we need it now.'

'Nice to see the intellectuals of Maribor taking pleasure in such activist ecstasy. So, you're done with 2 × 2 × 2?'

Dorfler smirks.

Rosa notices an unusual expression on his face. '*Was bedeutet zweimal zweimal zwei?*' she asks.

'That was a traditional game played by the young intellectuals of Maribor,' explains Bely. 'It requires two players. They get locked into a room where they have to stay for two whole days. Their goal is to assume the mental age of a two year-old as quickly as possible, not only in terms of their speech but also behaviour, from walking, crawling and thumb-sucking to floor-licking. Sooner or later the players relax so much that they fall into some sort of state of regression, taking off their clothes, looking at their genitalia or chewing on each other's bibs. Jostling for toys and the pooing of pants is normal. They're allowed to do everything, as long as they stick to the purpose of the game. They're being filmed the entire time, so that they can see themselves in action once the game is over. If they recover, of course.'

'Some people still play the game, although it's lost its popularity. Internet's a bitch these days. The recordings began slipping into the wrong hands and were easily used for blackmail.'

Dorfler pulls tobacco and some cigarette papers out of the desk. A big piece of hash licks the lighter flame. Dexterous crush and roll. Dorfler fires it up, inhales deeply and passes it on to Bely. He holds it for a while without taking a puff and hands it back to Dorfler, but Rosa's white gloved hand intercepts it. She inhales. She passes it on to Dorfler, who studies Rosa from above his round spectacles.

'Adam, you've got an interesting young lady here. Where do you come from, Rosa?'

'From Graz.'

'I mean, originally?'

'My father is from Havana; my mother is Austrian. I never got to know my father. We came to Austria when I was five, but my father left us soon after that. My mum always said he'd gone back to Cuba to dance salsa. I never saw him again,' she smiles scornfully.

'And you work as a journalist?'

'Yes. I'm working on a radio piece for Austrian radio about Maribor as the European Capital of Culture.'

'This is the European capital of nepotism and neoliberal manure, not culture. All the people hired to put together the European Capital programme are, as you'd expect, hirelings from elsewhere, from Ljubljana, who came here only to rechannel European money. If they were at all impartial, they would distribute the funding equally among every Maribor cultural worker. A thousand, fifteen hundred per head. At least that way we'd know where the funds were going. That would be the only fair model of democratic culture, not these golden plumes in operatic performances for élites. Although it's also true that culture should become more democratic and show more solidarity. The true cultural workers and intellectuals these days are proletarians, nothing like these self-professed art élites, these self-complacent, capitalist arse-licking cliques.'

Dorfler sways gently, stands up, scours through a pile of paper on the desk and pulls out a newspaper.

'You journalists should be the voice of the people's conscience, and not the herald of capital. Look at this! Look at the today's front page. "Mother sent to court because she had her one-month-old baby tattooed without the father's approval". What's this world coming to? Seriously, is this a headline that deserves the front page? As a progressive democratic society, you'd think we'd be enlightened enough to protect not only human rights but also the autonomous parental rights to a liberal upbringing. The Mother tattooed her baby with the Maribor football-team logo. What in God's name is wrong with that? Do we really have to call the fire brigade for something like that? Do we not label our children from birth onwards? What about personal rights? And what, a tattoo of Jesus on a cross would be fine? You two will say that this is just a matter of nomenclature. Very soon we won't be able to name our own kids any more. I've got a son. But there's nothing I'm allowed to say to him. He doesn't so much as look at me when I say something, he's glued to his iPad, firing away. Pirates, militiamen and sometimes Martians. All day long without interruption, shooting. Boom, boom, boom. For real? Are we really supposed to worry about a purple stain on a baby's butt, oh please! Shouldn't we instead focus on the wastewater treatment plant that'll gobble up babies' shit, not to mention our money, for the next five or six decades and mess up the entire ecosystem of Calvary? Or on money that was lost to the construction of the Marx Centre? Talking about your friend Andreas, the dream vendor, we just got rid of him, we threw him out of this city, and before you know it he's back with this developmental-cultural centre of Maribor called Marx. You get me, Adam. You worked alongside him for so many years, or at least you tried to. And do you know where he drew inspiration for this name, Marx? The name that defines this city's culture? From his wife's skunk. You don't know about the skunks? Yes, three. He's got three. Marx, Groucho and Harpo.'

'OK, but as far as I know there're many people here in Maribor who have skunks as pets,' says Bely.

'I've got nothing against them, don't get me wrong. My sister owns them, too. She had their glands removed, but they still stink. They make me sick to my stomach when I step into her apartment. They're all over you, those creatures, they crawl under your trousers, your shirt, they climb onto your head. Horrible. And what's even worse is that you have to trim their claws so they don't destroy your furniture. It takes at least two to trim the claws of a stinky-arsed skunk. You cut, while the other person holds the animal down. I love my sister, there's no question about that, but holding her skunks every Tuesday afternoon so that she can trim their claws, that's one step too far.'

'What does Evelyn do?'

Dorfler gets up and fills the glasses again. From beyond the walls comes the sound and rhythm of dull and steady blows accompanied by groans. From the other side of the soundproofed door leaks the softened sounds of booming death metal.

'She works at some firm in investment management,' says Dorfler curtly.

'I see. Didn't she work at a bank? What firm does she work for?' asks Adam Bely and pulls a fountain pen out of his pocket.

Rosa straightens her back, her gaze firmly fixed on Dorfler's exaggerated fumbling.

'She works for the town hall. Not for the mayor, not for that scoundrel. She's the head of the investment department that deals with social services.'

Sighing and groaning, louder and louder. Banging on the other side of the wall.

'These aren't easy times; it's a struggle for all of us. The college is in complete disarray, a total lobotomy. You can't imagine the things I must do to retain my autonomy there. We were cut from the city budget years ago. Now we're on our own. Some income comes from the café and some from rentals.'

The banging against the wall gets harder and faster. Laborious breathing, followed by a wheeze. Now only soft death metal from beyond the door on the other side of the room.

'You've got some lively tenants,' says Bely as he swings his fountain pen back and forth.

'You've got no idea. There's a swingers' club for pensioners back there, possibly the most profitable club in Maribor right now. All the ordinary brothels have gone bankrupt but not this one. They've gone about the business professionally, with discretion and business ethics. It doesn't bother me. We're all liberal, right? And we'll be members before you know it. That counts for something.'

Dorfler forces a smile, rummages through his jacket, pulls out his wallet, slides out a credit card then a plastic bag. He shakes some of the white powder on a newspaper. Chopping motion of the credit card, lined powder moving back and forth across the paper. Rosa looks on intently. Bely tries to attract Dorfler's attention with his swinging pen.

'Come on, Bely, you don't think you'll hypnotize me with that pencil of yours?' Dorfler jokes. 'Here, have a line instead.'

Bely puts the fountain pen back into his jacket and scratches his thigh. He takes the little tube that Dorfler has just rolled out of paper and brings it up to his nose. The thin line of white powder disappears up Bely's nose like water in the desert. Dorfler offers the other line to Rosa, who shakes her head and lights up another cigarette. Dorfler snorts the second line and clears his throat. The third line vanishes into Bely's nose again.

'Why did you come back, Adam? What's your real agenda here?'

'I'm here to help.'

'Who, me?'

'You, too, Ivan.'

'No offence, Adam, but we don't need your help. You're no longer one of us, Adam. You're Austrian now. Go back to where you came from.'

'Exactly my intention, but before I go back I've got something important that needs tackling.'

'You've always found everything important. In fact, so important that you didn't give a damn about who was going to pay for your mistakes.

You left me hanging; everything was set up. With your support I would've made the Maribor Theatre Board. Instead, you gave your vote to your dear Andreas, who was nice enough to abandon you in return. Bely, Bely, you've got a bright name, but lots of black under your nails.'

'You're drunk.'

Dorfler jack-knifes up in outrage. The glasses tremble on top of the rasping table, cigarette butts fly through the smoky air. Drifting confetti through the grey mist of the carnival ball. Dorfler lands on Bely and grips his throat. Surprised, Bely wheezes and flaps his hands, resists, but Dorfler is stronger and determined.

'You call me drunk? You rat, you're calling me drunk? You should never have come back, do you hear? Never!'

Bereft of breath and strength, Bely stares at Dorfler's flushed face, coldly intent eyes that bulge even more from under his magnifying spectacles. On the ceiling above Dorfler's head he sees a crack. It winds like a snake, like a road on a secret map. What a banal end. Who would have thought? Any moment now he will close his eyes and throw down his arms.

Suddenly Dorfler releases him. Bely catches his breath, coughs. Dorfler kneels on the filthy floor next to him. He gasps with pain and crouches over the table. He looks like a criminal just disarmed by the police. Rosa Portero rises above Dorfler, her left hand clutching the back of his neck. Big Dorfler tamed by a tiny woman, bizarre. Tears of pain pour down from under Dorfler's glasses.

Bely picks himself up, pulls the E-meter out of his bag, forces the cylindrical electrodes in Dorfler's hands and turns on the device. The banging against the wall picks up again, sighs, hard breathing.

'Ivan, why did you attack me?'

'I knew that you were coming and that nothing good would come of it. Your chatter here got me thinking about our past, about everything you did to me and my sister.'

'Evelyn? I did nothing to your sister.'

'That's what you think, Bely. Sometimes doing nothing is the worst of all crimes.'

'You're taking this too far.'

'Could be. Surely prigs like you know how to be impartial about these things.'

'What does your sister do?'

'I told you, she works in the municipal administration.'

Bely keeps his eyes on the E-meter needle. The wall is struck and shudders harder and faster. Clenching her teeth, Rosa keeps Dorfler pinned to the ground. She seems to be unbelievably strong.

'Ivan, tell me everything.'

'Fuck you.'

Rosa squeezes Dorfler until he moans.

'My sister and I run a company. Actually, it's run by the two of us and Don Kovač, the ECoC director. But the owner is somebody else.'

'What sort of business?'

'A retirement home. A specialized retirement home.'

'Specialized in what sense?'

'It's a luxury retirement home.'

The needle on the E-meter swings hard. Bely nods at Rosa, who pinches Dorfler even harder. Her grip is like a vice.

'We perform euthanasia for those who want it, even though it's illegal. We relieve the weak of their suffering. Adam, would you let go of me already?'

'Is that all?'

'Yes.'

Bely refers to the needle, which sways all the way to the left.

'You're lying.'

'Well, we allow the relatives of our clients to express their interest in euthanasia. Most of the time they're the ones who are really interested. You know how it is, Adam. You never wanted to take care of your demented father. We try to resolve such predicaments in a way that's very discrete.'

Adam Bely whitens. He kicks Dorfler in his abdomen with all he's got. Dorfler collapses.

'You'll never mention my father again. Do I make myself clear?'

Dorfler spits blood. He nods and pulls himself to his knees. Bely hands him the electrodes.

'Have you heard about the Great Orc?'

'I know nothing about it.'

'You're lying.'

Bely kicks him again, this time in his crotch. The E-meter cylindrical electrodes fly under the table. Dorfler doubles over with pain.

'I don't know who the rest of them are. All I know is that sometimes the select members gather in the city theatre for the premières. Maybe you should ask the theatre director?'

Dorfler utters these last words with unusual contempt. The banging against the wall comes faster. Screaming. Soft death metal.

'Pass me the oyster crackers.'

'*Schön jetzt?*' asks Rosa.

'Give them to me.'

Rosa pulls out her silver compact.

'Not those. Give me the dark ones,' hisses Bely excitedly.

'Are you sure? Wouldn't you prefer ...'

'Just do it!' shouts Bely.

Rosa nods and opens up a special compartment in her compact. The oyster crackers there are like the rest, only a shade darker.

Bely picks one up. 'Let your souls be absolved,' he utters and slips the cracker under Dorfler's bloody lip. His body starts shaking uncontrollably. For a moment Rosa feels as though she can see shadows that scatter through a thick curtain of smoke hanging in the room. Dorfler catches his breath again. He looks like he is about to fall asleep, when suddenly he opens his eyes, gets on to all fours and starts licking Rosa's boots.

'We must leave as quickly as possible,' says Bely.

They slow down only once they are halfway across the bridge. Snowfall sparkles by the lights of the Marx city gallery. Rosa points straight ahead. Beneath them, swaying from a long rope, inflatable human-sized dolls with the mayor's picture on their faces.

'They were put up by Dorfler's activists while we were in there,' comments Bely.

Back and forth, the plastic dolls rock in the breeze like human beings, eerily yet effortlessly.

'Swinging souls,' says Bely.

'You shouldn't have had all those drinks. You don't take alcohol well, let alone cocaine,' Rosa says.

He doesn't reply. After a few minutes' silence, he says to Rosa, 'As a student Dorfler had a special fetish for the ashes of dictators' dead wives. One night he stole the fresh contents of the urn that belonged to the wife of a former head of the Slovenian Communist Party. He loved to cook. We often went to his dorm for dinners, and on special occasions he would whip up his special dish with a pinch of his sacred spice, the ashes. Then, one evening, we'd drunk a lot, he accidentally spilled the precious content of his small saltcellar and, to save some of the ashes, he threw himself on the floor and licked up as much as he could.'

Rosa lights up a cigarette, the breeze blows away a few sparkles, tiny ghosts, into the darkness.

'Adam, why did you decide to give Dorfler a black cracker? How is it different from others?'

'The black oyster crackers take effect right away; there's no delay. In terms of their final effect they're no different from the lighter version,' says Bely. 'The souls get informed regardless of the colour, and it's only through being informed that they can move up a level. The body shell preserves its physical functions, but without the souls it's caught in a mental programme that's formed in early childhood, if not before, and is specific to each individual body.'

Bely stops talking. A gust of freezing wind steals the scent of Rosa's hair in a twirl of snow. Fatigue slowly seeps through every sinew of his body. Newly whitewashed empty streets unfold before their eyes, as they carefully tread the slippery pavements back to the hotel.

# European Approach

There's no one in this city who doesn't know about Laszlo Farkas, the famous prosecutor, who made a career for himself with a number of very widely discussed anti-corruption proceedings. His name is a fearsome metaphor for all convicted criminals who ran schemes involving the illegal privatization of public property during the time of transition to Slovenian independence, who laundered money, who intentionally debilitated firms, trafficked fictitious equity certificates and shares or who, in any other way, very quickly and illegally accumulated a significant amount of wealth. Farkas. Directors on trial tremble at his name. Farkas, renowned for cases such as Patex, Botox, Pimpex and many others that resulted in long-term prison sentences for the cream of Slovenian management. He's also well-known to the wider public because of his physical appearance. For many years Farkas has suffered from glaucoma, which contributes to his slightly insane appearance. A glance at his red, unnaturally bulging and puffy eyes, eyes that never blink, might send shivers down your spine. He left Lendava, a small town on the Hungarian border where he used to practise law, many years ago. He gave up his private practice upon moving to Maribor, where he assumed the position of prosecutor in the State Attorney's Office, in the department specializing in serious economic crimes.

It's around 2.30, early Friday afternoon. Farkas walks out of the court. His white BMW is parked just around the corner. As he does every Friday, he drives across the Tito Bridge, past the hospital to the Ball Bar at the foot of the Pohorje Mountains. The head of the Volley Football Fan Club is already there. Fifteen minutes later Farkas leaves the bar and drives back to his house at the foot of Pyramid Hill in Maribor. He opens his garage door with a remote control, parks the car.

Once at the front door he notices that the house alarm has once more been disarmed. 'I'll have to call the maintenance crew again,' he sighs and unlocks the door.

'Vila, where are you, Vila?' Farkas calls out.

Nothing. Farkas is surprised not to see his poodle, who usually greets him at the front door.

'You lazy little slug, are you asleep again? Vila, come!'

Instead of the dog he is greeted by a horrible sight: on his living-room floor Vila lies motionless. Open drawers, things scattered across the room. On the table, a bottle of whisky. On the sofa, Rosa Portero, revolver in her left hand, unlit cigarette clenched between her lips.

'Finally! I thought you'd forgotten about me,' she says in German and lights up. 'You don't mind, do you? Relax. Vila's asleep. She'll wake up in a few hours, probably with a horrible headache from all the sleeping pills she's had with her food. A very greedy little thing, that dog of yours.'

A door bell.

'That'll be the flower delivery. Come on, let's open the door.'

Farkas, his hands in the air, slowly walks to the front door, Rosa behind him.

'Ask who it is,' orders Rosa.

'Flower delivery,' resounds from beyond the door.

'Maribor doesn't do flower deliveries, except to the cemetery,' says Farkas abruptly.

'We call this the European approach,' says Rosa.

Farkas opens the door to Adam Bely. A couple of minutes later Farkas sits tied up on the living-room floor, holding the cylindrical electrodes. Deep snoring of Vila the poodle next to him.

'Is this his personal trick, or is it some common Maribor folk tradition to paint a poodle's tail purple?' Rosa addresses Bely as he frisks Farkas's coat and bag. He finds an envelope and counts out at least thirty thousand euros.

'What's this?' he asks as he turns on the E-meter device. Rosa turns on the Dictaphone and lights another cigarette.

'We don't smoke in this house,' says Farkas quietly.

'Where has this money come from?'

'I lent it to a guy, and now he's paid me back.'

'I see, says Bely', keeping track of the E-meter needle.

'You come from Lendava, is that correct?'

'From the way you speak, you could be from Maribor,' replies Farkas. 'Do you have any idea how long you'll be put away for this? You're good for ten years, and you'll beg me to call in a favour with my prosecutor colleague when they tear you apart in court.'

'The motto of your legal office was *Suum cuique*.'

'To each his own. Correct,' says Farkas.

'I assume the envelope with all that money adheres to that slogan, too.'

'You can have this conversation with the police, or, even better, from solitary, where you'll have plenty of time to think things through.'

'That's enough, Farkas. Tomi gave you the envelope, the head of the Volleys. Where would a kid like that get so much money?'

Farkas says nothing. Softly and steadily, Bely taps his fountain pen against the palm of his hand. Farkas's bloodshot eyes bulge further as he studies Bely's palms, one of which is injured. His eyes dart from the pen to Bely to Vila's purple tail. The dog's fur rises and falls with heavy breaths. He hears the ceramic fountain pen as it hits flat against Bely's wounded palm, the vibrations that spread evenly across the room and bounce off him back to Bely. Bely feels the vibrations as they settle into his body. Watchfully he stares at Farkas's big, bloodshot, never-shut eyes, which stare back at him. Tired, his corneas look like cocoons of heavily interwoven capillaries. As if the tiniest of the spiders were about to nestle in, the purple tail of the fountain pen, bloody trail, ceramics, blood-filled pools, soft Persian rug, the beating of a canine heart, heavy look, vibrations, the arching ground that opens up into the room, tick, tiring, they bend like sheets, tack, palm, eyes, tail, tick, pencil, breath, tack, pool.

Rosa's voice calls out to Bely to open his eyes. There's something soft underneath him. His nose and mouth are stuffed with purple tail fur. It's Vila, who lies on the rug beside him.

'What happened? Where's Farkas?'

'Don't worry, he's safe, upstairs in the bedroom. I put him there before I woke you up. He managed to hypnotize you while you tried to hypnotize him. Never seen anything like it before. All of a sudden you stumbled and fell across one another.'

'My head.'

'You were lucky you missed the table, but the dog broke your fall, and you probably broke all of her bones, poor little thing!'

'Come on, let's go upstairs,' says Bely, as he grabs the E-meter and staggers to the staircase.

The bedroom door on the first floor is wide open. Farkas, still tied up, lies next to the bed, his mouth Scotch-taped. Bely pulls Farkas up and over to the mirror.

'I should've practised more,' mutters Bely. 'I can't get the hypnosis to work, not even before the mirror.'

Bely leaves and returns with his coat, feels around the pockets and pulls out his little bottle of pills.

'You're not going to give him your fat-reducing pills, are you?' laughs Rosa.

Bely throws her a serious glance. He continues to feel around in his pockets. A small case, an ampoule, a needle, Bely attaches it to a syringe. Farkas tries to resist as Bely rolls up his sleeve. On his upper arm, a tattoo of the Maribor football club logo, a castle with a bird on the blossom of a violet. The needle pierces the castle, light tightening of the skin, a frozen moment. Farkas calms down, turns languid and mellow.

'We've got about twenty minutes,' says Bely. 'The serum only works that long.'

Bely tears the Scotch tape off Farkas's mouth and turns on the Dictaphone.

'Where did you get the envelope with the money?'

Farkas stutters incomprehensibly. Bely grabs him by his shirt and slaps his face.

'Answer me! Where did you get that money in the envelope?'

'It's a week's worth of earnings from my Volleys.'

'Your Volleys?'

'Nobody knows about it, they all think that the Volleys are a bunch of football fans. But some of them are also members of a well-organized group, which I run.'

'What group?'

'Well, we do personal protection, primarily politicians, but also businessmen. It's less likely that I'll ever see you in court if you have our protection. We also deal with other stuff, but on a much smaller scale.'

'Like what?'

'The brick trade, which has turned out to be especially profitable this year, because we're the European Capital of Culture. A perfect opportunity for the Volleys to sell bricks to masses of naïve tourists who visit the city.'

'What bricks?'

'Ordinary bricks. You offer tourists a Maribor brick in exchange for a hundred euros. If they refuse, you smash the brick in their faces. So they all end up buying one. But that raises the price threefold or more.'

'And what do the Volleys get in return?'

'A percentage of their sales; pretty basic economics. I also sponsor their travel to matches and performance-art events.'

'Their what?'

'Performance art during matches: volcano flambé, torchlight parades, pepper shows, choreographed with music and applause. The Volleys consider themselves to be urban artists. You didn't know that?'

During the interrogation, Rosa ransacks the wardrobes, pulling out long dresses, wigs, corsets, lingerie.

'Whose are these?'

'All mine. I love dressing up as a woman so nobody recognizes me. Of course, I can't afford to do that here in Maribor, but I often drive up to Vienna or Budapest to indulge in my secret little weaknesses.'

'What do you think of when you hear the name Great Orc?'

'I was a corn thief as a child. I got caught and beaten up. That's when I promised myself that nobody would so much as touch me again, that I'd be the one holding the whip. In 1945, as a special agent of OZNA, my father was sent to settle the question of the Hungarian and Slovenian Jews who survived the war. Within two months my father sorted out the problem; no more Jews after that in the Prekmurje region. They fired on them until they ran out of ammunition. After that they buried them, some still alive. My father never talked about it. But he had me dig, too, when he was upset or when I did something wrong. He gave me a teaspoon and sent me out to the garden where I kneeled and dug until the hole was big enough for me to lie in it. Sometimes that was mission impossible, when the ground was too wet, or too hard, or frozen in the winter. The teaspoon was inscribed with *ALL IST GEISTIG*. I still remember the blood oozing out of my blisters, but that didn't bother my father. I was happy that he let me live. Just like I'm grateful that the Great Orc lets me live. The Great Orc is my real father. It takes me into the corn fields, it gives me a whip and a spoon, and now I'm the one pummelling others. No, nobody will hit me ever again, nobody will hit me again.'

Farkas throws himself on the floor, unveiling a tattoo on his lower back. Rosa is startled.

Bely opens Farkas's belt and pulls down his pants. His buttocks are covered with a tattoo of conjoined twins, one body and two heads.

'What's this all about?'

'Leave me alone, and my arse. It hurts!' screams Farkas, foaming at his mouth.

'Farkas, we're not going to hurt you, just tell us where you got this!' shouts Bely.

'It's from my brothers. They're the only ones who truly love me.'

Bely scratches the back of his neck. Speechless at first, Rosa now strides across the room, about to explode.

'Have you been to Balatonkenese?' shouts Bely. 'Have you ever seen us before?'

'Only that night when you went through the initiation ordeal. The chief abbot should've killed you, both of you. But you had the symbol on your chest. It scared them to death, they were petrified, so they left you lying there with her. A big mistake.'

'What symbol?' Bely asks and scratches hard across his chest.

'The symbol of return. It coursed through you and kept you safe. Nobody else has it. Only the inner circle of the consecrated knows the stories about this symbol, but nobody had ever seen it in real life.'

'The return of what? Whose return?' asks Bely.

Tears mixed with blood burst forth from Farkas's swollen eyes. Two creeks of slimy blood run down his strained, screwed-up face.

'No, let go of me, stop hitting me. You've got your corn here, here … No, not me, kill her, she's the twin, she's the evil twin!' shouts Farkas and points at Rosa with his bound hands.

Rosa's rage washes off her secretly vulnerable face. She collapses and bursts into tears. Trying to appease her, Bely gently strokes her back. Rosa shrieks, shoots up and punches the wardrobe door as hard as she can. The door cracks under the force of her strike.

'Look at her. I'm telling you, she's a witch. Kill her, kill her!' screams Farkas, trembling with rage. His lips white with foaming saliva. Blood streams from his eyes, gushes down his cheeks.

'Shut up!' yells Bely and knocks him down. He wants to give Rosa a hug, but she pushes him to the ground. Then she crumbles on to the bed and cries. Bely picks himself up, takes the compact out of her pocket and grabs a dark oyster cracker from its separate compartment.

'What do you know about the Great Orc?'

'It's here. It's everywhere. It's here to beat you for your misbehaviour. All who misbehave are punished accordingly.'

'How many people in Balatonkenese know about the Great Orc?'

Farkas struggles to his knees. Soaked in blood, he starts to laugh like a maniac.

'You bad boy, you really have no idea. Didn't you listen to my daddy Orc? I am the Great Orc's only son. The Great Orc of Maribor. My daddy Orc has lots of brothers, one in every city. And each of his brothers has many little boys.'

Farkas is back on the floor, laughing hysterically. The blood from his eyes now pouring over his cheeks.

'Who are the other Maribor members?' shouts Bely, slapping Farkas across his face. Farkas starts coughing violently, his body writhing, blood pouring from his eyes.

'It's no use, the serum is wearing off,' says Bely, looking at Rosa. 'You absolve him.'

Bely lays the cracker on Rosa's trembling glove. She looks at Bely, her eerie gaze piercing through his eyes.

Soon Laszlo Farkas's body begins to spasm, and he loses his bearings. A dense form ascends from his body, and drifts across the room. Transfixed with horror, Laszlo screams his lungs out to a face straining with blue veins, bulging eyes and squirting saliva. His scream turns silent, his inaudible voice all that remains of the body shell of Laszlo Farkas, the state prosecutor.

# A Twin Sister

Back at the hotel Rosa heads straight to her room, slams the door behind her and turns the key. Bely knocks. Nothing. Once in his room, he washes down two pills with mineral water, then another two. An attempt to read through the articles on the front page of a local newspaper gives way to his fatigue.

He wakes to a cloud of smoke. Rosa sits on the sofa next to his bed and drags on her cigarette. Her left hand rests against a half-empty bottle of whisky.

'Tell me, do you also believe that?' asks Rosa, her voice unusually deep and gravelly.

'Believe what?'

'Do you also believe that twins are inferior because they only have one soul?'

'Rosa, where's this coming from? Don't be silly. You know the answer.'

'Then why were you there, Adam Bely? Damn it! Why the hell were you there to kill me that night?'

Bely straightens up. 'We're both here, Rosa, together, alive, safe and sound.'

'Alive? For all you know, you might be the only one alive here. I may not even be alive, not like you, you superior people, you perfect people with two souls.'

'Rosa, only the Twin Cult people believe that,' says Bely.

'What about you, Adam, what do you believe? That twins only have half a million souls, and you, normal people, a million? That we twins are a race inferior to yours?'

Bely says nothing.

Rosa bursts out crying. Bely first looks at her, paralysed, then strokes her hair. Rosa's wet eyelashes touch her eyebrows. Covertly, Bely flinches at the sight of her glassy eye. How could a face so familiar scare him like this? Rosa catches his reaction and steps away, abashed.

'You're no different from the rest. It's all my fault. You have no idea how many times I've asked myself why, why is this happening to me?

61

I'm locked up inside a glass case, Bely, away from the outside world, the world that's ordinary and relatively normal. In here I'm nothing, the barbarous experiments they've put me through, just look at my hand …'

Rosa tears the glove off her right hand. Under the translucent artificial skin metal fingers, joints, mechanisms.

'This is who I am. Look! I'm not a human being. I'm a remnant of a human being. I'm everything that other people throw out. These metal fingers may look like fingers, but they're not, even though I feel them and move them as though they were mine. Just like I still feel them, my two little girls and my twin sister. They're all a part of me, a part that is no longer mine. I'm dead, yet I live. Why am I still alive, Adam? People like me shouldn't be allowed to live. All this babble about the death penalty, how it should be abolished for its cruelty. This, this is the cruellest punishment, to live after you've killed the person you love the most.' Rosa buries her face into the palms of her hands.

'Rosa, it wasn't your fault.'

'What do you know? What the hell do you know, you double-soul fuck-up? What do you know about it? You didn't even have the guts to kill me, a creature inferior to you! Me, Rosa, who murdered my own twin sister and my own children! You bastard, you clever little bastard.'

Rosa tilts the bottle. They don't speak for a long time. Bely waits for her to get a grip on herself.

'It's all my fault. I've always been to blame. Guilt is my specialism. We were born on 1 June, Gemini. Blanca always surpassed me, in everything. She was always the better one and never to blame. I was the one always at fault. When we forgot to clean our rooms, or that time when our dog weed in the middle of the living-room because we'd forgotten to take him out for a walk. Blanca was never guilty. Never. She was more likeable than me. More attractive, cleverer. Boys liked her more. I was the leftovers. Finally, I killed her, along with everything else I had in life, my two little girls, who were born with the same curse. My two little twin girls, who were robbed of the chance to start living. I took my own children's lives, do you understand, Bely? My being a shit wasn't good enough for me. I had to incapacitate my children so that they wouldn't become the shit that I am.'

'Rosa,' says Bely quietly. 'It was an accident.'

Sure, and the car drove itself, right? I was the one behind the wheel, so it's my fault they died.'

'That's only in your head, Rosa. The court found you innocent.'

'What court? Whose court? Not my court! I am the only court I recognize. There's no court that can ultimately convict me, for life. Only I can do that. Bely, the only courts that count are in my head! They convict me when I look at myself in the mirror. They convict me when I cross a road and see the cars driving by. They proclaim me guilty when I see mothers with small children!'

'Rosa, we've talked about this a hundred times. You've got to stop torturing yourself. You survived for a reason. We might never find out what that reason is, but we both know that there is one. There's no way everything was just a coincidence.'

'I want to die, Bely, don't you understand?'

'Rosa, just imagine, you a twin, with everything that has happened to you during your lifetime. Then the Hungarian sect, the fact that they let us live, and now Farkas! Who would've thought that someone from Maribor would be one of the disguised cult members? Rosa, you must understand that that's not a coincidence. Like it's not a coincidence that we met, that we're in this together. We were brought here by everything that's happened in our lives. We have a mission, Rosa, and that mission is no accident. By the way, the Maribor football club logo is not random, either.'

Drowsy, Rosa looks at Bely and lights up the next cigarette.

'What's a football-club logo got to do with anything?'

'I never thought about it until I injected Farkas with that serum. We both saw he had two tattoos – the symbol of the Maribor football club, and something like a violet blossom with a castle and a bird on it. The moment I pressed the plunger, I knew what it meant. A violet, its enticing aroma, that's drugs. Its petals resemble big clouds of smoke, like an eruption. The castle symbolizes the old castle in Maribor, not the one here in the city centre but the one that once stood high above the old city centre, where there's nothing but a chapel now. For many centuries, following the demolition of the castle, a pyramid stood there, and that's why the hill is still called Pyramid. And on top of Pyramid hill stands the castle from the Maribor club logo. Most importantly, the shape above the castle is not a bird. I was convinced all of my life that it's some sort of a heavily stylized bird, but I was wrong. The symbol represents a bomb or some aircraft crashing into Pyramid Hill, something like that.'

'Fine, so you're saying that the aliens visited Pyramid Hill, the castle and this city and decided to raze them all to the ground so that Hitler would be spared doing that a few million years later. Am I close?'

'You're right on target,' says Bely, and he smiles.

'Adam, don't you think this is a bit far-fetched?'

'Rosa, have you seen the souls leaving the absolved bodies? What are souls? Souls are the remnants of different life forms in dimensions unknown to us. Still, occasionally we can communicate with them, or even help them. Do you know what the number-one secret and central ideology of the Scientologists is? It's a story about Xenu. Xenu was the ruler of a civilization that was supposed to have inhabited another planet about seventy-five million years ago. Because this civilization was over-populated and faced collapse, Xenu decided to preserve his planet by carrying out a genocide against his own people. He coaxed millions of them to board his spaceships on the pretext that he was going to send them to planets better and more beautiful than their own. He chose the Earth, but not to populate it. He chose it as the place where he would annihilate his people by hurling them into a volcano.'

'So?'

'And so he did. All of them, except for the few chosen ones. He killed off the majority of his people, but not their souls, because souls are indestructible. So he manipulated and deluded them to the point where they were suspicious of their own pasts but can no longer actively remember them. As a result, these souls are bewildered and petrified, with a tendency to gather, form clusters and exist in an environment that encourages mutual rivalry, a parasitic life. It is these soul clusters that represent our souls. We're made up of the souls of those that were killed, but we're not aware of it.'

For a long while Rosa stares at Bely. Then she tilts the bottle of whisky and takes another long sip.

'Which means our planet is ...' Rosa utters gingerly.

'... one big burial ground. Graveyards at every step, souls that can't set themselves free because there's no way for them to escape the dimension they've been trapped in over the millennia. When we absolve souls all we do is allow them to change dimensions. We help them leave their cages, we help them remember once again where they came from and how they ended up in these cages, our bodies.'

'And Maribor?'

'Maribor is one of the biggest burial grounds in this part of the world. The Pyramid, Calvary and other nearby hills are nothing but the monstrous burial grounds of those slain millions.'

'And you figured this out from the logo of a local football club?'

'It's logical. What's the hardest thing to notice? The thing right before our eyes. There're very few who have the insight that lets them read this symbol the way we can. For others, this badge is nothing but violets and birds and castles, all of which are long gone.'

Rosa Portero closes her eyes and grabs the bottle again. Gulping, long sips. Slowly, she releases the empty bottle on to the won-out hotel carpeting.

'I hallucinated while I was locked up. I was often left alone in complete darkness. There must have been two or three days when I saw no light at all, which made me incapable of distinguishing dream from reality. You lie there, waiting to be killed or devoured by the darkness that surrounds you. I often had this vivid vision – I don't know whether it was a dream, a hallucination or perhaps I was just imagining things. I was on board an enormous spaceship, flying away together with people full of expectation and hope. And the more often I called this image to my mind, the more realistic it became, and it was the only thing in that darkness that infused me with hope and the desire to live and pull through. Then one day they brought me out into the light. And there you were, appointed to sacrifice me.'

'I didn't know I was expected to do such things while being initiated into the cult. It's been many years since I left Scientology, it wasn't easy. They don't care for break-ups. I was high up in their hierarchy, and they made it very difficult for me to leave. They kept hold of me through my possessions, but I never wavered. So I left them with all I had and started fresh. For a long while I wanted to hear nothing about religion, souls, our past. I was in Leoben, happily working as a graphic designer and producer of short promotional films. Until the Hungarian businessman, the head of the acquiring company, came along and introduced me to the Twin Cult. I laughed at first. But every month he stopped by for an inspection, wanting to have lunch with me. Not with the director of our studio, with me. Like everybody else, I first believed he was gay, but it turned out I was wrong. He was a very intelligent fellow who kept telling me about this cult, and somehow he got me hooked. He truly believed that we all have two souls, apart from twins, who, as the fruit of error, are obliged to divide two souls between two people, which leaves them with only one soul. The sect encouraged its members to help each other out – financially, they were just what I needed. The timing was perfect, because I was pretty much broke at that point. I had no idea that all who were newly initiated into the sect were required to kill a twin.'

'And instead of killing me, you and I both ran.'

'Yes, but we didn't get very far. Lake Balaton, the swamp, remember? You were so fragile, having been locked up for such a long time, that you staggered more than walked.'

'I was sure that they were going to kill us both. No, they just drugged us and left us lying on the lake shore.'

'I never understood why they did that.'

'Adam, show it to me, show me the symbol that Farkas was talking about.'

'I don't have it.'

'I don't believe you. Show me!'

Bely stands up and takes off his shirt. Rosa touches him, her cold metal fingertips slowly feeling through his hairy chest.

Rosa presses against Bely's chest.

'You were right, there's nothing there. I don't get it, Adam.'

'Nor do I, Rosa, but this seems to be one of those things we have to believe in blindly.'

'What about us, Adam, do you believe in us?' asks Rosa.

'Rosa, I ...'

'Adam, don't say a word. You don't have to say anything. I know you don't love me. But if you can't love me as a human, then love me as the machine that I am.'

# Marx

Bely looks at the time: seven thirty. The exhibition opening at the new Marx city gallery had started at seven, so the speeches must have ended by now. The guests raid the snack-laden tables,; they scout about the new rooms. He should have been there long ago. If he doesn't catch Pavel Don Kovač, the director of the European Capital of Culture, a catastrophe is all but inevitable. Rosa's left cheek and her curls plunge across Bely's nude torso. The metal weight of her right hand rests below his navel on the buckle of his belt. No, nothing has happened, nothing will happen, nothing can happen. We recognize emotions that find their echo, and we know emotions that draw you deep into their precipitous pit. Rosa's breathing, the aroma of liquor, her strong yet miniscule body, an animal at rest, cloaked by exhaustion, by powerless resignation to evil dreams. At half-mast her quivering eyelids hint at the cruelty of her dreams.

Gently, Bely rolls from under her body and covers her up. He puts on his shirt. He pulls her silver compact from a pocket in her coat and drops it in his black briefcase. The squeak of the door handle, but Rosa doesn't so much as stir. In front of Hotel Eagle stands a group dressed as gypsies. Cigarette smoke, the pungent scent of pot, a few others who pass by. Drink stalls in Castle Square play Oberkrainer music. Occasional drunken shrieks, three couples standing around an accordion player. Teased bright hair, high-heeled boots sinking in the snow, intoxicating perfume cloud, dismal companions who see adversaries in all who pass by. It is the Friday before Shrove Tuesday. On the bridge, doughnuts are sold at half price. The smell of old oil drifts through the air. Inebriated laughter. Three young men on bicycles meander across the bridge. Behind them clatter a few bouncing cans tied to a length of string. The Festival of Lent. The echo of bell-strung traditional Kurent costumes paddling up the river. Flickering street lamps, slight rise in temperature, suddenly winter seems to be on its way out.

A desolate construction site leads up to the gallery. Wistful, snowbound excavators rest their rusty buckets on the ground. A narrow flame-lit white path. Poster panels for the European Capital of Culture, brick pallets and piles of sand behind them. Distant wasp-like buzzing. Lights, a spacious terrace, a view of the river and the illuminated city, people chatting and smoking away. At the last moment Bely gives way to a man who walks straight at him. Behind him is Pavel Don Kovač, who whispers something into his ear. The man shrugs his shoulders.

'We'll see,' is all that Bely overhears. He recognizes the man as Voda, the mayor of Maribor, who is just leaving the exhibition opening ceremony accompanied by a pair of bodyguards.

'Don?'

'Hey, Bely, long time no see. What've you been up to? Great to see you here. Isn't it lovely, this new gallery of ours? Too bad that the original plan to build a theatre next to it fell through. Well, it's not a catastrophe, although you might disagree.'

'You planned a new theatre?' asks Bely.

'Yes. Didn't you know? A theatre and some other stuff. You know how things are in our capital – on paper everything is plausible.'

'Living, yes,' says Bely.

'So instead of a five-star hotel you end up with an agrotourism farm. Who cares, so long as we've got a roof over our heads, right? What a victorious day this is: we've successfully launched our ECoC, opened the gallery … Bely, we're untouchable. Great to have you here. Let's drink to that.'

Pavel Don Kovač and Bely raise their glasses of champagne. Bely takes a sip; Kovač drains his glass.

'Is Andreas here?' asks Bely. 'As far as I know, the gallery is his baby after all.'

'It would be a miracle if he showed up in the city again. I know that you two had a rough break-up and probably haven't been on good terms, but no one deserves to be treated the way this city has treated him, especially not a director who's made a name for himself abroad, which none of these back-stabbing hypocrites can claim for themselves. Nasty, I tell you, really nasty! They were so stupid and shameless that they never even considered changing the name of his centre, which he named after Karl, of course. Just imagine, a city of clericalists across the river who'll be forced to look at Marx night and day. But, let's give Andreas a break now. Look, there's more champagne over here …'

Kovač takes another glass, drinks it down and wheezes with relief.

'I'm starving. I haven't had anything to eat today. Come on, let's grab something at the buffet ... Aaah, good evening, how do you do?' Kovač smiles, shaking hands. People tap him on his shoulder, short phrases of courtesy.

'Bely, you've met our Terminal 12 programme head – this may pique your interest, at least the international theatre programme side of it. Aleš Šteger, meet Adam Bely.'

Abrupt hand shake. Šteger pulls Kovač to the side and says something in his ear. Kovač's face grows dark.

'Fucking hell. Tell them to shove it up their scarlet back-ends, I'll give 'em their opera!' yells Kovač.

A couple of people turn around; Kovač forces a smile and raises his glass to salute them.

'Move, move, get this over and done with, go!'

Anxious, Šteger leaves without saying goodbye. Kovač puts on a wide smile again, embraces Bely, takes another glass of champagne from a platter and knocks it back.

'Adam, my friend, this is like having two premières every day of the year. Do you know what this means, 365 days? It's not just my nerves and soul, I'll sacrifice everything for my country.'

'Everything?' smiles Bely.

'Including my liver, if necessary,' grins Kovač. 'Do you know Šteger? He's our Minister of Foreign Affairs. He's a little social butterfly, loves to hang out with foreign diplomats and cultural people, but to what effect? None, nothing, zero, zilch! You know how it is. Everybody screams teamwork, teamwork, but in the end you're always alone when cleaning up their mess. How about you, where have you been all these years? You should stop by some time; we could do another project together, like in the good old days. Ah, those were the days. How long have you been in the city? By the way, have you been to Off?'

Bely looks ahead and shrugs his shoulders.

'You haven't heard? *Mon dieu*, Adam, Dorfler went mad. Not too big a loss. The guy's a cheat, there're no words to explain how he screwed me over the last few years. But still. His sister Evelyn, you know her, she called, all hysterical. My kids are babysitting her skunks as we speak. She was completely crushed. And the skunks, you won't believe how sensitive they are, they immediately felt that something was wrong, and now there's no way to get them under control.'

'And Dorfler?

'That's the thing, nobody knows what happened. The guy never seemed unstable; rather, the contrary. There's been a rumour that the mayor had his hand in it. Dorfler was in charge of a team that organized protests and tried to destabilize the mayor's position, mostly because of his plan to build this wastewater treatment plant. Dorfler was a dark-horse candidate for mayor. If you ask me, he couldn't have gone insane for no reason. I bet it was drugs. I've heard that he's lost every last marble. They found him all bloody and with a cut-up tongue. Adam, rumour has it that he was on all fours, licking the metal threshold in front of Off. Horrible! I wouldn't wish something that grotesque on my worst enemy.'

Kovač stops the waiter. He takes two shot glasses of Williams-pear schnapps off the platter and consolidates their content into a long drink. He blushes slightly and takes on a more melancholic expression.

'Well, whatever. Today is the day. Today we celebrate. The exhibition is beautiful. We've got a new gallery, and the mayor has a big venue for diplomatic events. Did you see how pleased he was? Were you here for his opening speech?'

'What else do you have planned other than the gallery?' asks Bely.

'Weddings and other receptions,' says Kovač. 'Just wait until you see the upper room! *Exceptionnel*! Between the two of us, I find the mayor's private elevator that links the underground garage with his office unnecessary. His office measures three hundred and fifty square metres, it's got two bedrooms, a bathroom with a Jacuzzi and a view of the Drava River, but let's not get bogged down in the details. I'm content. All I care about is that we have a venue for our extensive programme. Maribor is the capital of Europe, and we have hordes of foreigners who swarm to our city not only to see its beauty but also to come away with a memorable experience. Just imagine if we had no space to showcase all the highlights of our programme – *une catastrophe*.'

A young lady, who has been waiting for the right moment to approach them, says hi. Accompanied by a pair of elderly ladies, fashionable eyewear, silky shawls, the young lady addresses Kovač.

'Mister Director, may I ask you, the ladies are from the European Union delegation, we've encountered some difficulties with their accommodation. They're staying at a four-star hotel with no swimming-pool …'

'Adam, I must run, I'll be seeing you around, OK?' says Kovač, visibly tired, pushing up a laborious smile for the ladies.

A waiter supplies Kovač with drinks, champagne and Williams-pear schnapps. They make a toast.

Bely walks to the banquetting table. Baskets brimming with bread, decorative fruit on tablecloths fill the gaps between the platters, the occasional slice of salami. Behind a big door an exhibition entitled *The Antique Aqueduct from Maribor's Twin City of Malja*. Three enormous empty-looking showrooms, a few photographs, panels. Vitrines, displaying copies of shovels and tools from two thousand years ago, which were used on a kilometre-long conduit channel that supplied a village on a Croatian Island with water. Slogans on the wall announce that Maribor is a twin city of Malja and that the exhibition was the fruit of a personal friendship between the two mayors. At the back, a Styrofoam mock-up of a tunnel segment. In it, children at play. A breathless guard with a corpulent belly runs towards them, shouting, 'Get lost. No destroying of culture here, even if it's Croatian!'

Bely steps back on to the terrace. The crowds gradually disperse. The magical sight of the city across the river appears to float almost within his reach. The breaking light from under the street-lights, the snow-lit darkness, give birth to a new city, a stage illusion, a city behind a city. The Maribor before him is the lead actor in a piece that has yet to be written by its participants, their fantasies, fears, reactions to things that don't exist. Or to things that exist as mere consequence, never as a script written in advance, a plan or reality. Does Bely have a plan? Is he also just a reaction without a plan? Can a plan be plausible, in a situation where all the variables are subject to constant change? And is it not the destination that is equally, if not incomparably more indefinable than the journey itself? It's snowing again. Small, firm, Styrofoam-like snowflakes crumble into the dusk-clothed river beneath the terrace.

Every crime contains its fatal error. One of the souls must have escaped the destruction of Xenu. It must have evaded the soul-memory deletion that ensued, following their mass-destruction on Earth. After millions of years, somehow, in an unknown form, the information found its way to Bely, to the constellation of the here and now. Maribor 2012. Imagine a snowflake that drowns before Bely's eyes. Imagine this snowflake surviving the plunge, the torrential river currents, the melting of other snowflakes, meandering water, emerging unharmed after millions of years. Where has it been before it emerged here, today? What keeps it alive? What makes it different from other souls that were subject to mutilation, deletion? Was Xenu's plan flawed? Were the souls equipped with a secret self-preserving programme, which has only been activated now?

'Adam, is that really you?'

Adam recognizes the voice. It is a voice from the past that never passes. Its echo runs through his veins like the sparkling of some distant fire. Ostensibly long extinguished, it flares again, the all-embracing fire, instantly burning down the time between now and then. Sixteen years burn before the flakes can hit the water, glimmering with the flame of lights from across the riverbed.

Suddenly, here she stands, as if she has stepped out of fire, in a crimson dress and silk pitch-black shawl. Anastasia Green. Sparkling eyes, skin visibly made-up, a short almost masculine hairstyle like that of a roguish little boy.

'This city of yours looks magnificent from a distance,' says Bely.

'Did you forget, Adam, this is your city, too,' replies Anastasia.

'I didn't forget anything. But I'm no longer that Adam you're talking about.'

Anastasia looks deep into Adam's eyes. Silence. Then she turns back to the city before them.

'I see no difference between the two of you,' says Anastasia. 'I guess I'm wrong. I could be wrong,' she adds. Lightly, like a cloud of warm breath, her words paddle over to Bely and he smiles. Her breath now swells into an embowering white cloud.

'Have you been in the city long?'

'A few days.'

'How long are you staying?'

'Depends.'

'On what?'

'Business.'

'Since when have you been back in business here in Maribor, Adam?'

'I'm here with some Austrian journalist doing a piece on Maribor.'

'Where is she? Is she here?'

'She stayed at the hotel. Not feeling her best tonight.'

'Is she your girlfriend?'

'Yes, my girl. Why do you ask?'

'I thought that you were committed only to religion not to flesh. Aren't you the head of that Scientology club of yours? I read it in the news …'

'Anastasia, Scientologists are not like Catholic priests. They can marry without restriction.'

'I know, I know, I remember those debates. They are advised to marry fellow Scientologists. Especially if they're ambitious and want to climb up the ladder. And you've always been ambitious, haven't you?'

'What are you trying to say?'

'Well, our last break-up was, how should I put it, pretty turbulent. You claimed that you'd found the big secret of your life and that you became clear or something to that effect. I imagine that must have felt like a divine revelation. Or even an ascension? Then I turn around and find that you've packed and left the city. Nice to see you again before this life is over, Adam.'

Bely's lips remain sealed. He watches the snowflakes sink into the precipitous humming dusk beneath them.

'I left Scientology.'

'Did you?'

'Yes. I steered clear of them years ago.'

'How come, Adam? I thought that was your life, I thought that your being clear was more than you could ever ask for.'

'I wouldn't put it that way.'

'It sure meant more to you than I did, than we did, Adam. You were the deputy head of Scientologists in the Styria region you were their élite. You'd made the inner circle, or whatever you call it. All that so you could leave?'

'All that so I could leave.'

'But why, for God's sake?'

Bely takes a sip of warm champagne. River. White city. Its reflection undulates in the river like flame.

Snowflakes strike the geometry of the water.

'I fell ill,' says Bely gently. 'Which should never have happened since I was clear. It should be impossible to get ill if you're clear. Which means you're either not clear or there's something very off about this Scientology doctrine.'

'You were sick?'

'Cancer, chemotherapy. I made it with the help of fasting. I starved it to death. But I never returned to Scientology. They did write for a while, sent other esteemed members. Then they called in the middle of the night, they even threatened to sue. Gradually it all quietened down. But as we parted, they made me pay for ten years' worth of training, with interest, too, so I went bankrupt. Fortunately I owned an apartment, which I was able to sell.'

'And now you live with this journalist of yours?'

'Anastasia ...'

'Why don't you bring her to the theatre this Tuesday? For the grand Slovenian première of Andreas's adaptation of Tolstoy's *War and Peace*.

I saw the play at the première in Zagreb, and it's absolutely wonderful. Our good old Andreas is obviously at the peak of his career. Then you have these knuckleheads who chase him out of the city. Have you heard about that? This is the second time that they've dragged him through the mud, driven him out of his city, and they were awfully smug about it, too. Rats. It was pretty awful. The media pursued him so relentlessly that even his mother doesn't feel like leaving the house. If not today, I wonder if he's going to at least make an appearance at the première. It's hard to believe that none of the speakers even mentioned his name when everybody knows that without his efforts the gallery would never have been built. It's even named after Marx, his favourite actor from the Maribor period.'

'I see you're still a fan.'

'Look, we're all professionals here, and I truly appreciate all that he's achieved in terms of theatre. In contrast to those who did nothing but disparage and slander him, which may very well be the biggest achievement of their lives.'

'Fascinating that, in spite of it all, you're still loyal to him,' says Bely, smiling.

'Talking about loyalty, Adam, who are you loyal to now that you're not into Scientology any longer? At least to yourself, I hope?'

Bely forces a smile.

'Listen, Adam, I'll put aside two tickets for you and your Austrian friend for Tuesday evening. Come and pick them up at the theatre on Tuesday at three in the afternoon, OK? If you don't show up I'll give them to someone else. There're plenty of people out there who are willing to kill for these tickets because of Andreas's scandalous departure. It's late, I really should go now. It's going to be a rough weekend. Tomorrow we're hosting a show from Croatia.'

Anastasia brushes her lips softly against Bely's cheek. For a brief moment, Bely can taste the warmth of her body. He watches her leave. Her shadow, a fire amid white snowfall. Before him an abyss, agape and roaring. Snowflakes, devoured by night without exception. A view of a dormant city nocturne. Suddenly, well before the dawn, the street lights go out, probably an error or an economy. The water beneath him hums. The flames turn to ashes rippling in the darkness.

The gallery is nearly empty. Drained glasses are cleared off the tables. Bely puts his glass down and heads for the exit, when he hears a call. He looks back. Pavel Don Kovač and his crowd wave at him from behind a column. Bely joins them. As usual when drunk, Kovač starts singing, launching into 'Non, je ne regrette rien', and everyone around him feels compelled to listen.

'Adam, you're a real citizen of Maribor. We, Maribor folk, always overstay our welcome. Before we go, let's sing to brighten the night,' mumbles Kovač before he hums the next chorus.

Kovač goes silent. He staggers violently.

'I know another one.'

*In einer Kaserne vor dem ...*

At that moment a waiter walks by with a tray and a half-empty champagne bottle at its centre. Kovač stops singing and dashes for the bottle.

'We're not pouring away good taxpayers' money, are we?' grins Kovač and tops up everybody's glasses.

'Ah, how we used to sing back then. Today everybody's embarrassed to sing. The human voice is one of the most sacred things, not something we should be ashamed of. What's the world coming to? We're ashamed of what we have, and we crave everything we lack. A metaphysics of madness. Craptastic!'

*Nede mi več rasla,*
*Travica zelena,*
*Ge se mi je šetala,*
*Lubica liblena.*

Kovač fills up everybody's glasses, they toast and drink up. He upends the champagne bottle into his glass and tilts it.

*Ochi chornyye ...*

'It's the swine that's black in Maribor, not the eyes,' says a man standing next to Kovač.

Everybody explodes into laughter, except for Adam Bely, who is the only one who fails to understand the joke.

'I met him today in Castle Square. They were out on a walk, Maister and, a few metres before him, his black pig on a lead,' adds the man.

'How about that! This guy is a true mascot. I think he deserves to be immortalized, perhaps as a stuffed-animal souvenir for the European Capital of Culture? Or maybe as a postcard with the inscription *DAS IST MARIBOR*,' says somebody else.

'You're laughing, but I think that Maister is an artist with a sociopolitical agenda, who holds a mirror up to this city,' says Kovač. 'First off, Maister is a top attorney with top rates. Obviously he must've been at the top of his game during privatization, intelligent and resourceful as he is, otherwise he wouldn't own so many apartments in the old city centre. That's a fact.'

Quaking with enthusiasm, Kovač takes a deep breath. Everybody stares at him in anticipation, but there's no sequel to his thoughts. As if rerailing his lost train of thought, Kovač's eyes roam the room in a search of another bottle.

'I concur, Maister is a top attorney,' says the man who first initiated the debate. 'He got me acquitted on two charges, even though they were both hopeless. Still that doesn't erase the fact that he's a terrible stock farmer. Actually, I'd really like to know what he thinks about populating his sophisticated *fin-de-siècle* apartments with young pigs instead of people.'

'I know where he's coming from,' says an elderly lady with a brooch over her rather exaggerated cleavage. 'Do you even know the type of people who occupy such old *fin-de-siècle* apartments in the centre of the city? Most of the time they're the sort of people who transform one room into three caves. They lower ceilings, smash mouldings, burn old furniture, install plastic windows and doors; they put laminate flooring over parquet, convinced that they've finally succeeded in transforming the last leftovers of the bourgeois culture into something modern. All they aspire to is a socialist apartment. That's their level. Just look at how wrecked and dilapidated the courtyards in the old city centre are. I live on Jewish Street. Our courtyard was once a well-groomed flower garden, but today the downstairs neighbour uses it for storing gutters. How did he come by all those gutters? They're stolen, everybody knows it, but what am I supposed to do? The thudding of the rain against them forced me to move my bedroom to the other side of the apartment, in spite of my deteriorating hearing. And the pile just keeps on growing. It's now reached my flower troughs on the second floor, and it's only a matter of time before it breaks through my windows. Sometimes you see homeless people there, grilling road-kill kebabs, cats or rats, I don't know. One time I called the police only to be told that "guinea pigs are a common food in Peru" and that I should "take it easy". They also told me that "fighting hunger wasn't illegal" and that I should "be ashamed of not having the solidarity gene". Solidarity gene! Outrageous! Unheard-of!'

'I'm telling you, not only is Maister a top attorney and one of the wealthiest people in Maribor, he's also a true artist,' says Kovač. 'Who else would fill up every one of their apartments with pigs rather than people? And who else would defend himself against neighbours' complaints on the account of noise and stench caused by the pigs, by using notarized leases, in which illiterate pigs act as his legal contractual partners, complete with first and last names? I tell you, his work is the greatest performance-art piece in the history of this city!'

'I don't know about this performance of yours. The fact is that in the end he was forced to move his pigs out of the apartments,' retorts the lady with the oversized brooch, which tips over, holding on for dear life to her sweater, the pin inside out.

'Says who? He had some sanitary inspectors over, but they were pretty well handcuffed. The guy was so up-to-speed with all the loopholes in the law that he could easily be smuggling truck-loads of pork through those apartments and nobody would notice. Meanwhile, the pigs squealed, gnawed at the old wallpaper, scraped their hooves against the parquet. Eventually the apartments looked like pigsties with elegant ceilings. But then, one by one, the pigs started to disappear. My guess is that the neighbours got organized, or they hired someone, because the break-ins came one after another until Maister was left with one single swine.'

'Which no one had the guts to touch,' adds the lady, while readjusting her gigantic brooch, mildly smudged lipstick, sweaty furrows on her forehead.

'Because it's black,' shouts the man.

'And because, apparently, it chirps. Imagine, a black swine that chirps. Unbelievable,' says the woman. The brooch keeps on tipping over, so she decides to hold it up with one hand.

'The art establishment may theorize, put up installations, invent concepts and other crap that they call avant-garde, but it's all for nothing. It's Maister who is avant-garde. Walking with his black swine, Maria, around the city, that's what I call pure art. The sight of Maister and Maria fulfils all the postulates of the art experience, according to Ingarden,' adds Kovač, his lips billowing, as if laden with the shifting weight of his imbalanced frame. 'I've heard rumours that his black swine can fly at night. I don't buy that, but I do believe that black pigs excrete faeces as black as coal. They say it's so black that you wouldn't be able to tell whether there're black flies sitting on it. Their shit is supposed to be toxic, that's normal. I've heard that someone accidentally stepped into it and the sole of his shoe instantly melted away.'

'It's a good thing that the poor guy pulled the scorched sole of his shoe out of the boiling shit in time or he might have lost his foot,' somebody else chips in.

'They say he pulled it out in time all right. He kept his leg, but instead of a foot he's got a hoof now,' says another one.

Laughter all around.

'Bullshit! It's true, though, that people are scared of that black swine. They also fear Maister twice as much now that he's got the pig. Who knows why?' says the lady who unravels her finely knit sweater by pulling on the brooch.

*C'est payé …*

Kovač bumps his leg against a bottle, knocking it over so the champagne spills across the gallery floor.

'We seem to be pouring out the good taxpayers' money despite our best efforts,' says Kovač, watching the bottle as it empties into a puddle in front his shoes. 'Ah, how we used to sing back then! Bely, do you remember? Today everybody's embarrassed to sing. There's nothing more sacred than the human voice. You hear me? Nothing! Everybody should sing. Even if they chirp like Maister's swine. We live in times where not even swine are allowed to chirp any more. Awful! We're ashamed of everything we have. Why on earth should we be given more?' Kovač shrieks with rage, suddenly heading for the exit. 'It's on us to take what's rightfully ours. We have to stand up for ourselves. No one else will do it for us, remember that!' shouts Kovač from the doorway. 'We're on our own, left to our own devices.'

Bely catches up with him in front of the gallery.

'What a shitty city, Adam. So the guy doesn't have a white cackling dog for a pet, but a black chirping swine. And already people want to nail him to the wall. Can you imagine? Jesus Christ!'

Kovač waddles into the snow and urinates. He aims to extinguish a torch that burns on the ground but misses, carving a yellow depression into the snow around the torch.

'Come, Bely, let's go and grab another drink and then hit the sack. Tomorrow we celebrate culture. If only it would stop snowing! I'm sick of it already.'

'Same here,' adds Bely quietly and watches Kovač as he masterfully governs his evermore staggering steps.

'There is an upside to snow, however. It makes the city look much less messy than it really is. Although it made it really difficult for me to mount my spatial interventions. Look – there's my marker!' Kovač points at yet another huge balloon with the ECoC label and a pinwheel-like logo. 'They're driving me nuts, Bely, nuts. No, not the journalists or the artists. It's those scumbags at the Ministry of Culture and the town hall, not to mention the mayor. Every single morning he calls me before eight and screams at me, "Do you have any idea what you and your workers are doing?" Crazy! And if I don't follow through with every single order of his, then he has me audited. It's only mid-February, and I've already lost six weeks of work because of the bloody inspectors. *Merde!*'

'What does he want? To be part of the programme?'

'He's clueless about the programme. Every once in a while he wants something, like this exhibition on the antique aqueduct from Malja. You know, there's the twin connection between the cities. He goes to Malja every year for underwater fishing. But other than that, he's not at all interested in the programme.'

'What then?'

Kovač looks up to the sky and laughs boisterously. 'The balloons, Adam, the balloons!' He points at an enormous, slowly rotating pedestal mounted with an inflatable sphere. 'Do you know what a pain it is to relocate these balloons? There's electrical wiring under each pedestal that weighs several tons, then you need workers, cranes, permissions, road closures …'

'So?'

'He moves them almost every day.'

'But why, if they're visible from everywhere? Much too visible, if you ask me,' replies Bely.

'Because that's what his fortune-teller tells him to do.'

'A fortune-teller?'

'You don't know about the fortune-teller? You're really out of date, aren't you? She is Voda. She's the one who runs the politics of this town and decides where these balloons will stand. It's her damn tarot cards that dictate where we'll be moving the balloons, and it's a new location almost every single day. Other than renovating the roundabout, these balloons seem to be the only thing that holds the mayor's interest. I'm no manual labourer, Adam, moving his balloons all the time and checking why the fountain lighting is bust again. What's the point of having lighting in the middle of roundabouts anyway? Damn it, Adam, I'm the ECoC not the Maribor centre for road construction!' Kovač takes it out on an empty wheelie-bin, half covered in snow. Furious kicks, flying rubbish. Bely tries to intervene.

'Let me be, Adam, just let me be!' shouts Kovač. 'I'm no artist, not like my father who ran a symphony orchestra. I'm just a messed-up football player. Leave me alone.'

Bely remembers that Kovač used to be an amateur footballer. As soon as his club was eliminated from the regional league Kovač became a music producer, which later opened the door to his leadership of the ECoC.

'Come, let's move on.'

'Move on? Adam, you don't get it. In this city there's no such thing as moving on. We can only go down or stay where we are.'

'Let's move down then, somewhere warm. It's freezing here by the river,' says Bely.

Kovač and Bely cross the bridge and take a narrow street down to the river. Closed restaurants, a few windows lit up. Behind a restaurant window a woman sweeps the floor. A pit bull melancholically observes the broom as it dances across the floor.

'Last year', says Kovač, 'we announced a thematic contest on the Drava River. The winner was some young Dutch guy. He exhibited twenty-four thousand glasses that were filled with water from the river, all over the city. An interesting, original project. Not something people here are receptive to. For one week the city turned into a mountain of glassware. And then another artist from Maribor meddled. You know Šava, don't you?' Bely shakes his head. 'It doesn't matter. Anyway, Šava is supposed to be one of the leading Maribor artists, but because he didn't make the selection, he decided to do his performance art right here *in* the river. It was August, and it was hot, and he sat in the Drava River waist deep. Over the course of two hours he drank twenty-four bottles of beer in protest at Dutch artists stealing bread from out of the mouths of Maribor artists. Can you imagine? In only two hours the guy drank twelve litres, which of course he whizzed out into the river. He whizzed in the river, drank all the beer and then wandered around the city, completely wasted, shouting, "Maribor, art and manure. Kovač, a scoundrel and a pawn. This is my job, this is culture, this is Europe and we're the capital of all this shit."'

Kovač and Bely walk through an ancient door. A single graveyard candle flickers from amid snow-capped car parts strewn across a dark courtyard. Kovač draws back a carpet. Beneath the carpet is a cellar door.

'Bely, let's have one more glass, we'll sleep better. It'll be a long day tomorrow, I'm scheduled to move the markers again, and we're expecting Andreas and his team to arrive. Then we're doing the installation of a human fish with legs frozen in a block of bloody water in front of the theatre. On top of that, I'm being audited again, fucking hell.'

'What human fish?' asks Bely as he follows Kovač tentatively down the gloomy flight of stairs.

'It's these artists. They had an idea to freeze a blown-up version of a human fish in a cube of water adulterated by a few litres of blood. Their own blood, of course, which took a couple of months to collect. They'll set it up tomorrow and wait for the thaw to set in, which will let the fishy go free. More art bullshit.'

Cellar thick with smoke. Brick vaults hang low above their heads. Wall niches and candles, tables and benches.

'*Bienvenue!* This is my paradise,' says Kovač. Bring us a bottle of red.

Bely watches the waitress as she disappears into the thick of the smoke, as if swallowed by fog. Kovač hums quietly under his breath and flicks through his phone.

*Nede mi več rasla,*
*Rien de rien ...*

'This is about the only place where I feel safe, Adam. Five metres under, the river above us, no phone signal, and no one pestering us. This is what I call paradise. Oh, look who's over there!'

Kovač nods to a scraggy old man who sits alone by an empty table.

'See? Another grand blood artist. This guy is a city legend. He was featured in yesterday's newspaper. For forty years he's been donating blood at least once a month. Forty years, can you imagine? That's a Slovenian record. Allegedly his ancestors were all surgeons who were interested in breeding leeches. He says that it's his mission to donate blood, that every month he donates blood for Maribor and will continue to do so until the day he dies. He says that as long as there are people like him the city's got nothing to worry about. And what does he get in return? Nothing. A Kranj sausage for every litre of blood, calories to recuperate. Can you imagine? That's ten litres of blood a year, times forty, four hundred litres of blood for Maribor. Not bad, right? With four hundred litres you could fill up a child's swimming pool. I guess we all help to the best of our ability. Some give our souls, some blood. Just look at him. All skin and bone, but still his blood flows like butter. I forgot his blood type. If you ask him how he's doing, he'll say *"Blut und Boden"*. He says *"Blut und Boden"* no matter what you ask. People from outside Maribor may find that confusing, but we know he means blood and Maribor.'

The waitress unveils the curtain of cigarette smoke. A bottle of red wine. Glassy red, burning eyes. Incomprehensible muttering from the neighbouring tables. Bely and Kovač make a toast. Kovač apologizes and vanishes. Bely studies the catacombs. The blood donor at the neighbouring table sits motionless, leaning on a cane. Bely takes a sip of wine, strives to catch some oxygen. Burning eyes. Muttering. Light vertigo, eyelids heavy.

Bely looks up again. The old man is gone. Odd, where could he have gone? As if he's vanished into thin air, Bely thinks to himself, swirling a cork in the palm of his hand. A few drops of wine ooze through the bloody pores of the cork and stain Bely's trousers. The red of the wine undulates through immaculately clean glasses. No air, a mild vertigo. Incomprehensible voices pierce from beyond the cellar vaults. The bricks move with softness and elasticity, as if the earth behind them has sprung to life. The red, sticky liquid spills over the rims of both glasses, creeps across the table. It claims the bricks, painting the grout red. Strange, thinks Bely. No one seems to notice the red puddle crawling across the floor. It's ankle-high, thick and warm, viscous like blood. Bely dips in his hand and licks his fingers. Tastes of blood. The slimy, thick liquid overflows the cellar, drowns tables, drowns people. Strange, thinks Bely, I can breathe, and I'm submerged. I can breathe with more ease than before. Cane, slowly gliding on the red surface. Past the cane floats the waitress. Her bloody hair. Behind the waitress comes a giant human fish. Its strong eely swing pushes the brick vaults until they split open, revealing a pile of bones. The human fish swims past Bely through the sinking thicket of glasses and bottles, then to the table, its blind inquisitive eyes staring at him. Now numerous tiny octopi propel themselves through the blood, their sucking legs everywhere. Bely calls out to them, but instead of words only bubbles of air come out of his mouth. He swings his arms and follows an octopus to the bar. He's disgusted. The blood is warm and sticky. Through the murky red blood Bely notices Rosa Portero at the bar with her Hungarian man. He swims closer. Rosa raises her brow at seeing him, while the Hungarian kisses her neck. She shuts her brown eye, tilts her head back and moans with pleasure. Her green eye continues to stare. The man's hand slides down to her crotch. He touches her. Bely tries to get closer, but a riptide of blood defies his every stroke. Again he tries to call out to Rosa, but only voiceless bubbles of air surge to the surface. The Hungarian takes Rosa into his arms, and together they swim to the toilets. Bely conquers the rip current and dashes after them. Sucked into a whirlpool, he grabs hold of a metal pole to keep his bearing. Afloat beneath the ceiling, he watches Rosa as her metal hand clasps the toilet flush handle to resist the Hungarian's violent thrusting from behind. To oppose the blood current, the Hungarian pulls on Rosa's lush hair and continues to thrust. Deep and hard. Rosa groans with pleasurable pain. The Hungarian's grip intensifies, Rosa screams as he stabs his fingernail deep into the flesh behind her right ear. More blood. Their bodies come to a halt. They're gasping while being lightly tossed about by the whirlpool. Bely notices that, like Rosa's hand, the Hungarian's cock is made of metal. They form an engine that is taken apart and put back together as they fuck. One engine made of flesh and metal.

'Adam, Adam, you fell asleep.' Kovač shakes Bely. 'I'm sorry, I got held up,' says Kovač. 'You drifted away while I was in the other room with the mayor of Malja and our municipal councillors. Come on, let's drink up and go.'

A narrow flight of stairs. With each step closer to the surface Bely breathes more easily. The streets are shrouded in darkness and snow, red crosses hardly noticeable against the black of the posters.

'Back to culture tomorrow. To hell with it. I've had it. Where are you staying, Adam? I'll crash at my office. It's warm, and I'll wake up ready for my first morning appointment with the cultural workers of Maribor. Do you know what the definition of a Maribor cultural worker is?'

Bely walks silently. He shakes his head, still submerged in images from his dream.

'First, he talks a lot. Second, he does a whole lot of nothing. Third, all that he creates is genius. Fourth, he's saddened and hurt because his genius goes unrecognized. Fifth, he protests because his unrecognized genius goes unrewarded. Sixth, he lives with his mother, he's an alcoholic and he sometimes screws his best friend's wife. And seventh, he's validated only when those who put him down and whom he despises do better than he does. Pretty good, isn't it? My own definition.'

'Don, do you believe in absolution?' asks Bely, as he tries to clear his throat.

'Jesus, what sort of question is that? What do you mean?'

'Do you think it's possible for people to truly absolve others for something that hurt them?'

'Of course not! Absolution is nothing but a fairy-tale for bad Catholics, Adam. You find me one person in this entire city who's truly and wholeheartedly willing to absolve others, and I'll call you a hero. It's more the other way around. People live off of hard feelings. People feed off resentment, not Kranj sausage or art. That's what we do best.

We all specialize in how to make an insurmountable mountain out of a molehill. Absolution? Don't be silly, Adam.'

'Don, what's the Great Orc?'

Kovač grinds to a halt and looks at Bely. His face grows solemn. 'Adam, where did you get that from? Don't you ever bring that up again, do you hear me, not with me, not with anybody else. It'll cost you your head. Here we are. This is the Vetrinj Mansion, and this is where my warm office is. It's time. Do you have a cigarette by any chance? I've been without since this morning …'

Bely looks at Pavel Don Kovač. Is this really the person with whom he played football as a child and later worked with on their first theatrical projects? Is he really that same enthusiast, the top music producer in the city, who continues to whistle chansons despite the variety of jobs he's taken on, despite the many political alliances?

Bely pulls the compact out of his jacket. 'Here's something for the road, Don.'

'What's that, Bely, a drug for schoolgirls?'

Bely draws a box of pills from the other pocket, shakes a few out into his hand and swallows.

'A fistful of crazy pills for me, and one gentle pill for you. Don't worry, with this you'll wake up a new man tomorrow,' says Bely.

Kovač looks at the white cracker in his hand. Light dusting of snow. Extinct city, grave-silent. Only a faint glimmer of street-lights and neon signs. Barking dog somewhere in the distance, a chirp, perhaps that of the pig.

'Why not? The night is still young, and so are we,' says Kovač and swallows the cracker. 'Sleep well, Adam.'

'Good night, my friend,' replies Bely and watches his friend's silhouette as it crosses the square and vanishes through the door of the Vetrinj Mansion, the headquarters of the European Capital of Culture.

# Death Comes from Pohorje

Bely browses the city newspaper's website during breakfast. Nothing, nothing at all has changed. He hadn't been in the city in sixteen years, but he couldn't shake the feeling that he already knew all the news. Like the repertoire of some provincial theatre with largely predictable, only slightly varying dramatic plots, just performed by a new cast. But three articles grab his attention. The first one an account of a long-married retired couple who were acquitted by the Court of the Third Instance, the highest of the courts, after having been convicted of tax evasion while trafficking in waste candle tallow, which they scraped off of graves and sold on to chandlers. The two pensioners are now suing the state for severe emotional distress for a sum equalling 2,666 average Slovenian pensions. The second article is a horticultural ode to the city's tidiness during the Nazi occupation, especially in the period before and during Hitler's visit to the city in April 1941. Maribor holds the dubious distinction of having been the southernmost point in the Third Reich. The fact that the Führer held a public speech here is something of which the citizens of Maribor, according to the writer, are still openly proud of, at least from the horticultural perspective. Prior to the Führer's arrival, the city was planted with hundreds of thousands of tea roses, pelargoniums, hortensias and even avenues'-worth of sycamore trees. An exuberance of flowers, which, during the later industrialized period, never bloomed again in such vast numbers, not even in honour of Marshall Tito, not for Yugoslavia. The city declined even further following the independence of Slovenia, when it became a dead zone, horticulturally speaking. With a heaped measure of nostalgia for the good old days, the writer concludes the article with a surprisingly daring thesis that draws on the philosophy of history: that human history is a continuous process of negative repetition, a circular regression, and not what the linear logic of technological advancement tries to impose on us. The third article in the crime section mentions two outbreaks of unusually aggressive psychosis that led to an intervention by the relevant authorities and mental-health professionals as well as the forcible commitment to the appropriate institution of the influential Maribor CEO Tine B. and the renowned professor and dean of the University of Maribor Ivan D. So far it has been impossible to determine whether there is a connection between the two cases. Both subjects were considered to be relatively stable personalities, and their psychotic breaks occurred almost simultaneously, which is why the possibility of a reaction to an undetermined illicit substance cannot be excluded. The investigation is still under way, concludes the article.

Half an hour later Bely exits the Hotel Eagle. Rosa exhales smoke and flicks her half-smoked cigarette into the snow. Absence of words. Dim light and the smell of petrol in a subterranean garage a few blocks away.

'To the cemetery?' Rosa asks dryly as they approach the garage exit.

Bely nods. Rosa heads east, towards the Maribor cemetery, then further south, towards the industrial zone.

Bely's thoughts keep returning to yesterday's dream. Could it have been brought on by exhaustion? Too much stale air in that cellar? Are dreams like a butterfly net that catches invisible images as they flutter around our collective consciousness? For all he knows that might have been a case of Rosa transferring her trauma to him through the medium of dreams. Why else would the cellar of a restaurant transform into the bar in Graz where Rosa first met the Hungarian a few months back? According to her, they had sex the very same night. The next day she woke tied up in a cellar. They incarcerated her there for weeks on end, prevented from communicating with the outside world. That dream has to be some form of communication, a message, not just a dream.

On the other side of the car windows flash giant shopping-mall signs, a road perforated with potholes, industrial suburbs. Rosa's gloved metal hand on the steering wheel. As if it were yesterday, Bely sees Rosa lying on the Balaton lake shore, tied to four stakes driven into the mud. He still feels sharp impressions of the knife handle in his palm, in the same place where Butcher bit into him. Silence, as the car comes to a halt. The chauffeur takes off his blindfold and leaves him in front of an unfamiliar villa by a lake. The door opens to a dim living-room. Crackling embers in the fireplace. Some twenty masked people, cloaked in black habits. Latin plainsong. Following the ceremony and allocution by the sect leader, they hand him a small wooden chest carved on its side with a two-headed human body; a long, sharp knife inside it. When he pulls out the blade, he's informed of his task for initiation into the Twin Cult. The deep, coarse voice of the cult leader, who speaks perfect Oxbridge English. The masked members of the cult surround him and escort him on to the terrace. A stone's throw from the terrace by the lake a fire crackles, a sacrificial offering beside it. He remembers the heat that flooded him beneath the weighty habit, heavy steps and the bound body of a woman trying to pull free, her eyes wide and frightened. The members of the sect on the terrace struck their staves rhythmically against a log. Cutting through the bonds, a strange feeling as he grabbed a hand made of metal instead of the soft hand of a woman. Running through the night. Reeds, tadpoles and frogs, silt, a lake-bed, mud clutching them by their feet. Barking dogs all around, hefty steps. Then shafts of light and drovers, shouting words in Hungarian and German. He remembers a dull blow to the back of his head and a slow dive through tepid darkness.

Why did they spare them? Why did the sect take such a risk? He was blindfolded during their ride back to the villa, but, considering the size of the lake, he could easily retrace their steps back to the place where it all happened. Bely remembers waking up, something warm and slimy dripping on his face. He opened his eyes to a snout, a large fleshy tongue that licked his face. A grazing cow, and the two of them, heavily drugged. He, who betrayed their trust, and she, an inferior and sinful creature bearing only one soul not two. The incomplete, that's what the sect called the twins who, by extracting only half of the human fate from the uterus, were destined to serve those complete with a pair of souls.

The Pobrežje cemetery lies on the outskirts of Maribor. By comparison with the city's population it is disproportionally large. From the front portal a long, paved, tree-lined lane leads to the main building, which houses a florist, a small shop, mortuaries and the cemetery's administrative office.

'Wagner. Wagner is like a cemetery. Only in Wagner do we find the *Gesamtkunstwerk*, an indivisible unity of all the arts. Everything from music, word and sculpture to theatre. Only in Wagner and in cemeteries. People are the best evidence of this. The cathartic experience of the Gesamtkunstwerk is one of the main reasons why they love to come here so often.'

Rosa Portero checks if her Dictaphone is working. Meanwhile, Magda Ornik, the director of the Maribor Funeral Parlour, readjusts her short skirt and smiles at Bely. Classical music in the background.

'*Lohengrin*! I choose the background music for the cemetery myself, based on the weather, the colour of the treetops and the proximity of holidays. If it's bothering you, I can ask them to turn it off.'

Bely shakes his head.

'If you need photos for the interview, I can email them or give you the link to my website,' says Magda Ornik.

'Thank you, but it's a radio interview,' says Bely.

'I know, I know, but sometimes even radio people like to have photos to put on the web. You know, in this digitalized world visual representations are more and more important. Which, of course, is wrong. We all know that true spirituality isn't material, but you can't stand in the way of technological development. You know, this was chosen as one of the most well-ordered cemeteries in the entire European Union. Not only because of the beautiful landscape architecture, flower arrangements and professionalism in client relations but, above all, because of our extensive array of advanced services. With us you can have a tiny, discreet video camera installed in the gravestone that allows you to see your family grave online any time you like. We call it "Final Home Surveillance". Of course, this presents a challenge for our gardeners, who must keep the graves perfectly maintained at all times. And, of course, the service comes at a price, but we believe it adds to our clients' peace of mind. Another innovative service is a device that plays back voice recordings of the deceased. We had to cut back on it, although, because there were too many complaints, especially during holidays and in the pet cemetery. It was awfully popular with dog owners, but the sound of barking was extremely disturbing to the cat owners whose darlings were buried right next to the dogs. You may say this is all just technological monkey tricks, but today's technology provides us with better and better ways to mark the spot where a person is buried. As long as there is a place where we, the survivors, can be assured that our loved ones are well taken care of, then we can come to terms with our loss. That's the paradox of loss, don't you think? We miss the deceased as long as they have a grave. If they don't have a grave then they, and their death, are forgotten.'

Magda Ornik takes a sip of her chamomile tea, pondering her words. 'Before I took up my position here, I never spent much time thinking about our ties with the dead. But now I understand better and better those people who choose our condensed cremation service so they can be even more closely united with the departed.'

'Condensed cremation?' asks Bely.

'You've never heard of it?' asks Magda Ornik, throwing Bely a seductive glance from beneath her long eyelashes. 'It's a special post-cremation procedure that compresses the ashes of the deceased into a small graphite stone. Most survivors typically have it made into a pendant for a necklace. Some have it set in a ring or might wear it as a brooch. Thus, in the form of an aesthetically pleasing decorative stone they can preserve the most direct, material bond with the deceased.'

'Are you saying that people wear their ancestors as jewellery?'

'That's right. Many women here in Maribor walk around with their parents or grandparents around their necks. More frequently they go for their parents in combination with their pets. Especially popular these days has been the so-called extended-family memento, where daughters-in-law have their deceased mothers-in-law made into a central stone, with other family members set in the space around it. We've got an in-house jeweller who's an expert in this sort of thing. Swarovski crystals for little girls; ancestors for us adults.'

Magda Ornik shifts in her seat, her legs stretched out. In the room, a fragrant floral arrangement of magnolia and dried meadow grasses; on the wall, photographs showing Ornik with the president of the country, the president of the European Union Commission, the prime minister, the mayor and a Maribor showbusiness celebrity.

'So that means the ancestors that people wear don't have graves? Do they have some other kind of marker?'

'They do; of course, they do, but it isn't their remains that are buried there, but the memory of them.'

Bely leans toward Rosa in order to translate Ornik's last response for her. As he does so he glimpses a long cut behind Rosa's left ear that momentarily appears then disappears beneath the collar of her sweater. He flinches. Ornik notices the change in his expression.

'Mr Bely, are you all right?' she asks.

'Yes, right, of course,' mutters Bely. 'Where were we? Right, the memory of our ancestors. Your cemetery is also special because a part of it lies above an anti-tank trench from the Second World War. One subterranean survey has indicated that this trench contains at least fifteen thousand individuals; other estimates say up to fifty thousand, most likely soldiers from former Yugoslavia. These were people who were covertly slaughtered by the Communists at the end of the war. In a way this cemetery lies on top of another cemetery of the nameless, the unidentified.'

'Look, Mr Bely, let's ask ourselves what memory is. Memory is only what's tangible. Objects are memory. Houses are memory. Tombstones are memory. What we carry within us are simply our desires, our frustrations. That's not memory, that's our psyche. When we remove a memorial plaque, the memory is gone. And if there was no memorial plaque, then there's nothing to remove. Why not let the dead be dead? Why poison the younger generation with questions about events that happened more than half a century ago?'

'What about the bones of the dead, are they also tangible?'

'Ashes to ashes, dust to dust, Mr Bely. What's the point in uncovering what was covered? Our society has always been divided by the question of the post-war massacres. Every politician, left or right, profits from these unresolved questions, from discovering new burial grounds that only give rise to new phantasms and hatred. If you ask me …'

Ornik leans forward and turns off the Dictaphone.

'Please, turn *off the record button*. If you ask me, all the cemeteries should be ploughed through every fifteen to twenty years. Then we would have peace. People remember because they regularly visit cemeteries. We should limit their visits or prohibit them altogether. You can look at it from two perspectives. First, our entire country is nothing but one big burial ground. We all know that whenever you start digging with a shovel you'll hit a grave or even a mass grave. The Romans, the Middle Ages, the Ottoman invasions, the First World War, the Second World War, the post-war massacres. Slovenia is at a crossroads. Everything comes together and mixes here, and every era provides its share of the dead. From this point of view the only difference between an ordinary field and our cemetery is the way people perceive it and whether the graves are marked or not. In our cemetery you always know that you're in a cemetery, walking between the graves. That said, we forget that we also sow graves with wheat, plant flowers and lettuce on them and build houses over them. It's hard to admit that all the dead are, in fact, just fertilizer for future generations. A rather morbid perspective, I know. The second one is more optimistic. It focuses on life, on everything that's alive here and now. I don't know about you, Mr Bely, but I'm happy to be alive, to see the sun rise every morning, to do my wonderful work, to help people accept their loss through quality service. I'm happy that I can move freely, plant seeds and cultivate the land, that I can breathe, move around and be excited about life, the greatest gift of all, like a bird.'

'A bird?'

'Well, perhaps that wasn't the best analogy, but you know what I mean. We're no better than animals; quite the opposite.'

Rosa Portero discreetly grimaces. She leans over and turns the Dictaphone on again.

Ornik looks at her sharply. 'So, you understand Slovenian?' she asks Rosa Portero.

Rosa shrugs her shoulders.

Meanwhile Bely draws the fountain pen out of his jacket pocket. He begins swinging it in time to the strains of *Lohengrin* coming in from the reception hall.

'No, she doesn't understand. Only a few words, that's all. Tell me, is Andreas in one of these photographs?'

'Ah, Andreas! How did you come across him? What a genius he is. His productions are the closest approximation to the *Gesamtkunstwerk*, besides Wagner – and our cemetery, of course. Years ago, when I saw his *Babylonia*, I was inspired to create a number of special installations that even today ...' Ornik stops mid-sentence then continues erratically, 'accompany our visitors ... on their walks ... in our ... cemetery.'

The ticking of the ceramic fountain pen. Wagner's *Lohengrin*. Tick-tack, tick-tack. Rosa Portero waves her hand before Ornik's nose. No reaction. Bely and Rosa nod to each other. Bely withdraws the fountain pen and from his bag pulls out the E-meter, placing the cylindrical electrodes into Magda's hands. He turns it on. The needle sways and lands in the centre of the dial.

'Magda, tell us about who you were before you were born as Magda Ornik.'

'I can't see anything. It's all covered,' Magda says quietly.

Bely keeps a close eye on the E-meter needle, which swings to the right twice and settles in the middle again.

'Who's keeping your past away from you?'

'It's me.'

'Magda, who are you?'

'I'm many.'

'That's right, you're many. Tell me about them.'

Magda stares past Bely. She's in a deep trance. her hands, pressed between her knees, clutch at the cylinders. Taut facial muscles; frozen, protuberant eyes.

'It's all dark. I haven't been born yet, but I'm already alive. I often hide under the brushwood. I'm scared.'

'Scared of what?'

'I'm scared of Father Frost from the Pohorje Mountains. Father Frost never comes on his own. He always comes together with Death, and they always come from the mountains. I can hear his raspy voice, and he smells of schnapps. Any moment the palms of his giant hands will find me, they'll drag me out of my hiding place and push me into the chasm with the others.'

'Who are the others?'

'I don't know who they are; I only know they're dead. Like my mother. She's with them, too. Father Frost and Death came for her, too. Death always comes from Pohorje.'

'Go further back, before this life. What do you see?'

'I see that I'm a butcher. I work for farmers on remote mountain farms. The work is hard. I often have to walk a whole day to get to the animal I'm supposed to slaughter. The pay is bad. I'm forced to steal to support my family.'

'And if we move back even further, way back?'

'It's all foggy. I see soldiers, Roman soldiers. Bright sky, a fire perhaps. I have many children. One of them just passed away because of a back injury. My children often die. My man tells me I carry death inside me, that I feed my children with death, which is why they die. Every day I'm shrouded in the death of my children. Death keeps me warm, it's my gown, my body scent. I mourn my children, and I give birth to them again. I mourn, and I give birth again. I see matchwood. Someone is lighting a fire. I sell bread and pray to the gods that I never have to return to Earth. But I return time and again, and wounds that have only just healed open up somewhere else. Everything is full of wounds, everywhere.'

Rosa Portero leans over Magda's head, shuts her eyes and sniffs at her like a dog. *Ich möchte mehr über den Weihnachtsmann erfahren.*

Bely nods in approval. 'Right, tell us more about Father Frost from Pohorje,' he says.

'They say he's a Communist, but in reality he's just a poor little man whose family was killed by members of the Home Guard. He's one of the most avid machine-gunners, assigned to kill captured Home Guard members, German soldiers, political opportunists and others who don't conform. The war is about to end. He's been working non-stop for three weeks. He's got to be well-organized in order to liquidate so many people. They're herded in groups to the edge of a ditch. It's his duty to shoot them; someone else takes care of the transport, while another person operates an excavator. They cover the cadaver-filled trench with soil as they go. They call it killing with a human face. Those who are liquidated die instantly – if not, they die soon afterwards under a thick layer of soil. Nothing we do here can compare with, say, the Barbara Pit. There they strip poor babies and women naked, tie them up with wire and bury them alive so they slowly die of suffocation. Or in Rog, where many continued to live after they fell in and then played dead for weeks so they could survive among all those rotting bodies. The people lived because they became vultures, cannibals. We didn't have that here. Killing with a human face. The machine-gunner was a professional killer. He only messed up once. Only once he was so drunk on schnapps that he mowed down a few of his assistants as well, that's all.'

Magda stops talking, then continues where she left off, her voice soft and cautious. 'The sound of machine-guns scares me. I cover my ears; but it doesn't help, the noise drills right through me. I try to think of piano suites I know. I wait for Schubert to save me, but there's no music that would stifle the sound of the machine-gun. Father Frost has many machine-guns. The guns get so hot from shooting that he needs to switch between them. Three weeks of killing. After those three weeks of uninterrupted butchery, the machine-gunner finally becomes Father Frost.'

'How's that?'

'His hands tremble. He drinks much more than he did before the war with the foresters in Pohorje. He's delusional. The city is gloomy. The survivors want to forget everything that happened. He talks too much; he's violent. His superiors have two options, to liquidate him or give him another assignment. They put him in charge of Operation Father Frost 45. He brings spruce trees and moss to Lenin Square in Maribor, creating a magical ambience. It reminds many of his colleagues of the woods around the anti-tank trench, but not him. After all, he's the leader of Operation Father Frost 45, and he decides what's what. They decorate the trees, lights, red lanterns, snow. Next to the logs stand miniature models of fairy-tale creatures, dwarves, leprechauns and the like. This is where all the children from the city and its surroundings are brought on 24 December. Everybody is excited and enthusiastic. Then the engine begins to roar and the bells jingle. The machine-gunner drives around among the children. It's not reindeer towing Father Frost, it's a Russian tractor. He sits there in his red cape, dead drunk, with a long white beard made of cotton wool. The children stare at him with big eyes. If any of them laugh at him, he slaps their faces. If he can't reach them, he raises his golden wand, aims it at them and shouts "Rat-a-tat-tat!" I like Father Frost. All children like Father Frost. He brings us sweets and talks about brotherhood between the peoples of Yugoslavia.'

Magda's lips tremble, and her eyes pop out with fear. She pushes the metal cylinders of the E-meter into her abdomen, her back arched, and cramps up.

'Oh no, Father Frost, please, don't drive into the hill. I don't know, I'm not there, but the image is there, I can see it clearly. Father Frost feeds us sweets then drives off up the hill on his ramshackle wagon pulled by the tractor. He always comes from Pohorje. That's where the unspoiled nature is. That's where you'll find clean water, deposits of marble. That's where our past is. He comes down to the city and brings us gifts. And then he always drives back into the hill.'

'Which hill?'

'The Pyramid. He always disappears into Pyramid Hill. One time my papa and I ran after him. The foot of the hill suddenly opens up, and Father Frost disappears into it, then the hill closes up again. Oh I'm so worried about our Father Frost. Something bad might happen to him inside that hill. The Pyramid is his home. Papa tries to console me, but I see he's scared, too. Papa is lying. In reality, Father Frost must always return to the Pyramid, and there he forgets about us children. I don't want him to forget us. I want him with us all the time! But he arrives only once a year to give us our share of sweets and slap our faces, and then he's gone again. I want to know what happens to him when he's there with the worms, deep inside the earth. Isn't he cold? What does he eat in there?'

Magda begins to tremble.

'It's OK, Magda. Can you tell me something about the Great Orc?' asks Bely.

Magda stares ahead, shaking.

'Magda!' Bely calls out.

Magda keeps shaking, more and more.

'The Great Orc lives inside Pyramid Hill. Father Frost is his child. Just as we are Father Frost's children, so is Father Frost the Great Orc's child. The Great Orc can go anywhere he wants, any time he wants, while Father Frost can only go back to his anti-tank trench in the woods. And he can visit us children, but only at Christmas. Here comes Father Frost, and here comes Death to push us into the abyss.'

'Where is the abyss?'

'Everywhere.'

'Where is the Great Orc?'

'In the Pyramid.'

'In the Pyramid above the city?'

'Everywhere.'

'Who is the Great Orc?' shouts Bely.

'Everybody. We all are the Great Orc!'

# I Hate Carnivals

Rosa Portero and Adam Bely, the sound of pebbles beneath their shoes when they walk towards the car-park. Rosa holds Bely beneath his arm. His coat smells like mud, although it is wintertime and the coat seems to be clean.

'On the left is the pet cemetery,' says Bely. 'Years ago, it was in all the newspapers. The soil from the pet cemetery was sold as top-quality humus, marketed for the cultivation of bonsai trees. Ornik's predecessor was forced to resign because of the scandal. Bonsai enthusiasts didn't take too kindly to their trees growing in cemetery soil. I don't know what happened to the former director. Probably nothing too dramatic, just a change of jobs. That's an example of justice in this town. It's too small for people from here to simply disappear. If we applied the sort of rules that are in place in larger communities – one mistake and you're out – then no one would live in Maribor any more. Even if everyone knows that someone did something bad, such behaviour only consolidates the person's place in society. The fact that he was up to no good would just endear him to his fellow scoundrels. You don't have to be ashamed in front of these people because, as a citizen of Maribor, you know that they are no different from you. You know who you're dealing with. It's just like the ending of the story about the machine-gunner, the one Magda told us about. I remember him. I was still in primary school at the time. He was officially deposed from his role as Father Frost. Later on, they learned that he was a child-porn dealer. Apparently everyone knew what he was up to, but his past made him untouchable. When he died, his funeral was one of the biggest in the history of Maribor. They paraded Father Frost down the streets of the city in his old Ursus tractor. An open coffin, his long white beard laid out over his chest. Our whole school was dressed in Tito's Pioneers uniforms, standing like an honour guard at the main bridge when his corpse passed, accompanied by the police brass band and interred with state honours. It was magnificent. His two grandsons had taken over the family business a few seasons before, when he had stepped down after the scandal. They spent a lot of time arguing over who would be Father Frost. It came to a head on 24 December, when they both dressed as Father Frost, began fighting in the main square, right in front of the children, over who was the real Father Frost. They might never have settled their accounts if the country hadn't become more politically open back in the 1980s. The Father Frost of Maribor got a younger cousin, Santa Claus. To this day they both visit the local schools and haunt children together.'

Rosa drives, speechless. Bely stares at her profile. He finds her more beautiful than ever. Yet he's racked by an insuperable feeling of her being forbidden, coupled with aversion towards her. No, Bely knows very well that he can never be with Rosa. That would be a deadly mistake. Bely's mind fills with images of Rosa's body as it squirms with pleasure and pain while the Hungarian penetrates her, followed by the image of him, post-coital, when he marks her by cutting into the skin behind her right ear.

'I noticed you've got a wound behind your right ear,' says Bely.

'No, you must be mistaken.'

'Maybe,' says Bely, scratching his neck.

'You're the one with the wound, from when Butcher bit you,' says Rosa.

Bely lifts up his bloody tissue and examines the wound.

'Does it still hurt?' asks Rosa.

'A little, not that it matters anyway,' says Bely, applying a bandage.

'It's impossible to predict the future with your palm in such a state,' says Rosa. 'Your lifeline has been interrupted or obliterated.'

'Does that mean that fate holds no power over me? Maybe I've got time to alter my future, at least until the wound heals?'

'Maybe.'

'If there's one thing I hate, it's prophecies. If they come true, it's only because they were predicted. If no one says anything, then life will go in a different direction. When someone makes a prediction, we internalize it, unconsciously following that path. That makes us like animals! Just think about all that's been said about Lake Balaton. All of it was planned, you know?'

'What do you want, Bely?' asks Rosa nervously.

'I want us to save this city, Rosa. This fucked-up city that doesn't deserve to be saved. You know what's scary? That it's not at all hard to fall into a bottomless pit here. Every society has safety nets, like at the circus for trapeze artists. They hang above the ground to catch the acrobats who fall. You see them suspended in every society, but not in ours. People here will watch you with glee as you fall and shatter to pieces. Whatever might be solved with a handshake elsewhere is an impossibility here.'

'*Schadenfreude*, you say, ha? You're exaggerating,' replies Rosa. 'I think you're taking it personally because it's your city. Or at least it used to be. You've been gone for how long? Sixteen years? This city is no longer yours. Deal with it. This is not about this city anyway. It's about things far more critical than that. I wouldn't be here if this were only about this city, believe me. Rosa Portero isn't worth much, but let me tell you, she's too good for this. You say this city's completely indifferent? I think everybody plays Mikado pick-up sticks around here.'

'What do you mean?'

'The first person to move loses. It's as simple as that, right? But that's not the most horrible thing.'

'What would that be then?'

'It's horrible that you believe in nothing but your dreams. You don't believe in what you feel, Bely. Your head's got room only for your mission, nothing else. Sometimes I wonder about everything that's happened. My abduction, the weeks I spent locked up in a damp, dark cellar, you saving me instead of killing me and, above all, being caught but allowed to live – doesn't it all come together a bit too perfectly to be true? Aren't we only the tools of some greater plan that we know nothing about? A well-thought-out plan based on us being a threat? So, if we wanted to fuck this plan up, shouldn't we do exactly what's expected of us? What if all these expectations are fake? Maybe you should've killed me by Lake Balaton and been appointed priest of the Twin Cult? Adam, have you ever thought about that? Maybe you squandered your only chance to find the Great Orc? What do we do? Where do we go from here? We've got three more names and very little time. None of the Great Orc members knew the names of the others except for the restaurant owner who gave us more than half of them. What if none of the remaining three know the names of the missing four? What if we never find them? Very soon the Great Orc will realize that its legs are under threat and will strike back with a power that's far beyond ours, and you know it. God damn it!'

Rosa slams on the brakes. The car slides, and for a moment it seems as though it's about to skid off the road, but the frozen ground pulls it sideways so it stops at a crossing.

'What the hell is this?' whispers Rosa, ghost-pale.

A giant bestial face presses against the car windshield. A snout full of black teeth, a long fabric tongue, a human face staring out of its larynx, it sticks out its hands and squirts a red substance, maybe ketchup, across the windshield. Raucous laughter, the rustle of the moving sackcloth, a loud belch. A huge caterpillar, eight pairs of legs with flippers, intermittently kicking at the front bumper of the car. The snake slowly slithers across the crossing, vanishes behind the houses on the other side of the street.

'That's a Rusa costume, a rather long Rusa costume. Usually it's a two-person affair, but this one had more than two pairs of legs,' laughs Bely.

'Not funny. I feel horrible. I almost hit that creep,' says Rosa, before running her shaking fingers through her hair. The skin behind her right ear looks flawless, although Bely could have sworn that he had seen the wound there not half an hour ago.

'I hate carnivals,' says Rosa after a pause.

'Everything around you is a carnival. People who think they're something they're not. Everybody is a different embodiment, of course,' says Bely, touching Rosa's right hand. He feels her tension as she grips the gear stick.

A car beeps its horn from behind.

'Fuck off!' shouts Bely. Rosa looks at him, shifts into first gear and drives on.

'In Cuba, apart from our version of the carnival, we celebrate a summer carnival that takes place at the end of the sugarcane season. It's called Mamarrachos, and it comes from Africa.'

'What's the difference?'

'It's mostly people dancing and drinking, people dressed up. The biggest one takes place in Santiago.'

'Wait a second, didn't you say your father was from Santiago?' asks Bely.

'I grew up there. One time my father took me to the carnival. I got lost in the crowd. A few hours later they found me at some old lady's place. My mum was completely beside herself. She told me that the old lady had performed Santería on me. I sat on a chair in the middle of her doorway, completely frozen. Around me was a circle of petals and fruit and candles. I held a puppet, which was carefully wrapped in a delicate white thread. I was four and a half, but I can't remember anything. I wouldn't know anything about it if my mum hadn't told me. She wanted to leave Cuba after that. She took me and my twin sister to

Graz to live with our grandparents. After a few months she managed to get all the papers for my father. He joined us, but it didn't last. In half a year he went back. I never saw or heard about him again. Perhaps that's some sort of a carnival approach to parenthood, to be dressed up in your own disappearance. I don't like it, Adam. A carnival like this is simply not my thing.'

That afternoon the phone rings in Bely's hotel room. 'Inspector Maus is waiting downstairs,' says the receptionist, 'and he has asked for you and Rosa.' Bely puts on his jacket and knocks on Rosa's door. When he mentions the police, Rosa pales.

'Stay calm,' says Bely, taking Rosa by her left hand.

The air whistles by as they sit on an aged light-grey refurbished sofa in the hotel reception. The sofas are battered, and sink under the weight of their bodies. For a moment Rosa feels as though the leather surface is alive, about to swallow her body like quicksand.

'May we ask you for some information, Mr Bely?' asks Inspector Maus. 'First, I'd like to get your permanent home address.'

'It's in Leoben, Austria. I've lived there for four years. Before that I was in Graz for quite some time,' says Bely, examining the officers' uniforms. Similar black parkas, blue jeans, black shoes and painfully white socks.

'And Miss Portero?' asks Inspector Maus.

'She comes from Graz. She works for Austrian national radio as a journalist. I help her with translation and other work-related things. I come from Maribor but haven't lived here for over fifteen years. Miss Portero is working on a radio piece about the city and the European Capital of Culture.'

'I see, I see,' says Inspector Maus, nodding, satisfied. In the meantime his colleague, whom he introduces as Gros, takes diligent notes. Bely is surprised to see the binding of his notebook labelled '1980'.

'When did you arrive in the city, Mr Bely?'

'Wednesday evening. Three days ago.'

How long are you staying?'

'Probably until Wednesday morning. We want to see *War and Peace*, Andreas's première on Tuesday evening,' says Bely.

'Peace, if only we had more of it. We're so concerned about striving for peace that we never manage to achieve it.' Inspector Maus thinks out loud and laughs complacently. Long, crude laughter.

Gros, his assistant, smirks and greets the remark of his superior with a nod.

'Mr Bely, you're from Maribor. Surely you must be familiar with Mr Ivan Dorfler.'

'Of course. We spent a lot of time together as students.'

'Have you seen Mr Dorfler since your arrival in Maribor?'

'I met him at Off, on Thursday night.'

'Was Miss Portero with you?'

'Yes. Why do you ask? Is Dorfler in trouble?' asks Bely, looking Maus in the eye.

'Tell me, when exactly did you see Professor Dorfler?'

'It was around nine in the evening.'

'And how would you describe him?'

'What do you mean, how would I describe him?'

'Did you notice anything unusual about him?'

'I wouldn't say so, no. He was in a good mood.'

'Also when you left?'

'He seemed normal. We had a few rounds – you know how it is meeting someone again after such a long time.'

'Sure, sure,' nods inspector Maus, convinced. 'I gather you haven't read the newspaper today? Well, why would you? Anyway, Dorfler had some sort of a nervous breakdown the night you met. He was admitted to a psychiatric hospital for treatment. By the way, the staff in Off confirmed you were at the club Thursday evening.'

'That's horrible,' says Bely dryly.

'It's bizarre? Professor Dorfler was found licking the threshold of Off, his mouth completely lacerated. He hasn't recovered. If left unsupervised he starts licking the floor, regardless of what it looks like and what's on it. We probably wouldn't have thought much of this case if we hadn't heard just this morning of another renowned businessman, Tine Butcher, going insane on the very same day as Dorfler. He was in a meeting with his business partner from Abu Dhabi when he lunged at one of the guests and bit his arm. A nasty bite. The guest had to be stitched up, and he almost returned to Abu Dhabi with a paralysed arm. I don't have to emphasize that incidents such as this aren't exactly a recipe for success for Maribor companies abroad.' At these words Inspector Maus bursts into boisterous laughter. Gros, his assistant, snickers at the laughter of his superior.

'You also visited Butcher, didn't you?' asks Maus.

'We conducted a short interview with him this morning. We're trying to put together a profile mosaic of different Maribor residents, to acquaint the Austrian radio listeners with the city life here through as many eyes as possible.'

'Of course, of course,' nods Maus in satisfaction.

'How's Butcher doing?' asks Bely.

'He's got similar symptoms to Dorfler. Dorfler licks the floor, and Butcher, he bites everyone who comes within his dental range. He's really dangerous. The psychiatrists say that they've never seen anything like that. It's rather unusual for two prominent citizens to go crazy at practically the same moment, two people with no prior history of symptoms and nothing in common that we know of. Except ...'

'Except?' asks Bely.

'Except that they both met you and Miss Portero just hours before they went mad.'

'What exactly are you accusing me of, Mr Maus?'

'Listen, the doctors think they might've ingested an unknown substance. They don't know how else to explain their sudden loss of sanity. The results of the first analysis were insignificant, but they're doing a new batch of tests now. Anyway, I'm not accusing you of anything yet, Mr Bely, all I'm asking of you is to help me solve this mystery. A pair of normal, stable people who may never been in contact with one another, how is it possible that they both go mad like that? And on the same day that you visited them? You have to admit the whole thing is pretty odd.'

'It sounds like it. I'm shocked myself, and I'd like to help. But I can't, for the life of me, see how I can be of any use to you,' says Bely in a painstaking effort to ignore the itch on his right knee.

'I think it's in your best interest to help me, Mr Bely. It better be in your best interest. Because until we've proven otherwise you'll inevitably be suspected of involvement. I hope you know what this means for you and your friend?' Maus looks Bely in the eye and winks. 'One question, Mr Bely, do you know Voda?'

'Voda, the mayor?'

'That's right, the mayor.'

'No, I've never met him, never had anything to do with him.'

'Of course, that's what I thought. Why would you?' nods Maus, satisfied. 'Tell me, Bely, did you notice anything unusual when you met Butcher and Dorfler?'

'Unusual like what?'

'Let me put it another way. When you were in Off and Butcher's office, did you notice any traces of birds, pigeons perhaps? Bird droppings or anything else related to birds?'

Bely translates for Rosa Portero. She shakes her head; they look at one another, baffled.

'No, we saw no pigeons, and no bird droppings either.'

'What about Dorfler's office? Were you there, too?'

'Yes.'

'Do you remember seeing a poster with a white pigeon?'

Bely recalls a poster with a dove of peace. He nods.

'You know, the threshold that Dorfler was licking was full of pigeon shit. The window-sill in Butcher's office was, too. That's my number one lead: droppings. Then there's you, and I've got another one.'

'Another one?' asks Bely.

'Both of them, Butcher and Dorfler, are sworn adversaries of Voda. Or they were, to be precise. These days they oppose no one,' says Maus as he gets up. His assistant Gros also rises and scribbles something in his big notebook with '1980' shining yellow off its binding.

Rosa Portero and Bely watch Inspector Maus and Assistant Gros leave. Bely brutally scratches his leg and abdomen and signals to Rosa to follow him into his room.

'Don't worry, they've got nothing solid,' says Bely as he closes the door behind them.

'Are you sure? Adam, what about the tests he was talking about?'

'There's no test in the entire universe that can prove they've been poisoned. These tests are meant to look for certain substances, which isn't our concern since we're not drugging anyone. The members of the Great Orc are drugged on pure information not a drug *per se*. Information that awakens the souls whose memory was obscured. These souls constitute our personality. Bound together, they're as helpless as clusters of sleeping bats. Information about what happened awakens them like a ray of light. Souls that have slept for millions of years wake again and leave the human body that they've been hiding in. The human, animal to its core, becomes a soulless beast again. Hubbard, the father of Scientology, was right in this respect. There are no people. We're only human animals inhabited by flocks of murdered souls. Souls who settled in the bodies of human animals because they were disoriented. Our oyster crackers only inform these souls of who they are, orienting them once more, but in no way do we poison anyone.'

'But, Adam, this information must consist of something. It must be tied to some substance. It's not simply a word floating through the air? What are these crackers made of? Where did you get them? Adam, what if you were tricked into using them? You think that they're pure information, but what if, in reality, they're some kind of a drug?'

Bely's fingers dig hard into his scalp at these words. They scratch with disappointment and anger over Rosa's lack of faith. If her faith in what they do is so fragile, if she thinks that everything they've been doing is out of mere necessity, then why is she still with him? It makes no sense. Wouldn't *auditing* reveal Rosa's bogus intentions, if she had any? Bely allowed her to join him in Maribor only after she had passed three cycles of hypnosis and an E-meter questioning. Moreover, he's always had this oddly steadfast feeling that he could trust her, from the moment he laid his eyes on her bound-up body on the shore of Lake Balaton. That she is the one who stood by his side in his vision of the Great Orc. Whatever the case, Bely just has to trust her. If there's one thing he needs right now, it's a person he can rely on.

'Rosa, do you really have so little faith in me?' asks Bely, taking her by her hands. The feeling of her gloved fingers, metal mixed with flesh, seeps through his skin and builds into an image of a creature before him that is neither human nor machine.

'Bely, I trust you, and you know it. But I still want to know where you got those oyster crackers,' says Rosa sharply.

'I get them at Hofer supermarket,' responds Bely and smiles.

'Where?' Rosa's eyes widen with surprise.

Rosa's metal-flesh fingers shift in Bely's grip. Pliers filled with hope.

'The little edibles we give to members of the Great Orc are just ordinary oyster crackers, the sort you can buy at any supermarket. Flour, water, salt, emulsifiers and stabilizers. That's all. The only difference is that our oyster crackers are informed, capable of absolving. Much like homoeopathic pills that are charged with diluted information about the disease they're meant to treat. But keep in mind that our oyster crackers aren't about informing through their diluted compounds, our oysters communicate via pure consciousness.'

'Consciousness? Whose consciousness, Adam?'

'Mine, yours, the consciousness of all who let this consciousness manifest itself. Listen, as a Scientologist I went through years of self-interrogation and cleansing. I became *clear*, which indicates a very advanced stage of consciousness. But at the same time, almost simultaneously, I fell sick with testicular cancer. Two mutually exclusive events. The rules say no one can be *clear* and have cancer. And that's why I decided to leave Scientology. Still, a few things I learned from them were useful later on when I fought the disease. I fought it and beat it through fasting and meditation.'

'No radiation?'

'Well, some. I also had surgery. But the cancer was so advanced that they pretty much wrote me off. I wasn't ready to follow their example, so I meditated. Forty days and nights of nothing but water and meditation. I spent all that time trying to connect to a higher consciousness.'

'The consciousness of those murdered?'

'No, a different consciousness. This consciousness transcends time and space, it transcends murders, no matter when they happened. This consciousness transcends the great cataclysm in which Xenu ordered millions of his own people to be executed and thrown into volcanoes, two of which are the Pyramid and Calvary hills.'

'Right, but what's that got to do with our oyster crackers?'

'After twenty-one days of strict fasting I was starting to hallucinate. I travelled through my previous lives, through time and space. I was there when the Earth was born. I saw the first atrocities and the most absurd banalities you can imagine. One time I I tried to rescue a wagon that was stuck in mud with nobody there to help me. The cow was drowning in the mud. I was a young girl. I was on my way back home, wearing a traditional costume, frayed and covered in dirt. In the end I finally managed to save my cow and the wagon, but my bonnet was ruined, my white shirt ripped. I was practically naked. And the heavens kept on dumping dirty rain on me. That feeling, when I finally opened my eyes, was indescribable.'

'And?'

'And so I meditated night and day, drinking nothing but water. First, with laxatives, then pure and unadulterated. Forty days into my meditation the skies opened up to a bright light, I rose up above the clouds and suddenly everything made sense. But I was too weak to stand, I lay on the carpet in the middle of the apartment, surrounded by bottles of water. I knew that could very well be the end for me, but then a green light burst in from outside, unrolling like a long rug at a royal reception. I stood up with the last residue of my strength and walked along it. The window before me opened and, gently, as if I were standing on cotton wool, I stepped out into the skies above the city. There was the Mura

River, Schlossberg with its clock tower. With every step my legs moved with more agility, the green light kept me afloat and restored the strength to my body that I had expended through starvation and meditation. Soon the green carpet flew me down to the city streets. I remember how frightening I found the jingling of a tram that passed right by me. A door opened in front of me, and the green carpet led over its threshold. I stepped in. Then all I recall are faces that stared at me with wonder and horror. I saw them stooping over me as I grew conscious of the world around me. I clenched a bag of oyster crackers as I lay on a sugar pallet at Hofer. With no money on me, I was penniless. But out of fear or disgust, maybe both, the sales ladies let me take them, my oyster crackers, with me. Emaciated, barefoot and dressed in nothing but pyjamas, I must've looked strange in mid-November. They let me drag myself out of the shop. I can't remember how, but I found my way back to the apartment around the corner. I sat on the Persian carpet, not the green one, and so I fasted for forty days and nights. I took in a breath of fresh air that billowed in through the open window. No lights, no green cotton wool. Only clouds rushing through the skies. Bustling city and chirping birds. I entered the state of highest consciousness that does not know death. I tilted my head and emptied the oyster cracker bag into my mouth.'

'You ate them, Adam?'

'I didn't eat them. I let them fall through my body so that they became informed. Minutes later the oyster crackers exited the other end. I picked them up and put them back in the bag. I was so exhausted that I fell asleep. I slept through the night and the next morning when I woke up there were more crackers beside me. Only these were darker in colour than the first batch. Can you imagine a cracker that doesn't break down in the process of travelling through the entire digestive tract of a human being? We're talking ten metres of digestive tract. Rosa, that's a miracle, but everyone would call me crazy if I shared this with them. This must mean that the connection between the human body and the souls or consciousness that inhabits us has more layers than we think. The body of an animal can become the informant of that higher consciousness, its body leaves the prints of what comprises consciousness. Rosa, we're not just animals, we're godly animals, if you want.'

'And how did you know how the crackers worked?'

'I tested them, first on my dog, Hasky. Poor little muffin stopped barking and started scratching. Later I tested them on two people. With their souls absolved, Scientology has a much better chance of gaining trust and expanding its community. The crackers are otherwise all the same, light or dark. They function the same way. The only difference is that the dark ones inform and absolve right away, whereas the light ones take a few days to kick in. But I've told you this before, haven't I?' Bely scratches his right hip and tummy again. Rosa stares at him.

'Adam, are you all right?'

'Of course, everything is fine. I suggest we meet up again in about an hour. I need to take a rest now.'

As if to double-check with him, Rosa looks at Bely again then leaves. When she shuts the door Bely rips off his shirt, vest and his trousers. He walks into the bathroom and turns on the light. The mirror reflects a body covered in prints. They wrap around his body like scorch marks from the giant legs of an octopus.

# Father Kirilov

Sunday morning. Rosa Portero leaves the hotel. Grey drizzle over empty streets and damp, cold air bite to the bone. Rosa winds her way down to the Drava River. Few passers-by. A lonely, tiny boat moored on the river rocks wistfully. There's a bar on it, and Rosa tries the door, but it's locked. A few steps further, a European Capital of Culture balloon marker, air blowing from beneath to keep it afloat. A huge inflated ball with an unusual sign, a screw or a turbine, Rosa thinks. It reminds her of something, but she doesn't know what. The slow rattle of the mechanism under the balloon. Rosa sinks into her coat and walks uphill across an empty market. Two cars, flickering lights, an ambulance siren somewhere in the distance. In the middle of a crossroad a couple of pecking pigeons, which take off before a passing car and then land to peck again. The trace of vomit and urine in the snow. A football stadium to the left, corroded chains around a rolled-up fence. Villas and socialist apartment blocks further up the street. Techno music comes from one of the windows. A woman pushes a screaming pushchair. Rosa peeks in to see the baby, but it appears to contain only a blanket. Primal screaming on rattling wheels. The woman pushes it through the slush and snow, resignedly. Further on, a park. Fighting dogs, one runs off, the rest begin to howl while looking at the Pyramid. Hoar frost flies with the breeze, brown trails of droplets in the snow beneath the overloaded spruce trees. As if somebody had been lying there through the night. Rosa returns to the hotel. She knocks on Bely's door. Nothing. She lies down on the bed in her room and studies the ceiling.

It's midday when Bely wakes her.

'Since when do you sleep fully dressed with boots on?'

Rosa sits up and soothes out her hair.

'You missed breakfast, so I saved you some toast with a ton of Nutella on it and a cold double instant coffee.'

Bely places the platter before Rosa. She leans over and smells it, screws up her face, but drinks the coffee anyway.

'How many years did you live in this city? Thirty? I'd die after three months here. This city doesn't exist, Bely. This morning I walked around a bit; it's empty, deserted, no living soul anywhere.'

'It's Sunday. That means day zero for the people of Maribor. Sunday lunch, TV. In the summer they drive off into the countryside. In the winter they curl up and wait for the summer to arrive. Some of them break out of this lethargic circle by going to the place I'm about to take you to.'

Rosa bites into the Nutella toast, looking interested.

'I'm taking you to church, to mass,' smiles Bely.

The big church door is locked. So is the side entrance. Slomšek Square in front of the church is empty. Behind the church flashes a sign advertising the New World restaurant. The façade of the post office, the university headquarters, a Maribor theatre building.

'This is a symbolic centre and the heart of the city,' says Bely. 'This view captures the entire city.'

'This heart is in urgent need of a transfusion and resuscitation. What's heart without flesh?' says Rosa.

Bely and Rosa walk through the portal. A golden placard, MARIBOR ARCHDIOCESE, on the wall outside. Beside it several drilled holes, a dead neon sign, BLUE NIGHT, poorly attached to the wall, cables erupting and swaying in the wind, a door that opens widely on to the courtyard to the right. In front of the door is a van, loaded with wood, tools and junk. Beyond, two men put up a disco ball, another one a large mirror behind the bar. Cardboard, cellophane, rubbish everywhere.

'Isn't this the offices of the archdiocese?' asks Bely.

The men glance at one another in silence. One of them speaks to Bely, his voice soft, as if he were about to give away a secret. 'It used to be, until it went under, and now it's up for rent. Financial crisis.'

Bely looks around. 'And now they're renting out their offices?'

'Not them, the banks. To the highest bidder. It's tough with loans these days. You skip an instalment, and the banks have you by the balls. For now they're lucky they can keep the church. And then you ask yourself, who would want to rent a church anyway? But I've heard they had an Italian film producer who was interested in it because of its height, perfect for a film studio. Look, I don't know, I'm just an electrician here. The charity offices and the soup kitchen are still here, though, straight across the courtyard. You might want to ask there.'

A few homeless people sit on the benches amid the trodden-down snow. Plastic cups steam with soup. Slices of white bread on a plastic platter on the bench. The gaze of a few souls, eating while standing. It is three o'clock, the day is tipping over. A homeless man, a white shirt with a red sign, T100, over his parka. A Maribor F.C. scarf wrapped around the neck of another. Bely says hello. They mumble back. An old woman shrieks to Rosa, 'Do you wanna eat, too?' The shriek scares the pigeons off the adjacent roof. Rosa keeps calm.

No answer at the charity door. Grate of the key. A sister peeks out through a narrow slit window. Short and petite, her head barely reaches the door handle.

'Good day, sister, we are looking for Metod Kirilov,' says Bely politely.

'Kirilov is not here. Who are you?'

'My name is Adam Bely. My colleague is from Austrian radio, and I would like to find Mr Kirilov.'

'Father Kirilov hasn't given any statements to the media for over a year. He's not here. Please leave him alone.'

'It's not our intention to pester him, we only wanted to have a few words with him.'

'Listen, Mr Bely, I told you already that Kirilov isn't here. Please respect his privacy and leave him in peace. He told your colleagues everything. You journalists have tortured him enough. He lives in solitude, I don't know where. We're not giving any statements. I think that will be all. Have a good day.'

The slit window closes shut, the key grates.

Bely and Rosa look at each other.

'*Das ist kein gutes Zeichen*,' says Rosa quietly.

'No, it's not good,' mutters Bely. He pulls out his pills and takes one.

'Sister Magda is tough as nails,' says a man on a bench next to the door, chewing on a crust. 'I call her Cerberus, but that doesn't stop her from biting. And she still hasn't got a clue about classical mythology.'

'Well, yes, I do remember the nuns as slightly more approachable,' replies Bely. 'They don't mean ill. Clergy, what can you do? I'm happy with them as long as they feed me a warm meal every day. I tell you, though, it wasn't the financial meltdown that broke them, it was this story about their loss of 1.3 billion that changed them for the worse.'

'Do they really owe that much?'

'We were all surprised. You'd expect the Church to be more conservative about their investment policies. They got bitten by the stock-market bug. They wanted to multiply their wealth, so they invested with different companies, mostly the telecom sector. When the stock market crashed everything was gone, including their principles. According to the *Financial Times* they're the most indebted diocese per worshipper in the world. At least one thing we can claim to be at the top of, right?'

Bely looks at the rotten teeth that gnaw on white crust. White saliva in the corners of his mouth, dirty nails shoving in more bread. The disparity between the homeless man's appearance and his words astounds Bely.

'People find it most offensive if you don't meet their stereotyped expectations. If the Church were dogmatic and conservative in terms of its economic politics, as people expect it to be, then it would easily live up to its reputation as a predictably evil institution. Everyone would sleep peacefully next to an institution like that. But, because the Church was pragmatic, in that it mercilessly followed its interests to accumulate wealth in agreement with the neoliberal doctrine and because it denied morality in the face of greedy capital accumulation, it ended up being punished far more than it would have been otherwise had the 1.3 billion been spent in a more predictable and less intelligent way. Those who castigate the Church for choosing a cable provider that offers the same adult programmes as all the other private or state providers, criticize the Church through the very same dogmatic premise with which they reproached the Church in the first place. When, in fact, they should recognize this as a liberalization of rigid Church dogma, as their empathy towards secular logic and, subsequently, towards the end-users, the worshippers. That's precisely what would pose a threat to all those who live off the alleged opposition to Church ideology! Which, in this ideologically bipolar society, knocks out the more passive alternative, of course. The atheistic, quasi-left alternative at this stage exceeds the morality of the Church, because it conceals its moralism under the mask of the supposed stance of Enlightenment. The truth is, in Slovenia the Enlightenment never happened. I would say that it was only through their neoliberal market shamelessness that the Church moved closer to its calling, the preaching of the Kingdom of God on Earth. It was only through unscrupulous financial machinations that the Church transformed from previously untouchable into vulnerable, possibly erroneous and subsequently more open and friendlier to the people. The Church would not have undergone a complete transformation, the Slovenian social contract wouldn't have been redefined, if the Church's finances hadn't gone under with the stock market.'

Rosa leans over to Bely and asks quietly, 'What is he saying?'

Bely shrugs his shoulders.

'You seem to be quite familiar with the financial sector, Mr …'

'There were times when Citibank wanted me to be their broker. I drove to the Trieste stock market three times a week. Everybody read the financial analyses in *Neue Zürcher Zeitung*, the *Financial Times*, and so did I, but that's not all I did. I was probably the only one who relied exclusively on instinct. You can't control the stock market through psychology. You can't rationalize it, because the number of parallel processes are just too exorbitant to allow the application of logos. These processes can be internalized at a subconscious level, and that's the work of a poet. You work instinctively, your body, your neurons, all of your cells are the stock market. But you have to be careful here. The connection between the neurological and verbal body takes place through a handful of synapses with a significant delay. And because language is basic, conservative and partial, in contrast to your insight, which is much more comprehensive, you may often only be able to explain your own actions after the fact. Not something investors are enthusiastic about. They're not always willing to invest millions, if you can't argue why they should do so, even though you know, instinctively, that this would be the only reasonable and sensible thing to do.'

The homeless man slurps his soup, wipes the noodles off his beard, strips his bread of its soft core, presses it into a disk and stuffs it into his mouth.

'Let's go.'

Adam Bely and Rosa Portero look at each other.

'You must look at your situation through the lens of probability theory. You've got a better shot at learning about Kirilov with me than you would have tramping around Maribor on a Sunday evening on your own. That's almost like going to a kabuki performance in Hiroshima an hour after the bomb drops.'

Once again Adam and Rosa look at each another. They follow the homeless man across the market. Rosa notices that he wears plastic bags instead of socks. The outer edges curl over the top of his boots and swish as he trudges through the slush.

'Miracle, this bar hasn't closed yet! Shouldn't we be getting a litre or two, before going to my place?' asks the homeless man.

Bely walks into the bar, the man following him. They come out with a bottle of tequila.

'Don't worry,' says the man, '*audentes fortuna iuvat*.' He looks at Rosa. '*Den Mutigen hilft das Glück*. You've read Virgil, haven't you?

An alley leading down to the riverbed, a narrow, slippery path, loose plaster on the ground, a trail of dog piss in the snow. The man removes the sheet metal from an opening in the wall. It is pitch dark inside. They enter to a blinding light from a naked bulb. Naked walls, ice-cold air standing still in the room, a pile of rubbish in the middle, empty bottles, wooden crates, damp paper. They take a squeaky narrow stairway. Door. Small room, bed, a pair of chairs, electric radiator, small table and an ashtray on it. Newspaper taped over the window. The dim light of a waking day illuminates the space between the letters.

'*Bienvenue*. This is my den. This is where I live in peace and write. No one bothers me; I bother no one. Paradise on Earth.'

The man grabs three plastic cups and fills them.

'What happened to you? I mean, how can a broker end up here?' asks Bely and takes a sip.

'Predictable questions, Mr Bely, are never good questions. Well, I can give you an equally predictable answer: poetry.'

'Poetry?'

'That's correct. Poetry. I was a top broker. I made a fortune from money that I borrowed. Not all of it was mine, of course, mostly it went to those who loaned me the money in the first place. Still, my share was nothing to sneeze at. It was smooth sailing for as long as I was a slave to the stock market. And then came poetry. I wrote some as a youngster, had some publishing success, but then it dissipated, and I thought I would never write again. So I just read and fed on wild, bold leaps of thought, on the complexity of a good poem with all its twists and images. And then, one day – bam! Deluge. Not even a deluge, a tsunami of words. At the end of my workday I used to hop in my Volvo and drive off to Trieste to lie on the beach. It was Monday, early September. I remember it like it was yesterday. That day I made tens of thousands in profit. I felt like a ruler with absolute power over my destiny. It was good. I was the magma, and the capital spoke right through me. I was its medium. Then something snapped, and, all of a sudden, something else appropriated me as its medium. It spoke through me like crazy. I ran to the first kiosk in my trunks, bought a copy of *Corriere della Sera* and a ballpoint pen and, in three hours, I'd filled every single page of the newspaper with poems. I didn't recognize myself. I was in a trance, and there was absolutely nothing I could've done to fight that spastic, absolute colonization of language over me. It occupied me, as simple as that, and it still pulsates when it comes to call. Look.' The man opens an old wardrobe. Neatly stacked school exercise books. Thousands of them. He takes one and opens it to pages densely packed with microscopic writing.

'This wardrobe, this is me. It's the only thing that holds my interest. Poetry, an accelerated translation of the complexity of the id into language. Don't get me wrong, I'm no genius. Truth be told, I'm only a series of muscle movements, nothing more. Would a man survive with no more than a few centimetres of colon? Maybe. Would a man survive with many decades' worth of delay between the id ...' The man licks his index finger and points it up into the air. He looks at it as if to determine the direction of the wind and then continues, '... and language, which he is able to articulate and understand? I don't think so. I want to minimize this delay. Everything else comes as a logical result of my absolute dedication to poetry, and I'm at peace with it. Of course, I'm intellectually superior to most of my fellow citizens. Of course, I can't find a normal person in this city who'd be able to discuss these matters with me. But that's nothing special. It's the fate my soul mates have seen repeated throughout history. That is not to say that I don't share this fate of a voluntary mental outcast with a few other madmen. But that's no solace – more like a point of orientation in an empty space, if you know what I mean.'

Bely drinks out of a plastic cup, grimaces and coughs. 'It's good, but I've had better.'

'Alcoholic drinks are controlled by the Dutch and Americans, in terms of global capital. While the producer of this tequila is, aside from minority stakes owned by two investment funds, still a family-run business, not publically traded,' says the man as he refills his cup.

'Will you read us a poem, Mr ... ?' asks Bely.

'No name. I had one once, and I still do for the purposes of the state and social care. But it's an empty shell, a social marker and completely worthless, almost annoying. Who I am, what I was or how I'll end up, none of this is important to me and my writing. Nothing in this wardrobe is a product of some pathetic desire to be cleverer than my time, or the need to leave my mark. I'm not at all interested in building fake identities. What interests me is the pre-Renaissance position of an anonymous artist. Possibly the only real monastic position, to be nameless, to consciously relinquish all the rights that, in our society, derive from our name. My poetry, like me, has no name; it's found no audience who might use it to solve their personal issues or outsmart death, at least symbolically. If you ask the poems in these exercise books they would tell you that I never even lived. If I were to read you a poem, you surely would understand that I'd do it not as the author but as an actor who's interpreting somebody else's text. And it's been over fifteen years since I last acted, Mr Bely. The first thing I did was to leave the act of my name.'

'All right, I understand,' replies Bely, 'but what if tomorrow you don't come back? Let's say something happens to you. And then none of the people who stumble on this wardrobe of yours recognizes the value of your work, nobody reads one single verse that you wrote?'

'Like I've said, predictable questions are best avoided, Mr Bely. A student of literary history would ask a question like that. Things aren't the way you imagine them at the other cognitive level. There's no obvious reason for our civilization, for life on Earth, to continue its existence in this equilibrium in which it's existed for millions of years. Every logical explanation speaks against it. Still, there's a remarkable flow of information that, even in the face of constant modifications, allows the system to preserve itself and all that vital information that is crucial to the system's long-term survival. It's a process we can't see. That small fragment of reality, which we can rationally perceive and translate into language, is much too narrow, Mr Bely. Our blinkers are set so close together that the reality we see is no thicker than a single ninety-gram sheet of paper. And we're surrounded by the whole Library of Alexandria.'

The man gets up and walks to the newspaper-draped window. Faint light gleams through it. His fingers softly brush against the yellowed letters, as though they were very delicate.

'How can you be sure that tomorrow you'll still be breathing, Mr Bely? When you tuck yourself in, how do you know that the next morning you will get up? That your heart will continue to pump hectolitres of blood and your kidneys will continue to do their work flawlessly? What assures us that tomorrow we will not become terminally ill, with cancer for instance, Mr Bely? Nothing, nothing at all. Still we go to bed in peace, thinking about unpaid bills, about who's going to water our plants while we're on holiday, about trivial errands, trivial problems. But in the meantime, the fundamental things take their course and we, dormant animals, even benefit from them. After years of studying the narrow passage between my blinkers, I'm not only convinced, but deep inside I know that everything that's of importance will remain. Not for our sake, we're completely unimportant here, but for the sake of the system alone, for its survival. I know that some things can't be eradicated, even if you try to destroy them by tossing them into an active volcano, for instance. But I'm sure, Mr Bely, that you know what I'm talking about. We should go now, because he's waiting for us.'

Bely rises, his face pallid.

Rosa, who has understood little of what was said, looks at him anxiously. 'What's going on?'

*'Haben Sie keine Angst, Frau Portero, Pater Kirilov wartet auf uns. Ich führe Sie jetzt zu ihm,'* says the man and slams the wardrobe door shut.

They all follow the narrow stairway back down into the dark anteroom. The man pulls open a few pieces of cardboard and a cluster of rusty wires to reveal a passage. They make their way down a short shaft into a narrow tunnel.

'Most people in Maribor aren't familiar with the city's underground tunnel system. We could be at the cathedral crypt in only a couple of minutes if we took this one. But we won't.'

Bely has to walk crouching. A tiny light in the man's hand casts shadows that wander beside him. Water drips from the brick ceiling. Steps echo. The mouse-like squeak of a dog in the distance.

'We've arrived,' says the man, and he pushes through a heavy curtain, revealing a door at the end of the tunnel.

A larger, gloomy space. In the middle, a desk crammed with junk, pieces of wood and other materials. A desk lamp, its pale glow distorted by a slender body that leans into it. An elegant garment that concludes with a clerical collar, a thick blanket over it. In the corner a humming heater, warm rays of air.

'Welcome. Thank God you've arrived. I was afraid my friend wouldn't make it. Please take a seat. Perhaps over there, I've got too much clutter here by the desk,' says Kirilov. 'I wish I could host you in my garden, a far more civilized and occasion-appropriate space than this, but it is what it is.'

Kirilov turns on the ceiling light, which brings the brick-clad vaults of the cellar to life. No windows. Walls covered in old carpets, a desk in the middle, a sofa and two armchairs in the corner, where they sit down.

'Five hundred years ago a Jewish jeweller had a workshop here. Today it's a space where I spend my exile and craft my miniature models. As you know, I don't live in Slovenia any more. Officially I'm in Poland, where I was banished by order of the Vatican. They are hoping that the archdiocese will be somewhat relieved of all that media pressure. Ever since Pope John Paul II managed to defeat Communism, Rome seems to be convinced that the solution to every issue lies in Poland. How naïve of them! I decided to respect the Church and retreat into seclusion, but I wanted to pick the place of retreat myself. If I can't share the streets of Maribor with my own people, then I might as well live beneath them, together with the city's rats. St Francis of Assisi converted only when he met the lepers. The only difference is that the Church not only thought I should convert but also believed that I was a leper who had to be expelled from society.'

Metod Kirilov lights up a cigarette then offers a smoke to the others. Rosa and the homeless man each take one and light up.

'Listen, I won't lie, I made mistakes. I sinned, God forgive me. I confess, I repent my sins. In contrast to many ecclesiastical authorities who are as guilty as I am for what happened but won't admit to it or regret it. At best, they're frightened of being excommunicated the way I was. Fear is a terrible thing and a fruit of divine providence, all at once. What would we do without it? And what can become of us because of it?'

Kirilov blows a smoke ring into the air and smoothes out his blanket, which, for a moment, looks like a cloak draped over a bishop's shoulders.

'I was also scared. Scared because of the money, because of my responsibility for the worshippers and my Church. You can't imagine the burden, once you're appointed chief financial officer of the arch-diocese. Needless to say, every decision of yours is secondary to the will of God, the fellow bishops and auxiliary bishops upon whom you're dependent. You know, I've always kept away from fear by believing that everything is a creation of God. Nothing would exist without the grace and providence of God, not even fallen angels, not temptations, not even sins. Without it we'd have no money, no monetary system, no stock exchange, no greed, no deception and no free markets with their barbarian laws. It's all part of a grand plan. His big plan, and He alone knows how things are going to resolve. I wouldn't be a Christian if I believed otherwise, don't you agree?'

Kirilov takes delight in blowing another smoke ring into the darkness, his hand gliding down his perfectly combed white hair.

'And if all of it is His creation, then the demonization of capitalism in today's newspapers is only another contemporary witch-hunt. After all that's happened, after all that's happened to me, I still believe that everything in this world is sacred and happens for a reason. The financial collapse of the archdiocese is no exception. That was His sign, so I repented, I changed and forgave all those who pointed fingers at me at the worst possible moments as if I were the only culprit, or even pushed me into this pit, to suffer as Joseph did. God have mercy on me. Let anyone who is without a sin cast the first stone. I've reconciled with my Church, but did the Church reconcile with me? No, they'd rather see me gone forever. God help me, a Church that isn't capable of forgiveness is not a Church.'

Kirilov's chin trembles. Then he composes himself and rises.

'That's why I'm here, crafting miniatures day and night. My love used to be bonsai trees, but that was back in the days when I had a garden of my own. I had a fabulous bonsai garden, you know. Must have been one of the most beautiful gardens in this part of Europe. When I wasn't occupied with the archdiocese or my duties as a priest I nurtured my bonsai trees. They were a balm to my soul during services and the seemingly endless sessions with the board of trustees. Plants are wonderful conversationalists; thank God you don't have to speak Japanese to talk to them.'

Kirilov smiles.

'I think our souls are like the souls of bonsai trees. Just like them, we've lost much of our spiritual core because of grafting. We've lost most of our branches, but we're still here, as people, in spite of it all. God keeps moulding us in line with his image. Anyway, it's too dark down here for bonsai trees, so I carve, like Jesus, who was a carpenter, only I do filigree miniatures, largely miniature Nativity scenes and sometimes Last Supper figurines. That's what I do to kill time in my underground exile. I sneak out at night every now and again, like some rat, and search for pieces of wood, moss or other materials, which I then use to craft miniature equivalents of everything that's defined my soul. You wouldn't believe the things that people throw out. I use it all for my little works of art. Look, this Nativity scene is made of mahogany, which belonged to an old bed that I found half eaten by worms in an attic. All that attire worn by Mary, Joseph, the Three Kings, shepherds, all these buttons, it's all made of waste material. The roof of the sty here is made of a Coke can, the shoes are from what was left of a glove and I could go on. Everything looks brand new, but in reality it's all made of rubbish. Pieces of old garments, wood, sheet metal, the only exceptions are the bodies of the figurines, which are always made from bones.'

'*Aus Knochen?*' Rosa leans over to Adam to verify she has understood correctly.

'You understood correctly, miss,' replies Father Kirilov. 'You must understand that I'm very fond of the works of art that my fellow Capuchins crafted out of the remains of their brothers. Have you ever been to the crypt of the Santa Maria della Concezione in Rome? You've got chapels there that are entirely clad in the bones of dead Capuchins, even chandeliers and doorknobs made of bones. Of course, people today think that's morbid, in spite of its cultural and historical value. My Church has thrived on relics for millennia. I know that my contribution is modest, but it's a contribution none the less. I'm not scared of physical death; what scares me is the death of my soul. And that's exactly what this city should be afraid of, the death of its soul, Miss Portero. That is your name, isn't it? Do you know its etymological origins? Does it derive from the Spanish verb "to protect"? From the Latin *portarius*? That would make for an interesting debate.'

Father Kirilov points towards the desk in the middle of the room.

'I use animal bones. I work mostly with pig femur and other larger bones. I chose them based on their shape, colour and the age of the animal. Pig bones are not all that I use. This Joseph, for instance, is made of a wild boar's tusk; the pair of Balthazars here are made out of a horse's rib. If only I could work with ivory! Not an easy thing to come by around here, although nothing's impossible. The only rule I strictly adhere to is that I always use human bones for the figurines of Jesus. Anything else would be an act of sacrilege, don't you think? Look at this box with a miniature set of the Last Supper, for example. It's almost finished. I must have spent several hundred hours on it –'

'Mr Kirilov,' Bely cuts in.

'Father Kirilov, please.'

'Well, if nothing else will do, Father Kirilov, why did you bring us here? And how did you know we were looking for you? We never enquired about you, and this gentleman here –'

'Poet,' Kirilov interjects softly.

'And this gentleman here who writes poetry, he was seated on that bench in the courtyard before we arrived.'

'Let's make this clear,' smiles Kirilov, 'this very gentleman was sitting there from yesterday morning onwards, so thank God you finally arrived and relieved him of his laborious duty. It's not easy to sit and wait out in the cold. He could've contracted pneumonia or something much worse.'

Bely and Rosa glance at each other.

'Mr Bely, I've got nothing to hide from you. I've got nothing left to lose; my only fault is that I'm still alive. With your help and the help of God that will soon no longer be the case. I'm not upset with anybody, I don't resent anyone. I will have no evil thought accompany me when I go under, Mr Bely. I forgave everybody, everything there was to forgive. My problem is that none of my brother priests are in a fit state to forgive me.'

'What are you referring to, Kirilov?'

'Mr Bely, not like this. We're not here to beat around the bush. There're plenty of rats in this city who do just that. I don't mean the rats down here but those up there who wear fancy clothes and drive around in flashy cars.'

Kirilov gets up again, lays down the blanket and walks to the curtain on the other side of the room.

'There's a small underground catacomb behind this door. Not many people in this town know about it, which shouldn't surprise you, considering most people know nothing about the history of their own city. Unless they're intentionally trying to know as little about all the unpleasant historical events as possible. The two of us, Mr Bely, couldn't be more different. History is our driving force, our veins pulsate with images from the past that others know nothing about. The moment I heard about Dorfler and Butcher I knew what was going on. I've done some research, and it appears that Laszlo Farkas has also been missing since Friday evening. He was expected at some charity event, but he never showed up. A touchy subject for a state prosecutor to disappear so unexpectedly. The NEW WORLD has closed down. Bely, I know your agenda, but relax, I'm not your enemy, I'm your ally. Your timing is perfect. Everything in my life happened so that we could meet down here in this pit, which I discovered only recently.'

Bely says nothing. Father Metod Kirilov, the notorious chief financial officer of the Maribor archdiocese, looks at Bely with relentless yet courteous determination.

'Everything I've done, I've done in good faith. I've always put our community, my Church, my brothers and sisters before my own interests. Curiosity is my only sin, and, as far as I remember, it's always been my sin.'

Kirilov bursts out in loud laughter. He sits back down and drapes the blanket over his shoulders.

'There wasn't much in terms of experimenting in the Pohorje Mountains where I grew up. I took whatever I could get. My curiosity drove me on to become the president of Tito's Union of Pioneers at primary school and chief altar boy at church. I thought things that seemed incompatible under Communism to be obvious elsewhere, even logical. Later, during my theology studies, I experimented with pretty much everything: magic, yoga and various breathing techniques, including hyperventilation. Dear Miss Portero, do you know what truly caught my attention?'

Rosa stares at Kirilov. She tries to pull on the cigarette, but it has already gone out.

'Regression,' says Father Kirilov ardently. 'As students we practised regression all the time, and I have to say I was rather good at it. Who knows, we might've met before, Miss Portero, on a Roman slave galley perhaps? I'm kidding, of course. Don't take me seriously. Some of my regression experiences, however, were far from amusing, like those from my recent past. It happened two generations back, here in Maribor. Every single time, with each regression, I got caught up in the same situation. I relived it a thousand times, the way you relive traumas. Would you like to hear about it, Mr Bely?'

'If you'd like to share it with us, sure,' replies Bely, somewhat distant.

'It's about me playing speed chess with Nikola Tesla. How can I forgive myself for not having recognized a genius in that filthy pig, who spent his nights sitting around in a sordid restaurant in Maribor railway station? He was a poor man, unkempt and miserable, originally from Lika in Croatia. Pungent and repulsive breath. And a pair of zealous, naughty eyes. We played. There was no doubt he was the better player. He played an unusual game, which made me think that he played against himself. Eventually, I saw that all of his moves were so well premeditated and far sighted that I was ready to throw in the towel after only twenty or so. But, in the end, I always won. My God, how I cleaned him out. I took him to the cleaners eight times a night. Yet I felt sorry for him. I knew he had no money. But he just smiled, slowly working his way through a hip flask filled with rubbing alcohol. Finally, after many nights, I realized that he was a genius in self-annihilation. Not only did he indulge in trying to find the most ingenious way to beat his opponent, he also sought a way to beat himself, to double the pleasure. He played neither on my side of the board nor on his. Imagine, Mr Bely, the guy played his game on both sides at once. Each time his victory was approaching, he began losing again. But he never did it in an obvious way, by overlooking a piece or by intentionally miscalculating the combination of moves. That would've been too simple. His defeats were always grand, part of his well-thought-out plan. Tesla was great, the greatest artist of loss. Not only did he steer his way through his own game he also steered it towards his own downfall, his own expunction from the game, if you will. Strange fellow indeed! And that wasn't his only eccentricity. Imagine, he was so engrossed in the game that he urinated under the table. As a result, he played only with the few of us who could put up with the smell. One night, when I finally realized his objective was not to win but to use me as a tool through which he planned to defeat himself, I decided to shift my tactics. The moment the tide turned in my favour, I began losing. Needless to say, Tesla saw right through me, so he stepped up his game. He managed to lose once again, only this time his game was so intricate and inconspicuous that I never suspected that he was actually winning. Besides, he had pissed on my military boots, which set me off so much that I forgot all about my suspicions. My rage and revenge had me rise again, but as soon as I cooled off a bit, he got me. I won. Again I won. I was desperate. That was the end of chess for me. Not only did he defeat me by forcing me to win he robbed me of my pleasure and love for the game. I've never played chess since then. See where I'm coming from? If I never play chess again, it will be too soon. The Buddhists celebrate nirvana, alienation from the cycle of perpetual return. Maybe that's what I want, finally to learn something useful from my past, my mistakes. I never understood why every regression took me back to the same seemingly unimportant scene from my past life. Until the stock-market collapse, the archdiocese financial disaster, the bankruptcy and the selling-off of the T100 company. Suddenly everything makes sense.'

'What makes sense?' asks Bely.

'The lesson of this story is not how to behave better when something happens again. The question is how to put an end to repetition itself. Your mission, Mr Bely, is to kill the Great Orc, of which I'm a part. Am I right?'

'You're right,' replies Bely, 'but it will take more than just you and me to fulfil this mission.'

'When I was told that I was part of the Great Orc, all I could do was laugh. I was a young ordained priest here in Maribor. I always made fun of secret societies of which, as we all know, there's no shortage among my brothers. I never pledged allegiance to this society, I'd never even heard about it. Farkas came to me one day and told me that I was one of the thirteen bodies inhabited by hundreds, thousands, millions of souls, which protect the world against change. I scoffed at him. Then one evening I felt octopus legs as they embraced my body, leaving red prints all over me. I've seen some stigmata in my time, but this was beyond that. I prayed, I fasted and I confessed my sins, but nothing helped. It was God's will, and I had no choice but to accept it, just as lepers must accept their condition. Mr Bely, I know you're here to absolve all thirteen members into the other world. You must absolve all of us, all of our souls, if you want to accomplish what you set out to do. And you're running out of time. I assume other members are as vigilant and watchful as I am. As soon as they can they will find new bodies, hosts for a new myriad of deluded souls, which will become new conductors, new additions to the group of thirteen. Do you know what Farkas said to me a few years ago, when I asked him who the head of the Great Orc was?'

Bely shrugs his shoulders.

'He asked me whether I used the internet much. He said that I would understand the machinery of the Great Orc much better if I used the web. There's no server, only a network of thirteen computers which aren't necessarily aware of who the other constituent parts of the network are. Only one of them is acquainted with everybody else in the group. That, however, doesn't necessarily make that unit the head of the network, because the entire network can be restored from any one of the thirteen computers. You may unplug twelve computers, but still the network will retain all the information, while the remaining computer will scout for new computers to add to a new network. So, in order for this to work, all thirteen computers must be unplugged, before one of them manages to find substitutes for those out of commission.'

Kirilov's face is draped with a stern, authoritarian look.

'Bely, I'd love to help you out. The pleasure would be all mine. But I truly don't know who the other members of the Great Orc are besides those you've already seen, myself and Mayor Voda. I assume you know about him. The rest I'm not familiar with. I have no idea where to get their names.'

Kirilov lights up a fresh cigarette, removes his blanket, stands up, straightens his elegant garment and readjusts his collar. 'Give me a minute. Let me just add two more figures to the set, so it'll be complete. I'd like you to have something from my workshop.'

Kirilov sits at the desk, repositions the desk lamp, sets up the magnifying glass, takes a pair of tweezers and moves the little fragments into one of the boxes on the desk.

The poet, who has sat silently on the sofa next to Kirilov and smoked cigarettes all this time, clears his throat. 'Father Kirilov is a saint, if you ask me. Of course, nobody in this city would agree with me. They mostly think of him as some criminal, but in reality he's just a man whose uncorrupted kindness and good faith managed to shake the foundations of the Catholic Church. From this day on the Maribor archdiocese will have to get by in poverty. It will have to return to St Peter's principle. Purification will be its next step. The T100 cable provider made people connect when it dug trenches to their homes, and because people are perverts they talked about the porn-channel-related stories. Let's be honest, Father Kirilov never had any influence over the cable programme. But it's thanks to him that some of its facets still work with great success. And that's what keeps the Church from going completely bankrupt. TV sales, for example, turned out to be especially lucrative. Their number-one hit is the sensor knife, which plays different sounds, depending on the type of meat you cut. If you cut up beef, autumn leaves start to rustle; fish brings about the swishing sound of the waves; and so on. The T100 is made of the right stuff; it's got the potential to make it big. I don't need to stress that the profits won't go the Church, they will go straight to the banks.'

The poet stops whispering. Kirilov is deeply absorbed in gluing and assembling the fragments of his miniature set. His eyes lean out of his skull, the tip of his tongue peeps out of the corner of his mouth in concentration.

'He mentioned the catacomb,' the poet resumes whispering. 'He knows what happened to Butcher and Dorfler. The moment the souls leave us, that's what becomes of us, I know. We, who still have our souls, find such existence indecent. So we agreed that once his soul is absolved I'll place his body among his brothers and sisters, where he'll rest in decency and peace. I'm telling you this so you'll be informed.'

'There,' says Kirilov as he stands. 'I wasn't able to perfect my miniature scene. That would've taken another day, but we don't have that much time. Mr Bely, I'm giving you this unfinished work as an art form open to interpretation and for your imagination to complete. In return, I ask of you that you immediately finish your work. The time has arrived for me to say goodbye and to thank you again for your visit.

Miss Portero, it was a great pleasure, even though we failed to resolve the etymological conundrum of your surname.'

Kirilov hands Bely the wooden box and bows to Rosa in farewell. He smoothes his combed-down white hair.

Rosa and Bely look at each other. Bely nods. Rosa pulls out the silver compact, opens it and offers Kirilov the oyster crackers.

'I suggest you take the one from the other side,' says Bely and opens the compartment with the dark crackers.

Kirilov nods, takes an oyster cracker, walks to the other side of the room, kneels down and sinks into prayer.

# Disinfection

Adam Bely lies on a hotel bed with his iPad, browsing through a newspaper's website. It's Monday morning, and most of the articles must have been written on Saturday, so not much is new. The crime section mentions no new cases of mental breakdown among the eminent people of Maribor. Further on, the section on local news invites Bely to an extensive article about the negative financial and ecological effects of the wastewater treatment plant construction beneath Calvary. The author's conclusion is that the city has too much wastewater and too little money and that the mayor and his team should try to invert this ratio. The cultural page contains a summary of the coverage on Maribor published in the German newspaper *Frankfurter Allgemeine Zeitung*. Maribor is described as 'a miserable city.' Voda replies to this statement with an offended letter to the editor, in which he lists some of the city's past achievements, such as the gold-medal winner from the 1924 Olympics in Paris, and Maribor being the world's capital of sautéed potatoes, where an astounding forty thousand people gather in the street just to fry up, eat and praise sautéed potatoes for days on end. Mayor Voda's objection against the biased German columnist ends with a long list of recent achievements, with a special nod to the fact that Maribor hosted the 2011 European championships in ultimate Frisbee and ju-jitsu as well as the European conference of hunters a year before. He also highlights that, in 2009, the city was given an award for having the cleanest public toilets in Slovenia. Further on, Bely lingers over a lengthy article that calls for a direct democracy, resignation of the city council and a new election. He notices that, unlike other articles that are signed with at least the initials of their authors, this one lists its author as an informal group called Chilly July. On their Facebook profile and their website the group calls for mass protests against Voda for having 'abducted their common shit', yet another remark on account of his wastewater treatment plant. Bely is stunned to see that the group has nearly seven thousand Facebook followers, which is quite an achievement for a marginal group with such radical views.

Saturated with news, Bely puts down his iPad. On the table by the window-sill stands the gift from Kirilov. A wooden box, in it a little hut with a comet over its roof and two groups of figurines, one on either side. Bely finds its composition unusual and not at all in keeping with what Kirilov told him about the use of bones. The small hut lies in a miniature landscape of tiny trees, moss, a manger, a meticulously crafted tiny tile roof, a fence and innumerable other details, among which there are no hand-made figurines. On the contrary, the figurines of people are plastic and factory-made, nothing that an ordinary toy shop wouldn't stock. The figurines adhere to the back wall of the box with thick layers of glue, blooming with tiny bubbles, which testifies that the content of the box was put together hastily. It is an obvious representation of the Nativity scene, possibly the arrival of the Three Kings, but what a representation it is! The manger is surrounded by seven figurines, some animals and three strange glass items: a shot-glass, a marble and a tiny glass lens. The manger lies empty in the centre of the box; there's no sign of Christ the Saviour. Bely doesn't know what to make of it. What's the gist of all of this? Is it all a hoax, with Kirilov mocking Bely from beyond the grave? Or was his creation only the act of confusion of a desperate man on his way to self-negation? Without an answer, Bely lies on a rather uncomfortable bed and stares at the tiny comet that glimmers above the box.

Did he only briefly close his eyes? The grey of this wintry day is still there. Ricocheting light on the firewall across the street, opaque and indefinite. The noise that woke him is more distinct by the minute. Bely tracks it down to the room next door. Moving furniture, dull conversation, muttering voices. Bely steps to the window. For a fraction of a second he sees a person in a diving suit and protective mask crossing the courtyard beneath.

Shrovetide carnival masks were not a tradition when Bely lived in Maribor. That is not to say that the carnival is the number-one event even now. The city is nearly dead and too down-and-out for that. People have no respect for real tradition any more; they're only interested in the Hollywood version. One way or another, the farce will soon end. Shrove Tuesday tomorrow, then Ash Wednesday, a cold shower of reality and finally a farewell to this masquerade.

A knock on the door. Bely opens. Two people dressed in white protective cover-alls, gloves, thick masks and goggles stand before him.

'You're on the list. We're here to take some samples and to disinfect,' says one of them under his breath and pushes past Bely.

The other person drags in a small trolley with a large device and two tubes with spray nozzles. One of them samples dust from each corner of the room and stores the cotton swabs in test tubes that lie propped up on the table. The other one sprays a white steamy substance across the floor and twice over Bely's shoes. Then he opens the window. Bely barely saves Kirilov's box from falling and shattering. A heavy cloud of ice-cold air takes over the room, overpowering the sugary scent of the spraying agent. The man sprays the outside windowsill.

'Damn parasites. There's an entire colony up here,' he says to himself. The sound of coo and flutter enters the room. The man scares off a pair of pigeons as he leans out, his legs dangling above the radiator. Bely is worried that he might topple over and fall.

Bely asks the men repeatedly about the list. The roar of the spraying device and the absent minds of the men yield no reply.

A few minutes later, they're both gone. The room phone rings.

'Inspector Maus here. Mr Bely, I'm down at the reception desk. Would you mind joining me for a minute? It's important.'

Bely heads to the reception desk and knocks on Rosa's door on his way down. A trail of spilled disinfectant that meanders from his door all the way to hers implies that her room was also disinfected. But there is no answer. Rosa must be out.

Inspector Maus greets Bely and gives a quick gesture to his assistant Gros to remain seated in the armchair. The two of them take seats at the outer edge of the reception area.

'Thank you for taking the time. I'd like to talk to you in private, Bely. I assume my men stopped by your room already? Did their job? Disinfected everything? That's my boys. You see, I've received the news from the lab, rather disturbing news that still needs to be confirmed. Before we begin, may I ask you to keep this strictly confidential? And by strictly I mean strictly. You will mention nothing to your partner, Miss Portero.'

Bely nods.

'Do you recall the dead swan case here in the Drava River seven years ago? Its death sparked alarm among the people, especially when it was discovered that the bird had died of the H5 virus, or the so-called bird flu. Soon the swan was followed by other birds, and some people even ended up in quarantine. Fortunately, we caught it just in time. Now the lab that examined blood samples from Dorfler and Butcher just gave me the results, which, I'm afraid to say, confirm my expectations.'

'And what did you find out? That bird flu was the reason they went mad?' asks Bely.

'Please, Bely, don't underestimate the parallels between both cases.' Inspector Maus shakes his head with pride. 'Of course, it's obvious this is not the same virus as seven years ago. But nobody yet excluded the possibility that this might be some sort of an advanced disease of non-viral origin. Whatever it is, it's very likely transmitted by birds, largely pigeons, and Butcher and Dorfler were the first two to succumb to it. There're also other things to consider, which I can't discuss with you right now. Anyway, based on what the lab has given us so far, we can't yet rule out a new form of virus or some other contagious disease. And, until that changes, I'll stick to my suspicions.'

Bely focuses his full attention on Inspector Maus. 'Then why are you telling me this, Maus?'

'Listen, we performed a preventative disinfection on everybody who came into physical contact with Dorfler and Butcher in the last forty-eight hours before the onset of their symptoms. At the same time, the state sanitary inspectorate authorized me to preventatively eliminate every pigeon in the greater Maribor area. Can you imagine what would happen if the media broke such a scandal? That would be a hard blow, not only for Maribor and its tourism but also for the European Capital of Culture, a disaster of unimaginable magnitude, which a small handful of people would take advantage of, for sure, especially now with local elections coming up.'

'Voda, you mean?' asks Bely.

'Who else? In the past he managed to dig his way out of what was a politically impossible situation by redirecting the attention from important questions to issues that only seemed to be important. As a former policeman, Voda's always felt at home in a crisis situation. You must know that if, all of a sudden, tomorrow there were an outbreak of some deadly virus in Maribor, endangering thousands of lives, then no one would show up at the protest against Voda. No media would pay any attention to his controversial projects, such as the wastewater treatment plant under Calvary. People would obsess about this mysterious virus long enough to fail to see the big picture. I'm sure that in such scenario he would be re-elected.'

'OK, but what do you need from me?' asks Bely.

'If there's one thing I don't trust it's the media. I know what will happen if my suspicions are confirmed. Voda has his own network of people who control certain newspapers and TV stations, not only local but national, too. Most of the independent media are either small or incompetent. If there's a scandal then I want the first report to come from outside Slovenia so that it will be presented in an unbiased manner. This would force the Slovenian media to sum up what the foreign press said. This is no safeguard against a malicious distortion of facts, but at least it reduces the possibility of manipulation. To do that I need a reporter that I can rely on, someone who's not on Voda's team and who's not from here.'

'Rosa Portero,' Bely says.

'That's it. As an institution, we find Austrian Radio more credible than our Central Bank. People like to say that we're a quiet Austrian province. That's not true. Even people who live in the backwoods have the right to a voice. We're just a lousy Austrian colony with zero rights. Anyway, I need you, Mr Bely, and I really hope you'll give me a helping hand here.'

'Fine, Maus, but on one condition.'

Maus looks at Bely.

'That you tell me how you got personally involved with Voda.'

Maus grows serious for only a moment, and then smiles again. 'I've got nothing to hide, Bely. I'd better tell you the story myself before you hear about it somewhere else. Voda and I went to the police academy together. We were room-mates, best friends, and we were equally fanatical about a hobby we shared back when we were only eighteen. Guess what?'

Bely shrugs his shoulders.

'We both bred pigeons. Not just any pigeons. I pulled some strings at the police academy, and soon I was involved in a secret project that was financed by the Ministry of Defence. Our goal was to breed a top line of pigeons to act as our intelligence agents. And I don't mean traditional carrier-pigeons. Breeding top pigeons that are trained to transport secret messages is a daunting task that requires time and knowledge. This was so much more than that. You know, much of our success with pigeons depends on what they eat, their food. So I discovered that next to their regular mixture of grains, they thrived on correct doses of dry garlic, powdered rose quartz and a certain chemical preparation. Armies invest billions of dollars into computer-run intelligence systems. And all I needed was a home-based lab, where I was able to raise kami-kaze pigeons. They were special pigeons that were resistant to potential hostile electromagnetic field disturbances, which is a big issue for them.

There's no aircraft or rocket in this world that can't be shot down. But how do you dismantle flocks of pigeons, tens of thousands of them, swarming in from different directions to strike the enemy all at once, and right on target? Especially when you're dealing with pigeons that are, just like modern viruses, contaminated with an intelligent biological weapon? But back then I hadn't even begun to think in these terms, although Voda may have, I don't know. I continued to breed pigeons simply because of my love of birds and sport. I wanted to raise the smartest pigeons in the world, and that's what I did. My training them for special missions played second fiddle to my love for the birds themselves. Voda was in my shadow. He was pathologically trying to copy everything I did. If I listened to punk music, then he chose punk in spite of his unconditional love for folk polka and traditional Dalmatian *a cappella*. And because I bred pigeons he decided to breed them, too. Soon he realized that his work was never going to measure up to mine, his room-mate, his mentor. He must have hated me for that, but this was something I didn't grasp until much later. It was a morning late in April. I drove out to the Pohorje region, where I kept my pigeons. It was a few days before we were going to test them in front of the ministry committee. If the pigeons passed the test, then the Ministry of Defence would invest considerable sums to develop the project. That would mean that the two of us, Bely, would have never sat here face-to-face because I would have left the police to work as an innovator and a top expert on biological weapons. In which case I would've lived somewhere in the States or Israel, for sure. So, imagine the scene that opened up before me when I got there on 27 April, one of the most horrible moments in my life: 201 out of 214 of my sweethearts lay on the ground. A massacre! Their bodies were still warm, some of them still kicked their little feet and flapped their wings. I felt as if somebody had poisoned me, my life, and my future. I knew that Voda was the only person who knew where my pigeons were. A few times he'd gone up there instead of me to feed them. Anyway, I returned to the dorm. I wanted to kill him, I wanted to punish him for everything he'd done to me. But his bed and his wardrobe were empty. He returned to the academy only after I had left, so we really only met again a decade later when he was a young member of parliament and I was a criminologist.'

'And what happened to the pigeons?'

'The project fell through. The research team went their separate ways. And it never occurred to me to breed birds again. The whole thing was far too traumatic, and I was just too young to be able to sleep on it and put it behind me. Besides, we were never able to resolve the mystery of the thirteen missing pigeons. Did they escape? Did he finish them off somewhere else? Or did he continue to breed them and plans to take advantage of them when the time comes, which I find to be the most probable explanation.'

'You are aware that these accusations are unproven, pretty damning and may have consequences? You're too involved to be working on this case. What about the rule of impartiality?' asks Bely.

'I know what you mean,' Inspector Maus grins so enthusiastically that the echo of his laughter floods the reception area and prompts Gros on the other side of the room to raise a smile.

'Bely, do you really believe in impartiality? In a small country of two million victims, many of whom are often also persecutors, and persecutors who are often the biggest victims? Oh please! The only way we can survive as a society is to be firm and relentlessly open about our partiality. There, I should be going now. The boys and I are performing another disinfection at Off. Don't forget your promise! Don't spill the beans. Is that clear?'

On his way out, he meets Rosa and takes off his hat in salute. Rosa is carrying a plastic bag. She and Bely go to her room on the first floor. Window wide open, messed-up room – someone had ransacked the drawers and her suitcase. Rosa lays a two-litre Coke bottle, instant chocolate porridge and a packet of Gillettes on the table in front of her. Bely takes a banana out of a bowl and practically inhales it, eating another two immediately after binning the peel of the first.

'What was that all about? What did Maus want?'

'Don't worry, he's got nothing. He doesn't have a clue. Voda is his enemy, and whatever happens, he'll blame Voda for it. And the more Maus is occupied, the better for him,' mumbles Bely with a mouthful of banana.

'Who's been in my room?' asks Rosa, checking her stuff. She spots a wet trail on the floor that runs the length of the carpet all the way to the window-sill.

'Maus's pigeon hunters.'

'Did they also stop by your room?'

'They did. They rummaged around and sprayed the whole place. I hope that whatever they sprayed wasn't too toxic, but I'd still rather be safe than sorry. I'll ask for different rooms.'

Rosa nods. 'I wandered around town for a bit. I can't get my mind off Kirilov's box. I can't help but think that it's a scam. This would be the time to resolve whatever secret clue it may contain, if there is one.'

'I looked but couldn't find anything,' says Bely, opening the door.

'I'll come with you and look at it again while you're down at reception.'

Rosa examines the box. Just like the night before, she carefully inspects each of the seven figurines. Left of the empty manger stands a plastic figurine of St Matthew with a pen and a book; next to him St Paul with a sword. The postures of some of the figurines suggest that they came from a Last Supper set, as if they had been seated at a long table. Adjacent to St Paul is Balthazar, the king with dark skin. Between them graze a gestating swine and a mole. Both animal figurines are oversized compared with the tiny people. Behind them, a small shot glass is glued into place. Right of the manger, Joseph, the father of Jesus, and a crocodile figurine playing a pan-pipes, stand deep in thick layers of yellow glue. Beside them, a larger Lego figurine of a zoo keeper with ZOO on its shirt, and St Peter with a pair of keys in his hands, as per tradition, and with glued-on wings, which must have been taken off another figurine. In moss next to these lie a glass marble with a red swirl inside and a piece of round glass, which is glued high on to the trunk of a tree so that it stands out from the rest of the figurines and objects attached to the moss. Rosa leans closer. The round piece of glass becomes a transparent eye that watches over the entire composition in unison with the other eye, the comet.

# War and Peace

In front of the hotel, Bely collides with a clown whose stomach protrudes out of his frame like a barrel. The clown laughs and tosses an empty bottle against a wall. Broken pieces of glass bounce off, and the clown laughs again. Suddenly a brown liquid squirts out of his mouth and punches through the soiled snow which, only seconds later, yields ground to his drunken clown suit, complete with stripy socks and clown shoes. For a moment, Bely is at a loss. He should probably help the clown and drag him off somewhere warm. But then a pair of clowns with bellies just as big appear out of the blue and scream in their compatriot's ear, slap his face and, after many failed attempts to bring their wrecked comrade back to life, grab him by his arms and haul him down the street.

It's a Shrove Tuesday. The clowns are gone. Bely sees no other masks walking the streets of Maribor aside from a couple of weary children dressed as cowboys, who lag behind their visibly agitated mother. The cathedral bells strike a quarter to three. Bely notices that the new neon sign above the former seat of the Maribor archdiocese in Slomšek Square is fixed to the wall. The sign will probably light up as the hazy afternoon gives way to the dark of the wintry evening. At last the snow had stopped. In the square, a worker in blue overalls shows Bely where to bypass the ECoC marker, which is attached to a crane. Yelling workers. A supervisor cursing, while three men move the electrical wiring from underneath the disembowelled cobblestone ground. Bely overhears a conversation between the workers who, leaning on their shovels, study the wooden pedestal, as it sways ominously above their colleagues.

'Whaddya they think they're doing, mate? Like we've got nothing better to do than move these damn balloons all day long.'

'If only they moved it somewhere worthwhile, once and for all. Just think about it, a digger, a crane, we've put up a road block, there're six of us, and for what, so we can move the damn thing by no more than a metre and a half? And it's not even blocking nothing where it is now! Do they know how much this costs? People can't afford, like, a glass of wine, let alone fix a busted mains line, the roads are a disaster, and we're moving bleeding balloons.'

'Crooks,' says the other worker.

'Maribor, a capital, yeah right. The gentlemen sit at the opera while we work all day for fuck all. Jesus, it's cold today. Throw him that shovel, would you, before the boss explodes. By the way, have you been to the Fašenk student masquerade? Today's your last chance,' says the first worker.

'That's for kids,' replies the other. 'I'm staying home with my old lady. She said she's taking me to court if I don't screw her at least twice in a row.'

'Only twice? My wife says that now that she's bought four new costumes I'll have to do her at least once per costume. And two times with the police costume to reinstate law and bleedin' order.'

'You lucky bastard!' yells the first worker.

All of a sudden a brown concoction surges from underneath the digger's metal bucket, dyeing the ground and patches of snow dark. The liquid manure gushes forth in a three-metre-high jet.

'Damn, he hit the sewage! We're fucked. You don't have to dig deep to find shit in this city.'

Supervisor, furious shouting. Chalk-pale, the operator climbs off the digger. Everybody forms a wide circle around the pipe that continues to spit faeces. Slowly, the pressure subsides, and the jet is brought down to a bubbling puddle.

'Franci, you're not gonna need to dress up today, you shitty fucker. Maybe your wife won't recognize you, but she'll smell you from way off.'

'I'm pretty sure that this new perfume of yours will earn you some arse, too.'

'Real cunts like a good smell not sterile white collars. My woman says it's best to fuck a skeleton, 'coz at least you see their boner, but to fuck a skeleton who's also dressed in shit, well, there's nothing better than that. A recipe for the fuck of the century.'

'You're too fat around your waist for a skeleton.'

'That's not me, it's my costume. Hey, Franci, if my dick had two bones I'd screw you too. But I'm afraid I'm taken now.'

'Your old lady?'

'For all you know you might be screwing a douchebag dressed as her.'

Supervisor fumes with rage. The workers grin and begin shovelling in slow motion.

'Careful you don't pull a muscle, Franci.'

'If it's gonna make it grow longer ...'

'Why don't you go and plug up that hole with that long dick of yours?'

'Shit won't stop shit from flowing, Lojs, you should know that. Your tongue is long enough to stop this shit, so why don't you put it to some proper use and help over there?'

'What use? That's a lost cause. I bought four masks with no holes in their mouths. My woman's a great fuck, but I wouldn't wanna lick her.'

'I know what you mean. Down there I would, but one storey up, no way. We don't lick no shitty soil, mate.'

'The digger guy should clean up his own mess. We know how it is. He'll plug it up here, and in one hour it'll blow up somewhere else. Mother Earth wants none of our shit. It bursts out everywhere you look, and we have to patch it up.'

'Only, Lojs, the two of us patch fuck all.'

'No, Franci, we're different. We stick to our shovels and keep our mouths shut.'

The workers grin again.

A large flock of cawing crows takes off from the treetops in Slomšek Square, draws a circle in the sky and lands again back where it started. Bely feels as though he never left the city. It doesn't seem possible that he was away for sixteen years. Was he on a short journey and he only just came back? It's as if nothing had happened. All across the square posters with red crosses against black backgrounds. Above the cross a sign in small letters: LEV NIKOLAYEVICH TOLSTOY – ANDREAS, and below the cross WAR AND PEACE in larger type. Fountain. In the centre of the fountain a huge cube of red ice. Opposite the fountain, a marble stairway, the entrance to the largest theatre in the country. Its façade, 1970s modernist, stuck in a corner of the Secessionist-style square like a foreign body. In front of the theatre a truck with a canvas tarpaulin that reads: CROATIAN NATIONAL THEATRE OF ZAGREB. Two angels with fanfares. Further on a theatre café, empty tables under the glowing patio heaters at its entrance. Bely thinks about the years that he spent in this coffee house. No memories of winter, only memories of hot summery days, together with his colleagues.

At the employees' side entrance, Štef, the doorkeeper, recognizes him and says hello. Hints of socialism, worn carpeting, an old scent of gloomy and musty air redolent of the past.

The secretary still looks the same as she did back in the old days when Andreas was the theatre's director and Bely one of the in-house dramatists. She receives him with a kiss on his cheek.

'It's been what, a billion years since we've seen each other?' says Dolores. 'The director's got a visitor. Wait a minute, she'll be right with you.'

Bely nods and takes a seat in an armchair. An unknown woman sits opposite him, looking like a theatrical prop. As he expected, she continues her monologue about the project she'd been rambling on about ever since he arrived.

'So I tell him, that's not how you handle things. "Offering", the event is called "Offering" and is about making an offering in honour of dictators: Tito, Stalin, Hitler, Mao. We make a true offering, and she thinks that a few old cars and a video projector will get her off the hook. We need blood. Hermann Nitsch-style, otherwise we'll get stuck offering nothing but ideas. I'm not saying we should slaughter hens, but we should slaughter at least one sheep per dictator, I told her. And then she asks, wouldn't I prefer a cow instead? Count me in, I say. She laughs, and I think we've got a good deal here. So you agree to something that's offered to you, isn't that a deal? And then she's trying to get out of it by saying that we haven't signed anything, that she never meant it and it was all a joke. Am I supposed to smell when someone's joking, or what?'

While listening to the unknown woman's dialogue, Dolores quietly checks her email. Every now and then she says 'Ah-ha'. It appears that she's used to performing two simultaneous operations, one secretarial, the other psychoanalytic.

'What's this all about?' asks Bely.

'It's about my production. You don't want to know. I've been working on this project for six years. Six years, can you imagine? I've finally received some funding from the town hall. I went to the mayor and told him that something needed to be done with these dictators, and he fell for it. I've got everything now, the team, a project that will kick ass, provided that I really do it well and not the way things are done here, half-arsed. A hundred-per-cent effort is what's missing from this town. Here everyone wants to stage reality. Theatre is reality! Sweat, sperm, blood, it's all there. Physical theatre is what gets to people not this symbolic shit for high-school kids and premières for some weary directors of state-owned companies.'

'Ah-ha,' Dolores sighs, deeply engrossed in her email.

The unknown woman throws her a glance, but that doesn't divert her.

'Imagine an unforgettable spectacle. Imagine something that will haunt you till the day you die, that will take your breath away and leave you speechless, something that will forever change you. That's the theatre I'm interested in. The theatre of shock, the theatre that's ultimately just like our city, where shocks are an everyday occurrence. If people think that stuffing yourself with Wiener schnitzel every single day is normal, then why couldn't they handle a theatre that's as cruel as normal, everyday life? Nothing new, you'll say, but it's new for our city and the time we live in. Sir, do you believe in the new? Whenever I go to our theatre, when I see guest performances, I'm more and more convinced that new doesn't exist any more, that we used it up a long time ago, that everything is already here. Every era's got its own prohibitions, censorship and self-censorship, so it only makes sense to stage the slaughter of a sheep, if not a cow. Our high-society audience just doesn't get it. A farmer gets it – if theatre was full of farmers, they'd understand. The farmer would come on to the stage and hold up a bucket beneath the slit to catch the blood. And let me tell you, she's no farmer!'

The unknown woman rages and points to the door of Anastasia Green, the theatre director. 'If she were a farmer, she'd understand. But what can I do? If I held out for six years, I'll last another six. Sooner or later my time will come, isn't that right, Dolores?'

'Ah-ha,' says Dolores, as she types on, undisturbed.

'There. I'd better go back to work now.' The unknown woman gets up and leaves without a farewell.

'Don't mind her, she's just one of my patients,' says Dolores. 'Times change, but not theatre psychiatry. It was no different when you were in the house. Remember Marula, who wanted half a million dollars to stage a performance in a zero-gravity environment? Or Berzajev, who threw hot rotten eggs into the audience? This poor thing is still pretty innocent compared with them.'

The door to the director's office opens; a woman in a short skirt steps before them. 'So we're all set. Tonight after the play and tomorrow at three o'clock?'

'Consider it done,' says Anastasia Green, grabbing the unknown woman conspiratorially by the shoulder and then kissing her on the cheek in farewell.

Bely nods at the woman as she passes him.

'Adam, I see you've found the courage to come? I'm really pleased. Come in. Dolores, thank you, that'll be all for today.'

'See you in the evening at the première,' Dolores calls to Bely. 'You're coming, right?'

'Of course he's coming! Missing Andreas's latest play would be worse than arriving on time for a date with Beelzebub. He'll be here with his woman from exotic and far-flung Austria,' Anastasia teases.

Dolores and Anastasia begin laughing thunderously, to Bely's surprise.

Bely knows Anastasia's office well. Other than a white-leather sofa and new photographs on the wall, the space looks more or less the same as sixteen years ago. Bely stops in front of the pictures: opaque footage of the submarine world – coral, fish, the underside of ships – illuminated by a soft light that penetrates from above.

'My photos. Taken with a digital version of the classic camera obscura. That's why you see vignetting,' says Anastasia.

'They're lovely. That intangible blur at the edges adds to the sense of mystery. I remember your photos from your student days. Back then you did only black-and-white photography, mostly of empty courtyards. Those pieces provoked a similar feeling, as if they had some indefinable absence trapped in them.'

'I find photography relaxing. With every photo I take I feel that I get to save a piece of this fleeting world of ours. I don't do it to preserve past moments; that definition of photography is far too banal. I do it when I catch myself thinking that the past doesn't exist any longer, which is, of course, not true. The past has always existed alongside the present. Photography is living proof of this. It's photography that rights our often corrupt image of time. We talked about this a lot in the past. And now here you are again. Adam, I can hardly believe that you're here, after all these years. And that you rose from the dead just in time for Andreas's performance. Can you imagine, *War and Peace*?'

Bely looks deep into Anastasia's dark eyes. 'Yes, that was the time when you worked with Andreas on the *Thousand and One Nights*. You see how things change? When I suggested sixteen years ago that we should do *War and Peace* he mocked me, asking if I'd like to play Napoleon. I'd written the entire adaptation; I really loved Tolstoy. My God, how time flies ... I don't even know where that text is. No wonder, the number of times I moved. But I regret nothing.'

Anastasia touches Bely's hands. The tips of three of her fingers rest, for just a moment, against his palm, mapping a miniature symbol on his skin. Small flagella that attempt to escape. Their faith in one another calls up images from their past.

'I remember the number of times we came to this office to work when Andreas was away on tour,' says Bely. 'He had already divorced me of my duties here, which is the worst, cruellest fate in the world of theatre. I was completely devoted to theatre, I was even paid for being here, but I felt useless because nobody wanted my work. The whole theatre was aware of the fact that I was put on the back burner. I was nothing but a walking dead, a zombie. The only reason they paid me is because that's what the legislation told them to do when, in reality, they would've preferred if I had disappeared off the face of the Earth. But, hey, at least one of us won the lottery. You must have been the big director's favourite dramatist. You loved coming here to the director's office and rocking in his chair while he was away.'

The fingertips in Bely's palm come to a halt and turn mildly moist, as if they had just pierced through mist.

'Don't be mean, Adam. You were just as happy to come here, if you remember. You and Andreas were never compatible. He happened to listen to me but only up to a certain point. That was normal. We were just too young and inexperienced to understand that. Everyone's a genius at twenty, at thirty most of them are embittered, and by the time they hit forty, they have nothing but hatred for geniuses.'

'I was fortunate enough to learn quickly that hatred was not the right response. I wouldn't have been able to play that game. If I hadn't moved on, if I hadn't discovered Scientology, I'd probably be pretty pissed off to see that the director who ran me out of the theatre is now staging my old script. Now I understand that this is how some things turn out and that everything in this world is a seed that eventually sprouts something else – better a decent performance than hatred, or something even worse.'

'I think that the play is more than just decent, Adam, and I'm glad to hear that you don't care about hatred.'

Anastasia leans in dangerously close.

'You said that you'd been sick, Adam,' Anastasia whispers.

Her fingers push into his palm with a surprising strength, as if she wanted to reopen the wound from Butcher's bite. Her lips open and close like the mouth of a fish.

'That's history,' Bely whispers. 'Like many other things.'

'What about your future?' sighs Anastasia Green, smiling roguishly. She steps over to the cupboard, grabs two glasses and fills them up.

'I left two tickets on the table here, for you and your Austrian lady. I put you in the balcony, OK?'

Bely nods and picks up the envelope.

'I knew that sooner or later you'd become director of the theatre.'

'In the end, it's the world turned upside down in the upside-down city that gives you a realistic view. If our everyday life here is turned upside down, then it's up to the theatre to right the picture that's invariably distorted,' says Anastasia, as if reading from some script.

'That's not what I meant. I meant your straightforward determination. Like a real Maribor citizen, you're not going to let anything stand in your way.'

Clink of crystal glasses. The gin spreads through Bely's mouth, unearthing more images from their past.

'Great job, great leather chairs, great office ...'

'Not everything is as great as you think, Adam. We're all part of a wider story, and, in the end, no one writes their life alone.'

'In Scientology it takes years to analyse your past,' Bely says. 'After hundreds of hours of self-interrogation you recognize the events that gave rise to the processes that take control of you later in life.'

'Adam, the problem isn't about who's controlling me or who I'm controlling, the problem is with control itself – we can't live without it. We don't know how not to control or be controlled when, in a way, we all want to be controlled. The question is what we can do about it once we reach a critical point. Sometimes I feel like a prisoner in a crystal palace that I've built around myself. It's wonderful to sit in on performances, to enjoy the magic of the stage. But everything else is pure torture. Do you remember the good old days? We were young and ambitious, the world was our oyster. You could become an influential dramatist, or a world-famous director, or president of a country. Then, all of a sudden, ten, twenty years on, you run out of options. You chose what you chose, and, of course, you stray, and even though you know where you lost your way, there's no going back.'

'Anastasia, same old Anastasia, still indulging in the feeling of being lost, although that's not something you ever believed in.'

'I indulge no more, Adam. Indulgence is for the young. I'm just objectively analysing the situation that we all found ourselves in, including you, Adam.'

'I believe in beginnings. Every moment could be the start of something new, something fateful. If I didn't believe that it's possible to change the course of our destiny at any given moment, then I'd no longer be on this planet. And I'm still here. Here and now.'

'Is your Austrian lady also part of your new life?' Anastasia pours herself a fresh glass of gin, then drinks it in one gulp.

'Forget about that. I'd rather hear about you, Anastasia. What's life like for you? What are you up to? Why do you feel like a prisoner and why don't you set yourself free?'

'Don't be a smart-arse, Adam. It's hard to be creative in this city of miracles, in this theatre of miracles, surrounded by miracle-working geniuses. And, believe me, I'm here all the time, trying to change things for the better. I've got a lovely apartment under Calvary. Imagine, two hundred square metres, but I rarely get to be there. Well, that's also thanks to my horrifying neighbours. Theatre is my life and my home, Adam. I'm afraid that everything will fall apart, that the theatre will vanish into thin air, if I miss so much as a day here.'

Bely notes that Anastasia has morphed back into the person he met at college. The image of a young dreadlocked dramatist who can't stop talking about Sergei Eisenstein, Samuel Beckett and physical theatre. Suppressed passion. Eel-like body. The scent of sweet complexion. The soft sound of her whispering talk with tiny, carefully interwoven plots and intrigues. The shake of her hand, heavy breath and the taste of her tongue slowly pushing beneath his. The full feeling of bodies, comfort and security, when he penetrates her, when they press together and her nails burrow sharply into his scalp. Interlacing and thrusting. Blue skies through the frame of the window. The sounds of summer on the shore of the Drava River. In the evenings reading rehearsals, Andreas and others, the taste of foreign mouths, broken vinyl records, crumpled letters.

'Adam, where are you? You drifted off.'

'It's nothing, just a little *déjà vu*,' says Bely. 'We both know that everything we're talking about now has already happened long ago.'

'Not everything.'

'Perhaps not everything, Anastasia. There're still a few things that need to be taken care of. Listen, I was wondering if you could help me out? I'd like to know the story behind the wastewater treatment plant beneath Calvary ...'

Anastasia glances sharply over at him. 'Why would you want to know that, Adam? It's just another sad story in this city. You'll be better off if you know nothing about it.'

'People are very upset with Mayor Voda; they say he'll poison them.'

'Lies. A classic case of general hysteria, if you ask me. Nobody will poison anybody, Adam. You know that Maribor folk have posed a threat to themselves since the beginning of time when nobody else did.'

'Anastasia, what do you know about the Great Orc?'

She pales for a moment, approaches the table, and opens a bottle. 'Will you have another?' She pours herself half a glass. Slowly she pushes the stopper back into the bottle.

'Years ago a Finnish faith healer came to town. A friend of mine dragged me along to his lecture on the theory of traces. It sounded really bizarre at first, but it's quite logical if you think about it. If you imagine two people who fuck, the man always leaves behind a trace to the point where the woman's old hereditary lines get smudged. And because women are forever marked by the trace of all the men they've ever slept with, it is only reasonable to assume that that's how new human profiles are formed, at least according to the Finn's theory. And the more traces we preserve within ourselves, the fuzzier our hereditary potential becomes and what we pass on to our children becomes. This is the secret reason for mass rapes during war, for example.'

Bely pays close attention.

'You know perfectly well how this city rolls, Adam. This place is dominated by women, whose reign depends exclusively on whom they fuck. Yesterday I walked past a bar called Shakespeare, near the railway station, just opposite the high school. This guy came out of the bar with a woman running after him, shouting that he should wash his cock because she wouldn't suck a dirty one. In front of everyone, in broad daylight! They seemed sober. That tells you everything.'

'I don't know where you're going with this, Anastasia.'

'The apartment building where I live is owned by Voda. Well, it's owned by the city, but Voda had it built for his mistresses. His apartment is in the same building, and you're not going to find a single man who lives in it, only women, from the directors of public institutions to the deputy mayors, aged between twenty and fifty. Nobody ever comes to visit, certainly no men. Voda is the only one. When he offered me an apartment together with my directorship of the theatre, I naïvely thought that the apartment came with the job. The building is owned by the city, it's a five-minute walk from here and very practical for my type of work with unpredictable hours. Sounds great, right? But when I moved in I started to get suspicious, until …'

'Until?'

'Until one day Voda materialized out of nowhere.'

'Where, at your door?'

'Not at my door, Adam. He's got the keys to every apartment in the building. He comes whenever he likes to whichever apartment he likes.'

'Anastasia, you're not going to deny that for something like that it takes two to tango?'

'You don't get it, Adam. Just because we're women it doesn't mean that we don't aspire to achieve something, and not only in social terms. Something useful. Like erasing the line of traces to the extent where nothing can be seen any more. We should be able to get rid of old genealogies, old curses and nightmares. There's got be a way to cleanse yourself, Adam, you know what I mean?'

'I understand, Anastasia, but –'

'No but. But is a word for cowards, for those who bury their heads in the sand and think they're smarter than the rest of the world. Maybe this wastewater treatment plant in the middle of the city is not such a bad thing after all. Never mind the cost overrun, if nothing else it's got a symbolic value, calling on the city to cleanse itself.'

'Is that the goal of the Great Orc, to cleanse the city?'

'To cleanse the city of severe trauma,' Anastasia adds quietly, before taking a long sip of gin. 'The past is a serious thing, Adam, we know that. There's nothing worse than the past. Earlier you said that you believe in beginnings. That makes you one of us. I also believe in beginnings. But to be able to start from scratch you've got to erase the past. It serves no other purpose than to weigh us down, so we might as well tie it around our necks and plunge into a lake. I want to have a life without this shit, Adam. I want to be able to choose my own ancestors, my own performances, my own lovers.'

Anastasia drinks up and slams the glass back on to the glass table. Her hand reaches for Adam's hand again, their fingers interlace, her tongue penetrates his mouth and slowly draws a circle. Their images from the past fill up the room. Bely dives into the homely darkness of her eyes. Suddenly, her hand lets go, the flagella of her fingers no longer touch his hand. Anastasia smiles, steps to the door, opens it and vanishes. Bely gazes into space for a while. Before him a director's office, white leather, photographs. Starfish in one of them. Hazy light. Behind, the windows that open up to the view of the fountain with the red block of ice in front of the cathedral and the university building, nothing but greyness, drizzling. How long has it been? Millions of years? A decade, a couple of minutes? Where did Anastasia disappear to? Bely sees the open door as an invitation for him to leave the office and enter the theatre.

Outside her office, an empty anteroom with nothing but Dolores's desk, chaotically stacked with paper. The logo of the Maribor National

Theatre bounces off the edges of the computer screen. The reception and lavatory are empty.

Bely descends to the first floor. None of the doors are open. Once on the ground floor he heads towards the staff exit. Vertical beams of light, the door leads to the stage. More lights, singles beams, a column of chairs, theatrical scenery. Bely inhales the old, well-known scent of theatre dust. He would find his way blindfolded in the pitch dark. Nothing has changed since his days working here. Backstage he squeezes past a stack of spotlights and steps on to the grand stage. The auditorium before him, eight hundred seats, rests in darkness. A single spotlight illuminates the apron of the stage, which is nearly empty: nothing but two tall pommel horses. Above the stage, chandeliers made from long neon tubes. The scenery for Andreas's *War and Peace*.

Bely stands still, listening. Utter silence, finally broken by a noise under his feet, deep in the theatre's guts. He runs back on to the old familiar stage, which brings back the memory of the game of hide and seek that they used to play, mostly during final preparatory touches before a première, at three or four in the morning, when the last actors and technicians had already left the building. It was Saturday 9 March 1996, the evening before Andreas's performance of *Babylonia*. That was his last working night at the theatre, even though he only sat on the balcony the entire time and watched the rehearsals in silence. Unbearable and humiliating. But four days later, Wednesday 13 March 1996, came the day he would never forget. He emptied his one-bedroom apartment at Lent, left the theatre and Maribor, all for Scientology. And perhaps he should've stayed and reconciled himself to the fact that his theatre career was side-tracked and held as much promise as a ficus tree sitting in a corner of an empty office. Perhaps he should've waited, like so many other actors and dramatists, for more promising times, when Andreas would no longer be director and he could find himself useful again. But he knew that the theatre was overstaffed. The Maribor National Theatre is the biggest in the country, but most of the employees shared his fate. Had he reconsidered and stayed, he would have turned a new, incomparably more predictable leaf. If … If everything that is happening right now hadn't happened then, on that evening before the première. Who knows how many times it has been reprised since then, but with a different cast. Time is an insatiable animal that yearns for reprisals, thinks Bely to himself as he hears a noise again under his feet. He feels as though someone has sucked the silence from beneath him.

The door is open. The corridor leads past the old wardrobes, temporary storage for costumes. Bely finds himself surrounded by Giacondas and Fausts, wigs and swords, above him a big artificial phallus dangling off a hook, a golden goblet – further on a Roman shield and the white skirt of a dervish. Scribbles on a door that reads STORAGE. Battered risers, big screens with opera motifs, furniture from various historical periods, a staircase that leads nowhere. Is this time? Is this the way our memory works? Pieces of material from different periods, stacked one on top of the other, ripped from the rhythm of our lives, quick transitions, now we're here, now we're somewhere unknown, imaginary witnesses to events that we never were a part of, events that might never have happened? Or have they? A mausoleum and an Egyptian sphinx. The tower from which Tosca leaps into the abyss, night after night. The throne of Titus Andronicus, sprayed with artificial blood. And, on the very same spot as sixteen years ago, the tomb of Babylon. Shamurammata, the queen of Babylon, walks on to the stage. Right here, in this tomb, she gives birth to a son of Ninu, the king of Babylon. It was here, sixteen years ago. The last technicians had left the theatre, drained by fatigue. She seduced him right in this tomb. He, jealous and frustrated; she, insatiable, hysterical laughter, her gaze dangerous and contained all at once. Bely grabs hold of a handle and pushes open the tomb lid. Anastasia lies before him, naked, just like sixteen years before. Thighs wide open, vagina, pubic hair styled in the shape of a swastika. Bely kneels down. Anastasia's tongue buries into his mouth, unwavering, her cold hand reaches for his crotch, she laughs through her teeth, pressed against his mouth. Warm breath billowing down his throat. There's no time. This all happened a long time ago. And it will continue to happen time and again into eternity. Open tomb, surrounded by theatrical scenery, time broken in two and mixed up, stories scoffing at the attempt of a single story, no wholeness, no succession, no exit from moving in circles, from repetition. Anastasia's bony thighs wrap around Bely, groaning, pulsating, their movements repeating those of sixteen years ago. There's no difference between these moves and those from the past, only vibrations, saliva, fingernails, two bodies pressed together, the pursuit of and rupture from the other, from yourself into the other. Everything is beyond, around, wrapped into the other. Pleasure is red as blood. It flows in from everywhere, flooding the tomb. Bely and Anastasia undulate deep beneath the surface of time. No sound, only the muffled movement of a drowned pair, a silent journey in every corner around them, a resonance of voids. Pleasure, fight, tentacles, ever tighter around Bely's body, the sharp burning trace of her fingernails' suckers on his back. What amount of time is stored in a single look? How much of the memory that keeps us inside the box is still alive? For a moment, as in a camera obscura, her pupil reflects the image of Bely turned upside down. How many pasts hide in the eye, ever narrower, ever slimier and cooler? How many millennia hide in the eye of the octopus that looks at Bely, while he looks at it as if it were a mirror that closes, opens, closes, as if it were human? His neck and ankles submit to the muscular grip of her tentacles. All that we are, or may become, is a silent passage. Bely continues to thrust, pleasure and pain without edge, joined as one, with every breath, with every move closer to the end. What will introduce change to our millennium, to a system many millions of years old? What is the driving force behind these masked repetitions? Weren't all changes, no matter how revolutionary, part of an initial plan conceived at the very beginning? Aren't they merely the means, the exterior shells, to perfect a much more far-sighted and advanced plan, which is far more intelligent than the system of human thought? And aren't we, this thrusting, these tentacles, this firm handshake, these gasps for air, blood, nothing but consumable products of the system? Aren't the palms that crush the head of an octopus, the palms that fight to the death the indomitable, silent gaze of a creature with eight legs, aware of what they're doing? They don't hallucinate? Don't they misinterpret things to be the way they want them to be? The way they have to be, so that no change would occur in the world of constant change? That would have made the fight against sea creatures easy. But to fight people with good and evil within them ... To fight the system that people ...

Swings, grappling, the ultimate fight. Suddenly the water dyes black, thick inky darkness swallows the air in the storage room. Pulsating tentacles, smiling teeth that illuminate even in absence of light. A battle as fought in ancient Babylon, as fought time and again in each reprisal of Babylon. Tense muscles, bulging eyes, mouth open in silence, ink spilling over the most secret parts of the soul. To live. On and on. Only to keep on living. Even if in this world, even if in the theatre storage room. Even if in a reprisal. Again and again.

Bely regains consciousness. Anastasia's body beneath him appears cold and stiff. His neck, back and ankles smart with burning pain. He climbs out with the last of his strength, his body aching as if it had been bitten by a gigantic octopus. Blotches of cuttlefish ink on his skin, the pungent smell of urine and sweat. He feels around his flaccid penis, the scars where his testicles had been removed. He puts on his clothes and looks at her naked corpse, her crotch, the line of hair above it. He could have sworn that he had seen a swastika there. As if she were a girl, Anastasia's body is thin, pale, white with a hint of blue. Her tongue rests on her lips, her fingers curled as if they had been crippled during strangulation. Bely leans close to her mouth. In absence of her breath he picks himself up and examines the body in front of him. Nothing is what it seems. So much in common, yet so estranged. No memories, when he looks at her. No past. Only a perfect silence, a special vacuum, which no one else can enter.

Bely empties a bag full of transparent plastic wrapping that he finds in a corner. He wraps it around her corpse, dumps her clothes inside, ties it all up and drops it into the tomb. He slams the tomb door behind him.

How long will it take before they discover the body? A couple of days? Perhaps longer? The traces are too many to eradicate. Sooner or later they will identify the perpetrator, but that doesn't matter. What matters is tonight, Bely thinks to himself, as he turns off the storage light on his way out. Tonight, this evening, the time when time and past are no longer.

No past. Nothing matters any more. It's only me, I who create my own past, here and now, in this very moment, Bely ponders as he leaves the theatre. He glances around furtively and slips away down one of the streets.

Slush, slight drizzle. A small truck passes by him, splashing him with water. Bely curses, shoves his hands into his pockets and sinks deep behind the high collar of his coat. No warmth anywhere. A couple of kids in costumes, one of them dressed as Superman. This is where it happened. How old was he? Ten, twelve at the most? He, too, had a Superman costume, a red cape and a big letter S on his chest. A few older boys. Where did they come from? All of a sudden he found himself lying on the ground. It happened right here, in this courtyard. They made him eat worms. Soil full of worms.

Bely stops at the door that leads into the courtyard. He enters. The space is still messy and empty, just like back then, apart from a new set of window displays. Bely lingers before the window, a sign reads: RECREATION CENTRE FOR THE ELDERLY. On the other side of the glass, music plays for some fifteen pensioners, standing or sitting in chairs or wheelchairs. The old men and women raise their hands, and gently wave them back and forth, following the carers' instructions. The two carers stoop down to those on the floor and help them perform the knee extension exercise. Some laugh, some mutter to themselves, bored to death. Bely notices his reflection in the window and, beyond, a reflection of a man in a wheelchair. The man sits and stares ahead. Bely finds his face familiar, familiarly absent.

Father?

The carer turns off the music. The men and the women sit down to a meal of bread and semolina pudding. The carer steps over to the man in the wheelchair, strokes his pale, bald head. She brings food to his mouth. A spoon of semolina pudding drifts in. The man opens his lips it as if he were on autopilot. The nurse moves on. The man eventually spits out the contents. Sticky pudding slowly dribbles down his chin and on to his tracksuit.

An image in the window. An image of the pudding that dribbles off the tip of the man's chin. An image of viscous ink slowly growing clear. An image of a boy who brings Bely a fistful of worm-filled dirt and shoves it into his mouth. An image of Anastasia's fingers gently combing through his hair. An image of an absent old man in a wheelchair, the tip of his tongue peeking out from between mordant bluish lips. There is no past, yet everything speaks in spite of its absence. It speaks, it screams and it won't go away. Bely trembles. No, nothing, nothing matters. Bely slides down the glass, he leans firmly on his knees, his head falls into his hands. There is no past. He, Bely, is its creator, right here, right now in this wintry darkness. Moist tentacles slither out of his eyes. His face is flooded by quiet tears.

# Scheiße

'*Scheiße!*' screams Rosa Portero and hits the brakes. The car skids on the snow-covered road, nearly hitting a boy who has ventured into the street despite the red light. Had she not been distracted by his attire she wouldn't have lost control over the vehicle. Despite the fact that it's freezing outside, the boy is almost naked, dressed in nothing but jeans and a purple T-shirt. His face is covered by a gas mask. No mouth, just a long, rubbery trunk with a big cylindrical filter at the end of it. The writing on his shirt reads: DAS IST MARIBOR. The boy furiously swivels his head and bangs his rubbery trunk on the roof of Rosa's car. The last she sees of him in the rear-view mirror is his Maribor football team logo, ripped jeans and his blotchy skin, red with cold.

'Not again! What is it with my car and all the masks around here? I should've walked to the city aquarium. On foot, no victims, no shitty potholes,' Rosa mumbles angrily.

Back at the hotel Rosa tries Bely's door. Nobody. She returns to her room to dress for the performance when the telephone rings.

'Reception in twenty minutes,' says Bely curtly and hangs up.

Rosa slides into her black, 1930s-style evening-gown. Lavish puff sleeves and gloves that cover her metal hand. Short skirt, strong perfume. Every once in a while she breaks a piece off of a three-hundred-gram chocolate bar and washes it down with a long sip of Coke. One-handed, she dexterously ties up her hair. She works her powder brush across her face then stops at a long scar behind her right ear. She runs her forefinger across it. Rapt in thought, she leaves the bathroom and sits in front of Father Kirilov's box. She examines one figurine after another then pauses and starts again. Suddenly she dashes for her coat, pulls out her ticket and a small flier and holds them next to the box.

Some minutes later Rosa tries Bely's door again, knocking vigorously and without interruption. Buttoning up his white collared shirt, Bely opens the door. She takes note of the burns and bruises around his neck.

'What's this?'

'I saw Green,' Bely says softly and vanishes into the bathroom. Shortly after he emerges in a black turtleneck that rides high around his neck.

'I absolved her. She knew nothing about the other members of the Great Orc, but she did mention Voda. What might be important is that Green lives in a prestigious apartment building that is supposed to be something akin to Voda's harem. It turns out that his apartment building houses only ladies who keep key positions in the city institutions.'

'Where did the abrasions on your neck come from?' asks Rosa, her voice coarse.

'Before I absolved her,' mutters Bely, 'we jostled a bit.' He says nothing more, pursing his lips and turning away to look out the window. 'You don't have to worry. Everything has been taken care of. Green is no longer part of the Great Orc,' adds Bely after a pause.

For a moment, Rosa searches deep in Bely's eyes. Cold and infiltrating, her gaze penetrates where it hurts the most. He withdraws and looks into the night on the far side of the window. Rosa lays Father Kirilov's box down on the table.

'While you were away I was curious about the main tourist attractions here. I drove to the city aquarium, which, to be honest, is just a small dilapidated house in the middle of the park with a couple of spiders, snakes and fish. A far cry from a real aquarium. No visitors, only a guard and a few circling fish, some starfish and some sea anemones glued to the glass. Listen, I was about to leave when I saw something.'

Rosa sits on Bely's bed and tilts her head, her heavy hair cascading down her right shoulder.

'I saw a small aquarium with small octopi. Lots of small octopi that emerged from under the legs of a large octopus, which just lay there, motionless, on the sandy floor. It was practically invisible because it had taken on the colour of sand around it. I read on the explanation panel that octopi are one of the most intelligent sea species. I was intrigued by the information that their brain is located directly around their mouth cavity. Can you imagine, they essentially don't distinguish between feeding and thinking?'

'I don't know what your point is,' says Bely moving closer to her.

'Well, that's when their keeper brought their meal of bottled shrimp. He tossed the bottle into the water. The bottleneck was as narrow as it gets, and you'd never guess that small octopi, let alone the big one, could ever get to the shrimp through such a small opening.'

'So?' he asks impatiently.

Rosa smiles and takes up where she left off. 'What happened next was horrendous. In an instant, the big octopus sucked on to the bottle. Its legs were savagely feeling around the surface, and soon enough they found the opening. One by one, the octopus then pushed its legs through the opening until, finally, it also squeezed its head through it. What a sight.'

'Shall we?' says Bely anxiously, grabbing his grey high-collar winter coat off a chair. 'It's already six thirty. We only have a half hour till show time.'

'I can't get it out of my mind,' continues Rosa, as if she hadn't heard him. 'A giant octopus that is so flexible it can push through the smallest of the holes to get to its prey. That's not all I've got to tell you, Adam. Look what I discovered.'

Rosa pulls a commercial flier out of her pocket that reads THE AQUARIUM-TERRARIUM OF MARIBOR. Colourful photos of fish and other creatures, opening times, entrance fees, group discounts. She holds it up against Father Kirilov's box.

'What do you see?'

Bely looks at her.

'Look at the aquarium's logo, Adam. See the drawing of an octopus under the sign? Compare it with the comet in Father Kirilov's Nativity scene.'

'They're very similar,' says Bely.

'That's right,' says Rosa and leans close to his cheek. A cloud of musky perfume wraps around him. 'This is neither a Nativity scene nor a comet announcing the birth of the Saviour in Bethlehem, Adam. It's a portrait of the Great Orc. Count the rays coming out of the comet. Eight of them. Same as the number of legs an octopus has. Kirilov tried to tell us something he was not able to share with us in person. Now, count the objects around the empty manger together with the octopus, but without the comet above them.'

'Of course!' Bely exclaims. 'All this time we were counting only the human figurines, when in fact we should have also counted animals and other objects, the shot glass, the glass marble and this piece of glass here. That doesn't add up to seven, but twelve.'

'Right. Among those twelve, who do we know?'

'Hm, let's see. St Matthew with a pen, an intellectual. That must be Dean Dorfler.'

'Yes. The pig is also easy to identify.'

'Butcher, his Kranj sausages are made out of pork.'

'And car tyres,' adds Rosa.

'And car tyres, yes. Then there's this small shot glass.'

'Shot glass. Alcohol ...'

'The restaurant owner.'

'That would be Gram,' Bely whispers thoughtfully.

'And the mole? It digs into the soil. Hang on, digging, like digging graves? Could be Magda Ornik. If the mole represents Magda Ornik. I wonder who St Paul could be?'

'A swordsman?'

'A convert, the only non-Jew among the twelve apostles.'

'A judge over the Jews.'

'A judge. It could only be Farkas.'

'And Balthasar, the only one of the Three Kings with dark skin.'

'There're no dark-skinned people in Slovenia, much less in Maribor, and if any show up they're immediately banished.'

'Hm, what about someone with a dark-skinned soul?'

'Pavel Don Kovač?'

'Yes, Kovač has always been distinctive, special – a fallen angel. Good, and Joseph here next to the empty manger?'

'Not hard to guess at all.'

'Are you referring to Kirilov?' Rosa asks, glancing over to Bely. 'A quiet, godly worker who doesn't like to be the centre of attention?'

Their gazes lock for a moment. An invisible cobweb that tears a moment later.

'This green crocodile, playing the pan-pipes ...'

'Green. Anastasia Green,' says Rosa. '*Nomen est omen.*'

'There're four more left. A Lego figurine of a Zoo keeper, St Peter with his keys, the marble and this unusual piece of round glass. What's this anyway?'

'I tried to figure it out. It could be anything. It's like a mini magnifying glass.'

'Kirilov's Nativity scene presents the Great Orc's secret plan! It's been here all this time, and we didn't see it,' says Bely.

'Don't forget that this is also a representation of the Last Supper. Twelve apostles and the Saviour. It's just that there's no Saviour, the manger is empty.'

'Right, the thirteenth member of the Great Orc is missing. So, all in all, we still don't know who the other five members are, and we're running out of time, too.'

'One of these has to be Mayor Voda.'

'This town is a menagerie. Could the mayor be the zookeeper, then? It's got to be. We're down to three then, plus the missing thirteenth member, the Saviour, so four. There's only one way to solve this mystery. Voda. He has to reveal the names of these last missing members. He's the key to all of it,'

Outside the air is weighed down by the heavy scent of coal. Roads and pavements bathing in dirty slush. Night. Old city-centre alleys. It could be anywhere in Central Europe. Flickering lights from beyond the lonely display windows. A fence enclosing the ECoC marker in Slomšek Square. An inflating pump and its smothered wail and a slightly deflated balloon. Heaps of granite cobblestone cubes around it. The digger, its scoop half buried in black, muddy soil. A still-life of Maribor.

'A *War and Peace* performance poster,' says Rosa, pointing. 'This red cross on a black background could be a negative image of the Swiss flag and the Red Cross emblem. Although it's neither. If anything, it's the opposite of chocolate and bandages.'

Rosa's metal right hand coils tight around Bely's upper arm. The squeaking of her stilettos as she steps on a pebble.

'What if the horizontal line represents the Earth that turns red from the blow of the vertical? The red of the cross represents the blood of those killed. In Tolstoy's novel, these are the people who fell victim to Napoleon's insanity. What if they're the victims of crimes from millions of years ago?' says Bely, while struggling to trudge through the slush. 'Our civilization has been characterized by guilt. We're guilty even though we have no idea what we're guilty of and why. And there's a reason for all of this. Usually we associate guilt with religion. We're guilty because of Christianity, socialization, society. But that's just scratching the surface. What's essential is that, deep inside, we're marked by a distant echo of Xenu's crimes, a memory eradication in souls, their disorientation and repetitive history as a result. The Romans, Attila, Napoleon, Hitler, Tito. Only darkness, with a blood-drawn cross in the centre; a cross of bloody guilt and dark oblivion.'

Fine rain glistens under the light outside the theatre. People in coats, some huddling under the patio heaters in front of the theatre café, some smoking cigarettes on the marble entrance stairway. Silhouettes break through the thick dusk on their way to the theatre. A few protest banners sway in the darkness in the park. Bely reads:

ECoC – MISERY

CAPITAL DESTROYS CIVILIZATION
WE'LL CLEAN UP THE SHIT
ONCE WE CLEAN UP THE TOWN HALL

Bely recognizes a few activists from Off among the group of youngsters standing next to the banners.

The sky booms with fluttering. A flock of crows lifts up from the treetops, only to be swallowed instantly by the vast heavens.

The foyer buzzes like a beehive. Crystal chandeliers, people queuing for tickets. Above the cashier's desk, the prominently displayed slogan of the European Capital of Culture: THE TURNING POINT.

On his way to the cloakroom, Bely notices Aleš Šteger, angry at a girl for distributing only a one prospectus per visitor and not two as instructed. At the back of the foyer he spots Magda Ornik in a black glittery dress, enjoying the company of three men in military uniforms, an Englishman and a pair of Americans. Champagne. Magda's coquettish smile provokes the men to show off.

Rosa leans over to Bely. 'What about her, the oyster crackers didn't work with her?'

'Easy, the crackers were informed and will take affect when the time is right,' he whispers in return.

Bely takes Rosa's black fur coat and checks it in.

'It's really important that we find Voda before they turn off the lights,' he says.

'That sounds impossible. Look how busy it is.'

Suddenly, Bely and Rosa are startled by a camera flash.

'Bely, what the heck are you doing here?'

'Gubec!' Bely cries out and shakes hands with the photographer. 'When did you switch to photography? May I introduce you to my colleague, a journalist from Austrian national radio? Rosa, Gubec is a journalist for the Maribor newspaper *Večer*. The best investigative journalist there is.'

'Bely, thanks for your praise, but I left the newspaper years ago. There were so many spanners in the works that I could've melted them down for a profit.'

'So, what do you do then? How did you land a job as a photographer?'

'I opened my own agency. Well, it's more of a one-man band, but so far so good. The web works wonders. You can't imagine the opportunities when people let you work. I sell my photos and reports to other media now. What about you? You've lost a few pounds.'

'Blame it on the Maribor water system', Bely smiles, 'and the sewage.'

'I see you've done your homework, Bely. We're building what will be the most expensive and the best wastewater treatment plant around. It'll stand right here behind the theatre to clean up the shit that we've been drowning in, and every single corrupt politician with it. How long are you staying? We could go for a coffee some time.'

'I'm on a very tight schedule,' says Bely, 'but we're bound to meet again this evening after the performance.'

'It's a deal,' says Gubec, 'but give me one more smile to immortalize this moment?'

A storm of flashing light captures them before Bely opens his mouth to respond.

'You'll be able to see the photos on my website if nowhere else,' Gubec shouts after Bely.

'Who's that guy?' Rosa asks.

'That's Gubec. We used to hang out when I lived here, although he's the sort of guy who likes to build a wall around himself but obviously finds it easy to breech the walls of the other. Back in the day he was one of the best-informed people in the city. I don't know where he got his information, but it was always reliable, and very quickly he got a reputation as a Freemason among journalists. Unlike others in his profession he never agreed to publish something that was only half true. You know the way the media works. You give journalists information and in return they settle a score on your behalf. Truthfully, newspapers, TV, radio are nothing but the instruments of repression. They've even replaced the courts, that's how bad it is, but only in our country. Anybody who appears in a newspaper as a suspect for something is guilty by default. No matter how far-fetched the accusation.'

'We shouldn't have let him take our photo then, should we?'

'No,' Bely shakes his head. 'If we don't find Voda soon it's not going to matter much whether we make the media or not. But it looks like luck is on our side today. There he is.'

Voda stands surrounded by a crowd. An unknown man approaches him, drags him to the side while Voda listens and nods. The man leaves. Voda returns to his people, says something that makes everybody laugh and nod in approval.

'We'll not be able to catch him in private here,' says Rosa. 'We'll have to wait for the intermission or the end of the play.'

'I'm afraid you're right,' says Bely, taking in the surroundings.

'Bely, good to see you here. And this is your lady from Austria? Welcome. I'm Dolores.'

Dolores offers Rosa her hand and Rosa nods her head.

'If you'll excuse me, I must find the toilet,' says Rosa and disappears.

'So, Bely, this is your new companion,' Dolores smiles as if she had uncovered some highly confidential secret.

'We just work together. I'm helping her with a programme about Maribor as the European Capital of Culture.'

'Of course,' says Dolores. 'Well, I hope you enjoy the performance. Things are so chaotic around here that I doubt I'll make it inside myself. Andreas announced his appearance, so everybody is expecting to see him tonight, but I don't think he's coming. He must've been very insulted by the way people reacted to his collaboration with our theatre. It even dissuaded his own mother from coming. From now on, she says, she's only going to go watch his performances away from Maribor. I need say no more.'

Dolores pulls out her mobile phone, checks the display and puts it back in the pocket.

'The director should've been here by now. It's very unlike her; she's never late. I must've called her a dozen times, but her phone is off. All this while the Croats are in the house. Freaking chaos, Bely, you know how it is.'

'Yes, I remember,' says Bely.

'Do you miss theatre, this theatrical adrenaline?'

'Not really,' says Bely, glancing around. 'At some point I reached a turning point and began to see life as a complex theatrical production, and theatre as an exaggerated simplification of life.'

'It's really a shame what happened between you and Andreas,' says Dolores. 'You belong in the theatre. We can never really wash away the stage from under our skin, Bely. Of course, I'm just a secretary, but I can't imagine working anywhere else.'

'Maybe that's how you see it, but for me it's just one of many equally thrilling or boring ways to waste your life. I also once thought that art was a privilege, some sort of church or cult without a god. But I was wrong. It's no more and no less than fishing or mushroom picking. The problem is that we don't know how to think outside of the accepted norms, so we make art seem more important than it is. In truth, if we didn't fawn over art we wouldn't really know what to do with it.'

'I don't know, Bely. I for one get a lot more out of the theatre than I would out of fishing. But it's true that someone else may feel just the opposite. We have some very accomplished fishermen in this city, like our mayor.'

Dolores nods towards Voda, who is still surrounded by a group of people. Voda gesticulates with his fingers, as if he were shooting. Those around him laugh.

'Do you know what's hanging in the mayor's office, between the photo of the president of Slovenia, the Dalai Lama and the coat of arms of the municipality?'

Bely shrugs.

'A gold-plated speargun for underwater fishing. Can you imagine, Bely, a golden gun? He says that it was given to him by our twinned city on the Croatian coast where he spends his holidays every year. Word has it that he got it as a gift from the Austrian construction firm that will build our water treatment plant. There they are, those hunters of yours. Say what you like, but I'd rather be here in the theatre.' Dolores checks her telephone again. 'I wonder where Anastasia is,' she says. 'This is slowly turning into a code-red situation. Nothing unusual. Look, there goes your Austrian colleague. Well, I've got to go, Adam. See you later.'

A bell announces the start of the performance.

Rosa comes back, accompanied by Inspector Maus and Assistant Gros.

'There you are, Bely. Gros and I would like a word with you, in private. Ms Portero, if you'd be so kind ...'

The three men step aside. The theatre's giant windows, heavy drapes. Bely sees the sparrows hopping along the dirty window-sill outside.

'Bely, all of my predictions are coming true. The additional chemistry tests haven't excluded the possibility that Dorfler and Butcher may have fallen victim to some mysterious virus, which happens to be spreading fast. I'll ask that this remains just between us for now, but it's only fair that you and your Austrian colleague are kept informed. Pavel Don Kovač seems to be another victim. It was this afternoon, during the opening of the new fountain dedicated to the European Capital of Culture. Right in the middle of the ceremony, he suddenly jumped into the fountain. They barely got him out in time – he nearly drowned. Even then he continued to open his mouth like a carp and flopped his legs as if he wore flippers. Before the incident he had been complaining of chest pain. Some said that they saw shadows creep over his face just before he jumped in. We asked all the media present to remain discreet. They reported it only as a minor incident, but I doubt we can keep a lid on the news for more than another day. The fact that the director of the European Capital of Culture has gone mad – well, you can imagine how the dominoes would fall. I bet that's grist for Voda's mill. This city is headed straight for a state of emergency. Meanwhile, my men have captured over seven hundred of the city's pigeons to carry out the tests. It turns out a flock of pigeons were sitting on the fountain when Kovač lost it. If it were up to me I would've already arrested Voda, but we just don't have enough evidence on him. On top of all this, I'm afraid that Voda's men have also infiltrated the police force and are putting pressure on me.'

Maus stops speaking. He looks around to see who might be listening in, while biting his upper lip nervously. 'It's clear that the media will attack me if I arrest Voda. You were right. Our shared history is incriminating and would make my arrest of Voda look like personal revenge. This is why I've asked to be removed from the case. Gros is in charge now.'

Gros nods silently.

'I have complete faith in Gros. He's entirely competent to see this case through, that is to say, until we can establish a solid body of evidence that leads to Voda's arrest. If you ask me, we have more than enough reasons to believe our suspicions are grounded: three prominent citizens infected by Voda's virus, the European Capital of Culture is in peril and there's an illegally obtained construction permit for the wastewater treatment plant. If it were up to me', Maus says while clicking his tongue, 'I'd get us a search warrant and arrest him! But, as I said, the final say is no longer mine. But Gros should know what's bringing us our daily dose of poison. Isn't that right, Gros?'

Gros nods again.

'Did you see the clouds over the city this afternoon? They were as straight as an arrow between two or three o'clock. You never see a symmetrical phenomenon in the stratosphere. Given that they sprayed us again this afternoon, we can expect that the night will bring new victims of this mysterious virus.'

Inspector Maus frowns as the bell tolls three times, announcing the start of the play.

'In short, Bely, I want you to call me tomorrow morning at this number so that we can carefully craft a press release that will go out through your Austrian press colleague. Every word, every comma must be meticulously weighed and considered. Voda's corrupt influence is through the Slovenian media, so if we don't get this out first then the whole thing is lost, you understand?'

Bely nods in farewell.

'What was that about?' asks Rosa anxiously.

'They found Kovač,' says Bely.

'Absolved?'

Bely nods.

'We're doomed when they discover that you were seen with Don Kovač just moments before he went mad.'

'We must end this tonight,' says Bely under his breath, watching Voda as he enters the main hall of the theatre with his people.

Bely and Rosa make their way up the colossal marble stairs to the first floor. They take their seats on the balcony, first row on the left, which offers a great view of both the stage and the audience beneath them. Rosa leans carefully over the brass railing.

'I wonder where Voda is. I can't see him anywhere?' she whispers.

Bely silently surveys the space. 'He must be seated in the first row,' he whispers back.

The head dramatist emerges on-stage. He welcomes the audience and announces that the grand première of *War and Peace*, a co-production between the Croatian National Theatre in Zagreb and the Slovene National Theatre of Maribor would start shortly after a welcome speech by the mayor.

Voda takes the stage from behind a curtain and approaches the microphone, which crackles with feedback for a moment. A technician rushes on to the stage to move the microphone a couple of centimetres away from Voda's lips. The auditorium goes quiet.

'Dear Mr President, dear minister of culture, dear mayor of our twinned city Malja, dear citizens and guests, welcome. I am proud to say that Maribor is known as the tidiest city in Slovenia, and we are now introducing new gas-powered city buses. Our city hosted the Dalai Lama, who is returning for another visit, along with many other Nobel laureates. Maribor was pleased to host the World Championship in ju-jitsu and, next year, we will host the Universiade. Not only is our city home to the world's oldest vine, but we also have a brand new stadium, the People's Garden, in which we defeated Russia. Maribor is also the European Capital of Culture. And as long as I am mayor of this city culture will have nothing to fear. Some think we don't care about culture, but here in Maribor we do. Just look at the European Capital of Culture programme as well as the rich offerings of our cultural institutions, from the Maribor Museum of Liberation to the Slovene National Theatre of Maribor, to the Maribor Funeral Parlour, to the municipal services and so much more. Maribor is a city both cultured and clean. Investments into a new, completely clean wastewater treatment plant will see to a better future for Maribor and all of Slovenia. Likewise, the opening of the Marx Cultural Centre has brought a breath of fresh air to both the left and right banks of the Drava River. Dear Mister President, honoured minister of culture, ladies and gentlemen of Maribor. What the malicious media has printed is untrue. It is time to find a sustainable solution for our city and its sewage system. A few days ago, when I attended the anniversary of the foundation of the city cemetery – which is a fine example to many other European cemeteries – my heart jumped for joy. When I cut the ribbon at the opening ceremony of the Marx Cultural Centre my heart jumped for joy. These are projects that bring us all together. There's no future without the present and, as long as I am the mayor of Maribor, positive projects will be executed in a positive way for the benefit of us all. Thank you.'

Moderate applause, the auditorium grows dark in anticipation of the start of the performance. Bely and Rosa keep their eyes on Voda, who shakes hands with the president and the minister of culture. He takes an empty seat next to her.

A minimalist set design, some fifteen people on-stage, all motionless. The first to speak is a servant. 'You understand that the world has changed forever? Mm? Yes? No? All I want to say is that thoughts with long-term consequences are always easy. My thoughts are a one-way street. If corrupt people collaborate only to remain in power, then it is absolutely necessary that upright people do the same. It's that easy. Ah, the war has not yet begun, but just because there is no war does not mean that there is peace.'

'How long is the performance?' asks Rosa.

'Just under three hours, with two intermissions,' whispers Bely.

'Are you familiar with the text?'

'I know the novel very well. I don't know this adaptation, but a few years ago I adapted it myself. It was never staged.' After a moment, Bely once more bends towards Rosa and whispers, 'And it never will be.'

Countess Rostova, a top-hat on her head, enters the stage: 'I believe only in God and our beloved Tsar. Nikolai! (Kisses Tsar Alexander) You will rid Europe of this murderer and bandit. Natasha! This is madness. *C'est à en devenir folle. On dirait que le monde entier a perdu la tête.* We can't continue to suffer in this way, at the hand of a man who threatens everything and everyone. Nikolai! Natasha!'

'Stay here,' whispers Bely.

'Where are you going?'

'Look, Voda's leaving the auditorium. I'll try to catch him. You stay here.'

Bely slips into a hallway ablaze with light. An empty staircase, grey Pohorje marble, modernism, grand crystal chandeliers. He moves down to the ground floor and hears a voice from the cloakroom.

'Are you leaving, Mr Mayor?'

'You have it easy, ladies, prancing about this theatre all day, but some of us have real work to do. Pass me my overcoat. I left my cigarettes in there. You'll get it right back. Here you go.'

Bely sees Voda chatting to one of the attendants.

'What do you girls do when you do nothing? I mean, when you are not at the theatre?'

The girls giggle in reply.

Voda sticks the cigarettes into his overcoat pocket and turns toward the gents. Bely follows him and heads for the urinal right next to Voda's.

'Boring play, isn't it?' says Bely.

'I don't know. I'm no expert on theatre,' says Voda, dragging deeply on his cigarette twice before stubbing it out in the urinal and fastening his zipper.

He follows Voda to the sink.

'May I ask you a question, Mr Mayor? People say that you are an avid hunter –'

Voda interrupts him and narrows his gaze. 'What, are you some kind of journalist?'

'No, no, I'm a bit of a hunter myself, so I thought I'd ask you about your experiences.'

'What do you hunt?'

'Well, I'm just getting started …' Bely says, and pulls a pen from his pocket.

'Hunting is, above all, about caring for animals, about culling the animal population, keeping it under control. Just last winter I fed deer with more than twenty-wagons'-worth of hay and corn. Which hunting club are you a part of?'

Bely says nothing.

'You know what I think? I think that you're not a hunter but a journalist who wants to screw me over,' roars Voda. 'What's that in your hand, show me!'

'I have a pen,' says Bely, lifting it into the air.

'That's got to be a microphone. Give it to me, you bastard,' says Voda, lunging at Bely. They wrestle one another to the floor. Voda rifles Bely's pockets and pulls out the Austrian national radio business cards.

'What's this? You little bastard! You're following me? Me? It's obvious that you've never held a rifle in your hands. I'll show you who the real hunter is. You're begging to go for a dive, aren't you?'

Voda drags Bely across the floor to the toilet. Bely resists, but Voda holds him tight by the neck. 'Want to know how we used to play submarines back in the Yugoslav National Army? I'll show you.'

Voda shoves Bely's head deep into the toilet bowl, causing his nose to bleed. He flushes the toilet, waits a moment for the bowl to fill again, then flushes once more.

'This is a technique that the American Marines call water-boarding,' says Voda enthusiastically.

Bely swallows the water that runs red with his blood. Voda's grip is too strong for him to struggle free.

'Journalist rats like you deserve this. You, a hunter? Whatever next? Do you know what journalists did to me? You broke my family apart. I can't do a fucking thing without you following me. I've got birdhouses with cameras in front of my bloody house waiting for me every morning just to make sure I make the midday news. Shit-kickers.'

The water floods Bely's lungs again. The thought that it will soon be over cuts sharp like a razor into his flesh. He feels himself leaving his own body as though he were cut in two. The picture is calm and clear. Bely watches his helpless body as it resists, trembles and gulps water in an attempt to escape. He looks down casually over Voda's shoulder, as if he were not the one drowning before his very eyes. A whirlpool of water flushes the toilet again. Bely watches his body capitulate. His heartbeat recedes into the distance. Flickering bloodstained water washes over him. He tries to remain still, to preserve the very last of his strength, waits for the moment to collapse, unconscious. He watches as the eyes of his body slowly close, his hands grow limp.

Voda's grip suddenly loosens.

In the blink of an eye, Bely finds himself once more inside his own body, in excruciating pain. He pulls his head free of the water and gasps for air.

Moments later, when he catches his breath, Bely notices Voda kneeling next to the toilet bowl. Voda's eyes and mouth spread wide in pain. Behind him stands Rosa Portero, clutching his neck.

'Bely, *ist alles in Ordnung*?' she asks.

Bely nods, coughing.

'Listen, Voda, you're dealing with something much worse than journalists or the police, and you better cooperate if you don't want this to get worse. Get it?' says Bely.

Voda groans with pain and nods.

'Put your hands on the floor and slowly lie down, over here,' says Rosa.

Voda lies face down, while Rosa continues to grip his neck.

'Tell us about Calvary,' says Bely.

'What Calvary? What do you want?' moans Voda.

Bely gives Rosa a sign. She tightens her stranglehold on Voda while Bely stamps his heel on Voda's finger, causing the mayor to groan in pain.

'Tell us why the wastewater treatment plant is beneath Calvary.'

'Because of the dream,' groans Voda.

'What dream?'

'I dreamed of Calvary. It was a beautiful, sunny day. Then, all of a sudden, night came. Birds everywhere, millions of them, darting and flapping like crazy. Then a plane flew by. A huge plane that had something hanging off of it, these long pipes. I thought it was going to crash into Maribor, but it missed it by a hair's breadth. Instead, it crashed into Calvary. The explosion smashed Calvary to pieces, and a geyser of shit flowed out of it, tons of shit, a proper shit tsunami, and swallowed up the entire city. I knew when I woke up that I had to save the city. And the only way I could do that is by building a wastewater treatment plant there, OK? I checked, and the crystal ball agreed. Do you think the environmentalists have any clue about what's going on underground? And we're still stuck. We've got no money, and the shit still flows into the Drava. It's my city, and I care about it. You know what I'm saying?'

Bely nods to Rosa. He steps on Voda's finger and covers his mouth to muffle the screaming.

'Don't lie.'

'What the fuck do you know about the truth? All you people and the media are interested in are lies, better and more tolerable lies,' wheezes Voda. 'Truth, my arse. Animals are the only ones who possess truth. When I'm done hunting, and I survey them, all lined up, shot, that's the truth. When I spray them in farewell with their very own blood, that's where the truth lies, in rituals like that. Not media. What the hell do you two want from me anyway?'

'Tell us who the members of the Great Orc are?'

'You'll never find us.'

Once again, Bely covers Voda's mouth and stamps hard on another finger. Voda trembles with pain.

'Gram,' says Voda, as Bely releases his mouth. 'Samo Gram.'

'We know about him, and we know about Butcher, Dorfler and Farkas.'

'That's all, there are no others.'

Bely crushes Voda's third finger.

'Magda, Kovač and Green, me, and Maher.'

'Maher?' asks Bely. 'Maher who?'

'Janez Maher, the head of the construction firm that built the Marx Centre and is building Calvary.'

'Who else?'

'I don't know, I swear.'

Bely steps on Voda's thumb. More muffled screams. 'Who else?'

'I really don't know, ask the stars, you fucking motherfuckers.'

The sound of steps in the hall outside. Rosa closes the door to the cubicle. Bely grabs Voda's head and smothers his mouth. The sound of urine gushing. Long, an infinitely long stream of urine. Then steps exiting the toilet.

'What stars?' Bely hisses furiously, uncovering Voda's mouth.

'What, you've never asked the stars about the future? The past has brought us nothing but shit, nothing but dead people everywhere. Stick a shovel anywhere around Maribor, and you'll dig up a skull. What good is that? What am I supposed to do with the dead? They're no good for profit, they're redundant, just another expense. What we need is living people who'll spend their money on the dead, if nothing else.'

Bely blocks Voda's mouth, and starts on the fingers of his other hand.

'This is the last time I'll ask you. The Great Orc, who are the other members?'

'I've already told you all I know, dammit. Fucking hell, I'm going to tear your head off the next time we meet.'

More steps. Bely indicates to Rosa to pass him the silver compact with the oyster crackers. He takes one of the dark ones and shoves it under Voda's tongue. Voda resists, but Rosa only tightens her grip. Jostling. Voda collapses unconscious.

'Now what?' whispers Rosa.

'We must find Janez Maher. This is the VIP première, so he's probably among the guests tonight.'

'Bely, you're soaking wet and covered in blood, you can't go into the theatre like that.'

'Why don't you return to the auditorium, and I'll run back to the hotel and change. It's just around the corner, so I should be back in a few minutes.'

'What do we do with him?' asks Rosa as she knocks her metal fingers against Voda's skull.

At that moment Voda's body begins to squirm like a fish out of water. Blue-grey shadows leech on to his face and leave him pale.

'The souls,' says Bely. 'They left his body and made him harmless. Now he's nothing more than a shell, the body of a human animal.'

Someone flushes the toilet in the ladies' toilet; the hum of water in the sink, blow-dryer, steps. Rosa and Bely stand absolutely still.

Bely focuses on the sounds and, after a few moments, whispers, 'The coast is clear. Let's go.'

As Bely opens the door, Rosa notices something sticking out from beneath Voda's body. It's her business card. She grabs it and makes sure that no other trace is left behind. An OUT OF ORDER sign hangs over one of the cubicles. Bely grabs it and hangs it over the cubicle housing Voda's body.

A few minutes later Rosa reclaims her balcony seat in the main auditorium of the Slovene National Theatre of Maribor. The stage plays out a scene with Andrei Bolkonsky and Pierre Bezukhov. Drunken Pierre on one side of the stage, his dying father on the other. Bolkonsky comes to get Pierre and takes him by the hand.

PIERRE: 'Such a crucial moment, and look at me! What am I supposed to do? I've disappointed you. I must have also disappointed my father. But he has also disappointed me. He never married my mother … I'd sin if I were their legitimate son, and my behaviour would have been better received … You still resent me …'

ANDREI: 'I resent that you won't allow yourself to be the best that you can be, to become someone.'

PIERRE: 'To become someone? Who?'

Enter Napoleon, he moves past Pierre and Andrei to the centre of the stage. All the actors pause, evidently surprised by his appearance. Napoleon extends his hand, as if to touch the audience seated in the darkness before him and mumbles a few incomprehensible words. From the wings of the stage two soldiers emerge, each taking one of his arms and leading him off-stage. Pierre repeats his line.

PIERRE: 'To become someone? Who?'

Napoleon returns to the stage from the wings. He points up into the air and cries out.

NAPOLEON: 'Napoleon!'

All that may be seen from behind the curtain is the hand of one of the soldiers, who again pulls Napoleon off-stage. Laughter in the audience.

PIERRE: (Quietly) 'To become someone?'

ANDREI: 'You must have a goal.'

PIERRE: 'You're right. Every morning, when I wake, I find myself disgusted by what I did the night before. Then I say to myself, today you will change. I say to myself, this is the day when you become a saint ... Tonight I have come to the club just to drink a glass of water and to demonstrate that I can resist temptation ...'

ANDREI: 'There must be something you want to do.'

PIERRE: 'I want many things ... I want to explore the meaning of happiness, the value of suffering, why men go to war and what they think, deep down in their hearts, when they pray to God. I want to uncover what men and women really feel when they say, "I love you".'

A cry from backstage, 'Napoleon!' Then the sound of a slap. Silence.

PIERRE: 'As you see, I have a lot of work to do. All this occupies my time. It's hard for you to understand that. To you everything seems so clear. You know exactly what you are doing and why you do it.'

ANDREI: 'Well, not exactly ...'

PIERRE: 'Everything you set out to explore becomes clear to you, but when I do it everything grows murkier ... You believe in what you do.'

ANDREI: 'It would be great if it really were as you describe. But you're wrong ... Do you know why I'm going to war? Do you really think it's only because I think that Napoleon is a monster, or that Russia will come out of it as a great country? What do we have to do with Austria, a country that's a thousand miles away from us? I've already told you that I'm going to war only because this life here is not for me.'

Rosa scans the auditorium. The minister of culture shifts restlessly in her seat in the first row. Voda's seat beside her is empty, a gap in an otherwise packed theatre. Could Maher be in the audience? Will she and Bely be able to find him before it's too late? When Voda's body is found in the bathroom, the situation will turn chaotic. And then what?

Rosa catches herself caressing her neck scar, which has reappeared. Scenes from the night when she was destined to be sacrificed line up before her eyes. Images of her escape through the murky lake waters, slippery silt beneath her feet, barking dogs, darkness. She was convinced that she and Bely would be killed. And now she's here, with a task that seems too incredible to share with anybody.

Cannon fire interrupts her flow of memories. Smoke fills the stage, soldiers stray blindly. A lost flag bearer of the Russian army. Bolkonsky is shot, he falls, looking into the sky, peaceful, the ironic monologue of the dying hero. Scenes that are impossible to stage in a realistic manner yet manage to convince only through their excessive stylization and conscious recognition that they aren't reality but only part of a play.

Rosa once more loses herself in thought. She contemplates Father Kirilov's Nativity scene, the four figurines whose real counterparts remain unknown. If the Lego figurine of the zookeeper is Voda, ponders Rosa, then three others remain: St Peter with his keys, a marble and a piece of glass. Three still missing, plus the missing saviour. One of those four is Maher. Will she and Bely triumph? She can't afford to have doubts. She would have never agreed to join Bely and come to this city had she doubted. But did she ever really say yes to all of this in the first place? Wasn't that clear the moment he cut the ropes that bound her? Did she follow a script that was written in advance? Is it not true that we always make an active decision on trivial matters, while all important matters seem to happen as inevitable facts? At least in Rosa's life. All of a sudden Rosa sees an image of an old woman, fruit and flowers encircle her bare feet, candles blazing as the old woman murmurs unintelligible words and waves garlands of bones and shells. If Rosa's soul is really comprised of many lost souls, then what pasts did these souls have? What was eradicated and murdered in those souls in order for Rosa Portero to exist? And what came to life in her souls and made all that she had thus far taken for granted seem like a lie in the few weeks since she'd first met Bely?

On-stage Napoleon appears like a mirage before Pierre Bezukhov, seated upon one of the pommel horses. On either side of him stand the soldiers who had previously escorted him off the stage.

PIERRE: 'All that I see has the colour of false icons. The people I see are but poorly painted angels. Beauty has lost its shadow. The story I hear is nothing but an empty book filled with white pages, the majestic history of nothing. The vanity of false icons.'

As soon as one of the soldiers loses focus, Napoleon slowly slips off the horse and sways. It looks like he is about to fall. Sighs from the audience. Napoleon staggers off-stage with the soldiers in pursuit.

PIERRE (continues): 'Everyone says that I'm like a child ... I've never separated from my own childhood. I grew up, and I've grown old in it, creating my own time. Subsequently my life has no past, yet everything that surrounds me is the past. What have I done? What have I done? Is this what I want?'

Enter Hélène.

PIERRE: 'No. I don't know her ... I also don't like her ... she's got nothing to say ... but, then again ... she's as timid as I am ... She doesn't say much, but everything she does say is curt and clear. She's wonderful. Is she what I want?'

PIERRE: 'Yes. No. Where is my willpower?'

SERVANT: 'Seriously, where is it?'

PIERRE: 'Perhaps I don't have it?'

Hélène and Pierre.

PIERRE: 'We could go outside ... take a little walk ...'

HÉLÈNE: 'You go ... I can't ... I'm not feeling well.'

PIERRE: 'You're not ...pregnant?'

HÉLÈNE: 'Me? Pregnant? It would never occur to me to have children. What has got into you?'

PIERRE: 'I'm sorry ...'

Rosa reads the English subtitles and observes all that takes place on-stage. Everything that happens on the stage happens so that she can have these thoughts. Everything in her life took place so that she could be here, in the midst of this play. The play and her life are a pair of parallel mirrors; she's here and there. Above it, the intangible water's surface; beneath, the harsh grounding of her life. Strolling across the surface are the actors, reciting from the script; Hélène, the corrupt daughter of Prince Vasili Kuragin, who seduces Pierre Bezukhov for his inheritance. Rosa's own inheritance is an indelible memory, at its ground level a road. Rosa's hands grip the steering wheel. Left and right hand, she still has them both. Gently rippling fingers, her ring tapping against the steering wheel. Polished nails. Voices. Her sister sits beside her. People say that they are almost identical, but she thinks otherwise. At the back of the car sit her bored children, kicking at the seats before them. Blanca loses her temper. The girls interrupt her while she's on the phone. The atmosphere grows tense. Rosa looks past Blanca at the girls, '*Los ojos de mi vida*', takes a deep breath and says in Spanish, since she always speaks Spanish when with Blanca, '*Por favor, niñas,* stop it, leave Aunt Blanca alone, *o no vamos a irnos a ningún lado ...*'

PIERRE: 'Let's divorce.'

HÉLÈNE: 'Excuse me?'

PIERRE: 'Let's divorce.'

HÉLÈNE: 'Ah, what a horrible punishment. You found just the right thing to scare me with ...of course, we'll divorce, but only if you compensate me appropriately. It would be my pleasure.'

PIERRE: 'I'll kill you.'

HÉLÈNE: 'Oh, please ... Talking about killing.'

PIERRE: 'Get out! I'll kill you! Out!'

SERVANT: 'Get out! I'll kill you! Out!'

Enter Prince Kuragin.

PRINCE VASILI: 'Hélène! Hélène! My dear, my dear ... You two are like children. You are angry at my ... Hélène! She's angry with you, but you can't live without one another. That poor thing is probably sitting in pain somewhere, waiting for you to call her ... Just say the word, and I'll call her and everything will be the way it was ...'

Isn't everything that I do simply an attempt to get them back? So it would all be as it once was, even if only for a moment? But isn't that the reason is everything is destined to fail? The way everything we know about ourselves deep inside, secretly and with the utmost certainty, is forever destined to fail?

Rosa lifts her gloved right hand and examines it. Its cumbersome mechanism slowly moves the hard knuckles of the gloved fingers as in a dream. In the distance, beyond her fingers, stand Pierre and Hélène.

SERVANT: 'Get out! I'll kill you! Out!'

Just then, Bely returns.

'The receptionist at the hotel gave me a strange look. Nobody else saw me other than him, I don't think. I googled our Maher at the hotel, so I know what he looks like. Obviously one of the richest and most influential people in the city. He owns dozens of companies, most of which are in the construction field, but also investments, insurance. One of them sponsored this performance and, if we're lucky, our Mr Maher is somewhere in the audience. Rosa, what is it? Are you OK?'

Rosa clenches her fist and leans back in her seat, pale.

On-stage Lisa, Andrei Bolkonsky's wife, and Mary, her sister. Lisa is giving birth.

LISA: 'Maria ... I think ... I think that it's begun ... it's begun ...'

MARIA: 'Lie back, Lisa ...'

LISA: 'No, no ...'

MARIA: 'I'll call ... I'll send for the doctor, don't worry, everything will be fine.'

Enter aged and hard-hearted Prince Nikolai Bolkonsky in a wheelchair. He rolls past Lisa to the edge of the stage.

MARIA: 'Father ...'

NIKOLAI BOLKONSKY: 'Maria, what's happening?'

MARIA: 'Nothing, father ... I've gone into labour.'

NIKOLAI BOLKONSKY: 'Good.'

Prince Bolkonsky grips the tyres of the wheelchair to turn it around, but one of the tyres locks. No matter how hard he tries, the chair is stuck.

MARIA: 'We must send for the doctor.'

NIKOLAI BOLKONSKY: 'Right.'

The wheelchair leans dangerously over the edge of the stage. At the last moment the prince throws himself out, and the wheelchair falls from the stage and thunders towards the feet of the minister of culture, in the first row. The minister squeals and jumps out of her seat. The wheelchair comes to a halt just before it reaches her. Stagehands rush out and lift the wheelchair back on to the stage. The minister of culture, frightened, turns in the semi-darkness towards the audience and forces a smile. The audience thinks it's all part of the play.

MARIA (repeating her line): 'We must send for a doctor.'

Laughter.

NIKOLAI BOLKONSKY (once more in the wheelchair): 'Right.'

LISA (yelling): 'Andrei! Andrei!'

Lisa is dying.

SERVANT: 'Son, son ...'

Andrei approaches.

ANDREI: 'Forgive me, Lisa ... Forgive me.'

Bely smiles at what is taking place on-stage.

'Not everything is going according to plan tonight,' he whispers.

Rosa's expression remains unmoved. 'Yeah, some may find this performance funny, but I think it's dreadful,' she says. 'By the way, your description of Maher matches up nicely with the figurine of St Peter with the keys.'

'Peter, upon thee I will build my church, says the Bible.'

'Just so. You said that Maher is in the construction business,' says Rosa quietly without averting her gaze from the stage.

'I uncovered one other thing. Remember the marbles in Father Kirilov's Nativity scene?'

Rosa nods.

'What's a marble, if not a crystal ball?'

Rosa looks at him in silence. 'Voda also mentioned a crystal ball. He said –'

'It was the crystal ball that also suggested that he build a wastewater treatment plant at the foot of Calvary … Yup. And guess who, aside from the high-ups at the town hall, lives in one of the apartments in Voda's building?'

'That's the building where Anastasia Green lives?'

Bely nods. 'That's the building, yes. That's also where the fortune-teller lives. Her name is Nana Numen. She's in the news all the time.'

'How do you know?'

'Mister Google,' Bely says, smiling.

Applause.

'Intermission. Come on, we've got to be quick because they'll find Voda any minute now, and then there'll be hell to pay.'

Bely and Rosa drift into the foyer, along with the mass of spectators.

A crowd around the theatre bar. Bely sees Dolores. 'Dolores, you've got to help me. I'd like to speak with Janez Maher, but I don't know who he is.'

'Maher should be around here. He always comes to premières, and I'm pretty sure I saw him earlier. Look, if I see him, I'll introduce you. Sorry, I'm a bit distracted. Can you believe it? Anastasia Green has disappeared. Swallowed up by the ground. I sent someone to her home, but there's no one there. No lights, nothing, and I can't reach her by phone. I'm really concerned that something happened to her.'

Just as she says this, a woman with long blonde hair lets out a scream and rushes across the foyer. A white dove flaps wildly after her, trying to alight on her hair. The woman takes cover under a small table. The dove circles over the guests, excretes on the head of one of the waiters trying to catch it and finally lands on a high cornice. More screaming, this time from the toilets. Bely and Rosa assume that someone must have discovered Voda's body, but the screaming comes from the ladies' toilet. Three women run out of the bathroom pursued by Magda Ornik, her stockings torn and the heel of one shoe broken off. Magda snarls like a wild boar, as saliva winds its way out of her mouth. Everything stops as everyone's attention focuses on her. She is on all fours, snorting across the foyer. Suddenly, Magda stops in front of the American military attaché with whom she had been chatting before the performance. The attaché attempts to approach her, but she lashes out and bites his leg so hard that he cries out in pain and kicks Magda with all his strength. Magda skitters away but suddenly scrambles back and bites the attaché's British counterpart. The bitten Englishman howls in pain and jumps back, pulling Magda along with him. She refuses to unlock her jaws. Onlookers continue to stand, silent and stunned, until Magda, teeth bared, rips out a bloody mouthful of trouser. The British military attaché roars in pain and collapses to the floor.

Police Inspector Maus and Assistant Gros push through the crowd. They throw themselves on the rampaging Magda and only manage to control her with their combined strength. People emerge from every corner of the theatre to see the director of the municipal cemetery kicking like some feral beast as she tries to free herself from the grip of the police. Gubec squats beside Magda's bloodstained face, snapping a close-up. They finally manage to drag her away from the crowd. Ambulance sirens can be heard in the distance. Just then the bell rings, signalling the end of the first intermission. The audience is shocked, numb, but slowly returns to the auditorium. Theatre staff and paramedics encourage the crowd to clear the foyer. After a brief scuffle, two paramedics manage to inject Magda with a sedative. She is sprawled on a stretcher. A few people remain in the foyer and on the stairs to watch the goings-on. The bell rings once more, and they, too, go back in to see the second half of the play. Bely spots Maher at the bar. He and Rosa take seats on either side of him.

Maher is chatting with a waiter, who is wiping the surfaces with a cloth before loading the dirty glasses into the dishwasher.

'Poor Ornik. Everyone has their plate full of social responsibility, but when someone really needs help no one volunteers. You saw, everyone just stood there and waited. If those two policemen hadn't been on hand, she would've bitten half the theatre. No wonder every other person in this city goes crazy. Yesterday I went to the town hall, but it's still closed. Since November. They moved their offices, but they're still out of commission. Hopeless,' says the waiter.

'A few more months and the renovations will be complete,' says Maher. 'My guys are working their butts off to complete everything on time. But what can we do, the entire building was under water, which is not something to sneeze at.'

'But for the guy to lock himself to a radiator. I'm not saying there's anything wrong with expressing your political beliefs, but locking yourself to a radiator in protest, and threatening that you're not going to leave until someone sees to your demands … That's not OK.'

'Allegedly he was even tended to for the first few weeks,' says Maher, taking a sip of his whisky.

'My neighbour works in the same office where this guy chained himself up. I've heard he's a smart kid, too, has a doctorate in maths. At first people sympathized with him. Some ladies even brought him food. He slept there for a week or so. My neighbour said that they grew quite accustomed to having him, like he was a cross between an ornamental plant and an office pet. Then the cleaning ladies stopped cleaning around him just to be mean. The kid started to smell so bad it became unbearable,' comments the waiter.

'What about the garlic?'

'Right, the garlic. The employees from the town hall brought him garlic from the start. Did you know that the mayor grows garlic on his farm? Anyway, they learned that this kid, who was protesting against an ineffective and corrupt city administration, was allergic to garlic, so they kept bringing it to him. If he was making too much noise or chanting his incomprehensible slogans, they shoved fresh cloves of garlic under his nose. You can tolerate that for a few days maybe, but not for weeks on end. So he got all puffy and weak because of the allergy. Meanwhile, because the stench was so bad they moved my neighbour's office elsewhere. They completely emptied the space around him and left him to deteriorate. God knows how long this would've gone on if it hadn't been for that poor plumber.'

'It wasn't so much the plumber's fault, it was the decrepit pipes,' says Maher. 'They should've replaced them years ago, but they kept postponing because of the investment it would've required.'

'Don't you think it's weird that the guy had to fix a broken radiator right where the kid was?'

'There was a lot to fix. He just happened to start in that room,' Maher continues before drinking down the rest of his whisky and ordering another.

'And then the radiator exploded, boiling water everywhere, and nobody could do anything about it?'

'Old pipes can be treacherous. You only need one valve to burst and it all goes to hell. It took hours before they were able to plug the main conduit, but the hot steam was still in the system, and it just kept on coming.'

'Poor guy. I'm starting to feel sorry for him.'

'You can't imagine the extent of the damage. The floors, the furniture, the doors – the whole town hall went to hell. Well, it was old and run-down anyway. You'll see, when my guys finish up, the place will look downright American.'

'Poor kid,' says the waiter once more, pouring Maher two fingers of whisky.

Bely orders a glass of mineral water and wine for Rosa.

'And what happened to the kid?' Bely asks.

'What do you think?' asks the waiter, as he slams the dishwasher shut beneath the bar and turns it on. 'I heard that they found only his skin, hanging off the radiator. That's what happens to proactive intellectuals in this city.'

'The problem isn't intellectuals,' says Maher, 'because they don't exist. You can't point your finger at the educated either – those you can usually work something out with. The workers who are still at the factory are also not a problem – they've got no time to do anything but work anyway. The problem is that there's no order. Here everybody thinks they're cleverer than the people around them, who also think they're cleverer than everyone else.'

'And on top of that everybody here's related,' bemoans the waiter.

'Yes, this city has too small a population and too many relatives,' says Maher, taking a sip of his drink. 'People still believe they can count on their relatives to pull them out of deep shit. They will never rely on the courts, or their profession, or their knowledge. Relatives, it's always their relatives.'

The waiter grins. 'And we know perfectly well that's not how things work.'

Maher nods and points to his empty glass.

'Oh yeah, we know that a relative would be the first to put a gun to your head and sell you to the Devil half price. What we're missing is an elemental order. No wonder we're the most backward province in Slovenia, a Lower-Austrian Zimbabwe.'

'So we should blame Maister?' asks Bely.

'Maister who? You mean the attorney?'

Bely shakes his head. 'No, General Rudolf Maister.'

'Ah, General Maister. You mean our great liberator who took Maribor from the Austrians? Sure, he's the biggest criminal of them all. Without him we'd all be speaking German right now, we'd have lower taxes and higher salaries. Everything would be better. Without him we wouldn't be where we are today. People here go after you for working your arse off. I'm telling you this from my own personal experience. It's not easy to run a company these days.' Maher gets up and pays.

Rosa and Bely remain seated for a few moments more. They pay and follow Maher, who stands outside the door of the theatre and smokes.

Two girls walk past, the first dressed as a crab, the other with her blue-coloured face protruding from the mouth of a big fish made of cardboard.

'A fish and a crab. All that's missing is an octopus,' says Maher, glancing up at Bely and taking a drag on his cigarette. 'That's why you two followed me, isn't it?'

Maher offers the packet. Bely shakes his head. Rosa takes one and lets Maher light it for her as she stares off into space.

'No stars above us. Welcome to our Maribor skies. Tomorrow is Ash Wednesday. I'm not religious, but still … There's a time to reap and a time to sow. A man can't spend his whole life just reaping. Just as a man can't spend his whole life on the run. I've run long enough. Maybe we can't choose our own destiny, where and when we are born, when and how we die, but as long as we live we have the ability to choose. We can flee or we can stop running. That is the only real freedom we have.'

'How did you know that we're interested in the octopus?' asks Bely.

'It's written all over your forehead,' Maher replies, throwing his cigarette end into the slush.

Rosa notices the suction prints of an octopod leg on Bely's forehead, as it slowly coils, pauses and slides beneath his scalp.

'What do you want?' asks Maher.

'What are your thoughts on absolution?' Bely asks.

'You mean, absolving people of their responsibilities? Letting people go? That's easy. I dare say I'm the best there is at letting people go. If I could, I would have a doctorate in professional absolution. I'm not sure if you realize, but I hold the Slovenian record in letting people go. In just one day I fired 7,892 workers, and still the company didn't go bankrupt. I fired more than twelve thousand workers in a single month, but AFM still functions. That was just after Slovenia declared independence, at the start of the war in Bosnia. Overnight we lost our market for buses, but the division that produced weapons did better than ever. So I moved some people from our bus division to the production of automatic rifles, but I had to fire the rest. It wasn't easy. The union was tough as nails. I fired the first few hundred workers and bang, I had a revolution on my hands, right there in the factory yard. When I got home that night I found a rat waiting for me on the porch, impaled on a skewer, ready for the barbecue, with YOU'RE FINISHED painted on to it. Luckily I had no wife or children, or else I'd have been screwed. When I fired the next fifteen hundred workers I knew that I could no longer return home. I slept in one hotel after another, but each time they tracked me down. I was finally so desperate that I hid in one of our partly built buses that was parked on the assembly line for the night. The factory was guarded, so that was the safest place for me to be. I could easily have ended up with a bullet in my head if one of the workers I fired had seen me out on the street. They all had guns, naturally, as that was our product! Not to mention all those ill-fated new-money owners who tried to privatize the weapons factory, or the people from the foreign security agencies – any of them could've taken me out. So when I laid off the remaining 7,892 workers in a single day, I knew that I had to disappear. Back then we measured our business success in briefcases, not dollars or deutschmarks, not millions or hundreds of thousands, no, our currency was the briefcase. You know the sort, plain and black, the kind used by door-to-door salesmen. I had already received a suitcase the first day that I was appointed as director of AFM. A suitcase and a new passport. And when I fired twelve thousand people over the course of a month I got another black suitcase and another passport. Two suitcases and two passports, plus my real one.'

Rosa and Bely exchange glances. Bely notices the scar behind Rosa's right ear, which then disappears a moment later. For a split second Rosa once more catches the subtle suction-cup marks on Bely's chin.

'Are you listening?' asks Maher. 'To cut a long story short, I had money. I had done some dirty work, and I was scared to death, exhausted, unable to sleep. From the first day I was afraid that one of the workers might come at night and slit my throat. And come they did. As soon as I closed my eyes, one of the union heads, the one I constantly had to negotiate with, would infiltrate my dreams and wield his knife. After two weeks I was so terrified of falling asleep that I had to drink at least a half a litre of whisky just to knock myself out for a few minutes. Finally, I had enough. I hopped in my company Mercedes with the two suitcases and three passports and drove to the airport at Graz, sat on the first plane that I could get a ticket for and ended up in Stockholm.

All I remember is being sweaty and frightened. Next thing I knew the pilot was waking me up. The plane was empty. I was so deeply asleep during the entire flight that the stewardesses couldn't wake me. At first I thought it might've been from exhaustion, but it turned out that I had some paranoid syndrome, or God knows what. Once I was in Stockholm I went straight to the hotel, and as soon as I tried to close my eyes that union leader once again slit my throat then skewered me and put me on a huge grill. From then on I was only able to fall asleep in airports and aeroplanes. Anywhere else I closed my eyes that union leader would appear. And if I didn't immediately wake up from this nightmare I was forced to smell the scent of my own flesh, slowly turning and sizzling on a spit. So I spent most of the next three months in airports and aeroplanes. I'm incredibly grateful to the architects of Doha Airport, who equipped the terminals with lounge chairs facing the runway. A great place to sleep. The Germans don't have much style in this regard, only uncomfortable seats divided by those high metal armrests. The number of times I napped on one of them, completely twisted up, but that's hardly anything compared with being safe, where nobody can hurt you. At a certain point airports became my home, I never left them, and very quickly I became a real expert at travelling without luggage. Well, I had my two black suitcases. Eventually, only one. I came up with a technique of turning my underwear and socks inside out in a way that allowed me to fly without doing any laundry for two weeks at a time. I did it by regularly inserting toilet paper to the most sensitive areas. And with the perfume boutiques all over the place a man can go in and spray himself to his heart's content. When you can't take it any longer, you can always wash clothes in the bathroom or buy new ones. Are you following me?'

'We're listening,' Bely replies, 'but I'm still not sure what this has to do with –'

'The soul?' asks Maher.

'With the soul, yes,' says Bely.

'I don't have a soul. I'm inhabited by a few corrupt little souls, but this doesn't change the fact that I sold my soul, swapped it, pawned it, discarded it, ran it over, shot it down. Whatever was left of my soul, I left behind in the waiting-rooms and airport transit halls of the world. The soul, my dear friend, is an outdated concept from antiquity, later adopted by the Christians. We measure time in briefcases and forged passports while laying off people from work.'

'Then why did you come back?' Bely asks.

'Every black suitcase, no matter how full, empties out eventually. I had no other option than to come back to a place where people possessed what you call a soul. They called me back, cashed the bill of exchange and forced me back to work. And here I am. You don't believe that any of my firms are actually mine, do you? Or that I own anything more than what you see me wearing right now? If that were the case then I wouldn't be as exhausted as I am. I'm pretty much doomed. I can continue to star in their puppet show, or I can cut the strings they've got me hanging from. Or …'

'Or what?' asks Bely.

'Or I can leave it to you to cut the strings,' says Maher quietly. 'Ah, that smell of coal and sweat reminds me of my childhood. And it's Ash Wednesday tomorrow. Couldn't be more perfect. My God, sometimes I feel like I must be a few million years old.'

'Who are the members of the Great Orc?'

Maher stares at Bely from beneath his knit brows and lights a cigarette.

'Mm, these cigarettes are to die for. You've got to treat each cigarette as a luxury, as if it's your last. That's the only way to make smoking worthwhile.'

Maher blows a pair of smoke rings into the icy night air. He is quiet for a moment, then continues. 'You've already met our friend Magda, and I suppose you also know Ms Green, considering she's gone missing. Then there's Butcher and poor Gram, Farkas and Kovač – I haven't seen him tonight – plus Kirilov, you probably won't find him, and, of course, my tormentor, Mayor Voda. There're others, but I don't know who they are. Well, you probably know about the fortune-teller. Although she won't be here for long; she's about to fly off into the stars. Look.'

Maher points in the direction of a marker for the European Capital of Culture, illuminated by spotlights. Next to the marker a flashing neon sign that reads BLUE NIGHT DANCING. Maher awaits Bely's reaction.

'Some people think that everything that's happened to the archdiocese is just horrible. But, if you ask me, the strip club on their property just goes to show Maribor's true colours. Maybe we need more strip clubs. And I'm not talking about girls, but I really think that, as a society, we'd all benefit from a top-drawer strip club, just to see who's made of flesh and blood. You know what they say in Pohorje. It doesn't matter what she looks like, as long as she's mine.'

'What do you mean by that, Maher?' Bely asks nervously.

Maher shrugs his shoulders and unbuttons his jacket. A pistol with a silencer hangs beneath his armpit.

'I think, my dear friend, that the time has come.'

Bely and Rosa exchange worried glances. Maher laughs and flicks away his cigarette. Red ash flies into the black slush and extinguishes with a hiss. Just then the main theatre doors open and people emerge, cutting between the three of them. The second intermission. Maher laughs once more, nods and runs off around the corner of the building. Bely pushes through the crowd and follows him. Rosa looks for both through the throng of chatting people. Some go out into the night, others stand with glasses in hand. The atmosphere is solemn. Restless, Rosa runs up and down the stairs. People continue to leave until, eventually, the stairway empties out. A bell announces the end of the second intermission when Rosa spots Bely again.

'What happened?' she asks.

'I found him in the neighbouring square. He shot himself before I could get to him.'

'What do we do now?' asks Rosa.

'You'll go back in, and I'll try to find the fortune-teller.'

Rosa nods and looks after Bely as he disappears into a dark alley. She returns to the foyer with the last of the spectators. The theatre bar is shut and dark. The hostess gingerly lets her into the darkened auditorium. Many of the seats on the balcony are now empty. Rosa sits down at the rear. The stage is decorated in a modern, minimalist interior, with women dressed like Red Cross nurses and the men in tuxedos. On-stage, a white neon lamp.

COUNTESS ROSTOVA: 'War and bloody revolution, the destruction of culture and the fall of nations don't happen because of our evil desires. Revolution must see itself through, challenged by its own horrors and rage. The extreme triumphs. The victims are always the initiators. Such is the nature of an uprising.'

Natasha, pale, immobile. Even Nikolai wakes up. Sonya approaches.

NIKOLAI: 'Mother? Sonya? Moscow! Sonya!'

SONYA: 'Don't speak. You don't owe me any explanation.'

NATASHA: 'What happened? Mother, why do you weep?'

COUNTESS ROSTOVA: 'It's nothing, it's nothing …'

Rosa focuses on a large pair of glasses worn by Pierre Bezukhov. Every so often the spotlight ricochets off the tiny glass, its reflection blinding the audience in the balcony. Once again Rosa's memories come upon her like a flooding river. Voices from the bowels of the theatre glance off the dark, distant surface of water. On the rocky ground, two identical children's faces, two little girls. They giggle and run off, each in their own direction.

ANDREI: 'Maria … Thank you for coming, that is kind … That is kind … Masha, you …'

MARIA: 'Leave me alone.'

ANDREI: 'There's no need for tears here. We can't understand …'

MARIA: 'What?'

ANDREI: 'What love is. Love annoys death. Death is an awakening. I died. I woke myself once more. I dreamed that one day people might grow wings so that they could fly to their dreams. In these dreams the churches leap, joyous, out of their stone garments. From every droplet of colour and light new images emerge. Like a blizzard, a Roman candle of golden icons falls from the sky. Dying for me, for a creation of love means going back to our shared everlasting spring.' Andrei dies.

Maria and Countess Rostova.

COUNTESS ROSTOVA: 'Now I know … I finally understand … Man lives conscious of himself but also serves as an unconscious tool for fulfilling the goals of history. Everybody lives a double life: personal, wherein the more abstract your interests are the more freedom you have, and one uncontrolled, in which you exercise the enacted laws by fair means or foul …'

# Crystal Ball

Bely runs uphill in the direction of Calvary. Slush, the trickle of water in the gutter. A party in one of the apartment buildings; music and shouts. Bely sees a couple wearing white mouse masks smoking on a balcony and tapping ash into the street below. Soon the noise subsides. Urban villas, night. The pavement beneath Bely's feet is split like a gutted fish. Voda's building stands between houses at the base of Calvary, with only a grey forest behind it, climbing up the hill. The entrance is locked. Bely reads the names on the bells. Eight apartments in the building, two with no names listed. The bottom name is Green; above it the name of the deputy mayor and the director of the city administration. At the top the names Numen and Ornik are illuminated. Bely steps back into the street to get a view of the windows. The whole building is dark except the window on the far left, which produces a crystalline shine. Buzzing. The entrance opens. Bely steps inside. Cameras in the corridor. The doors to the lift slide open for him. The lift runs on a key, but the doors close by themselves. Fourth floor. The doors open directly into an apartment. Persian rugs, upholstered nineteenth-century French furniture, porcelain and silverware. Hunting trophies stare out from the wall, wooden statues of angels, dimmed lights.

'Come in, Mr Bely, don't be shy.'

The voice comes from the next room. The double doors leading to it rest ajar. Bely enters a living-room. A plush red sofa before a flickering fire on which sits a woman, dressed only in a nightgown, her face licked by the dim light, her bare feet tucked beneath her, a glass of sparkling wine in her hand.

'You certainly took your time, Mr Bely. Don't be shy, please, make yourself at home.'

The woman sets down her glass, stands and approaches him. Bely's eyes slowly accustom to the gloom. Up close, Nana Numen looks older than at first glance: bags beneath her eyes, the silhouette beneath her nightgown hints at the curves of age, the belly, slightly sagging breasts.

'Anastasia described you as less reserved, Mr Bely. Your star charts, Gemini in Scorpio, lead me to believe that beneath this façade lurks a much more resolute, eloquent man. I've poured you some champagne, and I'm sure you won't refuse, Mr Bely? Join an elderly lady who has grown rather bored awaiting your arrival. Our house is a ghost town today with everyone at the theatre. As if they don't have enough theatricality in their lives. One nail drives out another. Isn't that true, Mr Bely? Please, take a seat.'

Bely sits opposite the woman. He looks around the room: heavy draperies, shelves full of books, a large aquarium that illuminates the far wall of the room with a shimmering light. Many oil paintings and photographs, difficult to make out in the dim light. A round table, covered in a rich satin cloth. Beside Nana Numen rests a bowl of ice. Numen reaches out for an ice cube and lifts it to her eye.

'Please do not think badly of my indiscretion, Mr Bely. What must you think of an old woman who invites you into her home, wears only a nightgown and holds an ice cube up to her eye? I thought that you had forgotten about me, that you were not going to show up. I was just on my way to bed, but I am no less pleased to see you. How was the play?'

'It's still going on,' says Bely.

'My God, that Andreas! You know, I love him. His symbolism, which he draws from deconsecrated paintings, might not always click, still he's a character and has his charms. I remember his *Divine Comedy*, especially *Purgatory*. Did you see it? Really excellent. But these days, who could survive more than two hours in a theatre? I mean, please, that's like going to a torture chamber! If someone cannot make themselves understood in two hours then it's better that they keep silent. Even if it's *War and Peace*. I mean, just make one hour of war and one of peace, and you're all set. Or, even better, a ratio that's more conducive to peace. I suppose, Mr Bely, that is why you're here? To find peace? I may be able to give you a bit of assistance there. Will you have some champagne?'

Bely thanks her but leaves his glass on the table. His gaze hesitates over a large black-and-white photograph of a small girl with long blonde hair seated in Santa's lap.

'Are you looking at the photograph of me as a child? Perhaps you know that my father was known as the Father Frost of Maribor? My father was a special man, Mr Bely. He suffered much and that experience left its mark on him. Will you take some tea? If you like, we can perform a tea ceremony.'

'An oriental tea ceremony?' asks Bely.

'No, I don't do the oriental sort, it's a bit boring, but I can do the Pohorje ceremony. You don't know it? There's nothing better to release tension. Well, in truth it's not really about drinking tea. It has a more stimulating effect. You place fresh pine needles in your mouth. Then you pour ever hotter water on your feet. When you come just to the edge of burning yourself, special mouth enzymes extract healthy properties out of the pine needles. An excellent tonic for the immune system, I'm telling you'

'Mrs Numen, I didn't come here to drink tea or clean my feet.'

'I would gladly clean them for you, just as Mary Magdalene cleaned Jesus' feet, or the way I take care of my little hunter's feet.'

'Were you thinking of Voda?'

'Voda, of course, who else? Isn't it nice to pour water on Voda's feet?'

Nana Numen once again reaches into the bowl of ice and picks up a new cube, placing it against her neck. Meanwhile, Bely has grown sufficiently accustomed to the darkness that he can see the many bruises all over her body.

'My little hunter. My father was also a hunter, you know, just like Voda. The trophies displayed by the entrance are his. That was the only thing that brought him peace, being in the woods in his hunting blind, always on the lookout. He used to say that to hunt or to be hunted is the most human activity, a game. It's actually true, isn't it, that we're both hunters and quarry at the same time? I guess you're being hunted now. That's why you rushed in here. Time is not your ally, but it is mine. Do you know why? Because I know that we have no time; the only thing we have are ghosts, the ghosts that surround us. Ghosts that constantly whisper in my ear that there is no such thing as time. All that was and all that will be is happening now, at this moment. One would think that if that's the case everything had already been accomplished, but that's not true. That's the greatest mystery. Even though we have no time, even though everything has already happened, we can still intervene and change what has come to pass. Strange, isn't it? But that's how it is. Who are we anyway, as a human species, Mr Bely? We are at best only small animals who, every now and then, understand what the stars are trying to tell us, but that's all. And there's not much we understand.'

'What about the people who comprise the Great Orc?' Bely asks.

'The Great Orc is far more than the sum of its parts. It's a higher structure, a higher intelligence, if you will, that comes with a very specific task.'

'To keep everything as it is?' asks Bely. 'To keep memory erased and the ghosts in our souls forever in a state of confused blindness?'

'That's not all, Mr Bely, that's not all. It's much more than guarding things as they are. It's about us being ready for the new arrival of those who came long ago and who made us who we are today. We were created through death, through murder, if we're going to be specific, Mr Bely. Through the largest-scale murder that the world has ever seen. World wars, atomic bombs, revolutions – none of these can match the scope of the massacre wrought by the ruler, Xenu. We constantly talk about post-war massacres, but that's nothing compared with the density of slain souls who float freely around our planet. And you know what's interesting here? That all the major religious stories suggest a return. Take Christianity, for example, the return of the Saviour. You know, when I was a child I often went to church and prayed. Especially around the Nativity scenes at Christmas time. I was a restless child, but each time I was surrounded by a Nativity scene the shepherds and animals gathered around the newborn Saviour, I grew humble. But then, one time, as I was praying in the church, I fell asleep on the floor, even though it was freezing. The priest woke me up and punished me. I didn't know why, but it turned out that while I was asleep the invaluable statue of Baby Jesus disappeared from the manger. To this day I have no idea who stole it and how it could've happened. I just know that I was in a deep sleep when the theft took place, and I woke up with a high temperature. I was sick, but the priest punished me anyway. Afterwards I came down with a severe case of pneumonia. I hallucinated for several weeks, and they feared that I was at death's door. But I pulled through. I guess it was then that I was given a gift of extraordinary power. I never saw the priest again – and neither has anyone else. My father said that he was transferred, but I very much doubt that. I think that my father punished him for his behaviour. That's just who he was. A hunter.'

Nana Numen once again reaches into the silver ice bowl. This time she reaches deeper and pulls out a crystal ball, which she slides along her cheeks and neck, down to her exposed left shoulder, finally dropping it on to her nightgown.

'You see, there are millions, billions, of people out there who believe that Jesus will return one day. But if you ask me, that's reserved for Xenu and his descendants. Certain events need repeating, Mr Bely. And no matter how bloody, they're held accountable for keeping civilizations alive. There are entire civilizations that are still alive thanks to these events. That is a paradox for us, for civilizations to live thanks to killing, but that's just the way it is. So keep in mind that our unfortunate European Capital of Culture is also part of a broader constellation. The fact that the European Capital of Culture happens to be in Maribor and not some other European city is a unique historical opportunity that we had to take advantage of. My hunter put up thirteen new fountains around the city. You've seen how beautifully lit they are at night? We also installed a series of markers around them. People laugh at us, because they must be installed within one-tenth of a metre at specific sites, but there's a good reason for this. Did you know, Bely, that these fountains and markers make up a constellation? When they're lit, they replicate the constellation of Osiris, which is visible from space. It's for Xenu's orientation. He needs to know where to send his new shipment.'

'Do you really think that what happened millions of years ago can happen again?' asks Bely.

Numen laughs and takes up the crystal ball.

'I like how naïve you are, Mr Bely. History repeats itself. It always has, and it always will. We make up only a small fraction of one of the endless cycles.'

'But the souls …'

'Even souls have their own lifespan. Information is lost and must be refreshed. And talking about refreshment, you haven't touched your champagne.'

'Tell me, who are the other two members of the Great Orc?'

The question causes Numen to laugh. She slowly rises to her feet and holds the crystal ball closer to the fire.

'There are things I don't know, Mr Bely. I know about death. When I look at someone I can usually see when and how they will die. At night I dream of those murdered. My world is full of the living dead, do you understand? But there're things that even I and my crystal ball can't foresee.'

She runs her hand slowly over the crystal ball. A fine glitter flashes from under her fingers. It seems to Bely that he can see something inside it. He wants to draw closer but suddenly realizes that he is riveted to the couch and cannot move.

'Did you intend to hypnotize me, Mr Bely? You know that your hypnosis is novice-level at best. What you are experiencing now is a much higher level of hypnosis, although, to be honest, it's nothing special. I didn't hypnotize you as a mental entity. I hypnotized only the animal in which you reside so that you no longer have any control over it. It's quite easy. Now you are a soul without a body, Mr Bely, which is, in reality, what you are anyway.'

Numen gently places the crystal ball on the table before Bely. It radiates a soft blue light.

'You're probably curious about how the Great Orc came to be, Mr Bely. You're unable to speak, but I can read your thoughts and know that it interests you. It interests you just as much as many other things, none of which you'll learn, not during this lifetime anyway.'

Numen crosses to the window and pulls apart the curtains.

'So, the Great Orc, otherwise known as the large stellar formation of the thirteen, has existed since time began. But, every so often, it materializes at various places with one objective, to carry out a specific task. It appears time and again in different places and among different people, but we don't know much about that. What we do know is that the last stellar constellation of the thirteen started here in Maribor a good century ago, some time during our grandparents' era. It was just before the First World War, in 1913. A group of farmers from Pohorje went on a pilgrimage to the church on Calvary. It was a summer's day, Saturday 21 June. Night fell, and the farmers camped out under the stars in the grass around the church. At night, glowing mushrooms sprang from the ground, and, although the farmers all knew the mushrooms of the region very well, they had never seen anything like that before. They looked like colourless black trumpets, and they had a stale scent that woke the farmers from their sleep. At first the farmers just stared at them. Suddenly the mushrooms burst into a fine dust that was accompanied by a sound. At that they lunged at the mushrooms and started to eat them raw, as if they were possessed. Of course, none of them knew that they were on a huge hill made of millions of murdered bodies from another planet – that the mushrooms were not mushrooms but the extensions of all those decomposed corpses. The farmers who ate them rose into the air. It is said that some of them levitated three or four metres off the ground. They just hung there, helpless, suffering from hallucinations, one of which was common to all of them, as far as we know. It was of a giant octopus that had thirteen legs, not the usual eight. While the farmers hung there, the octopus shoved its slimy legs into their mouths and other bodily crevices, which caused them to defecate and vomit until morning, when the octopus finally let them go, completely exhausted, to lie in pools of their own bodily fluids. The mushrooms disappeared and have never sprouted again. Those who ate them agreed to keep this a secret so people wouldn't think they were mad. While many of them died in the upcoming war, those who lived kept this secret for generations. Among them a group was formed of thirteen guardians who safeguarded the knowledge of all that had happened: the so-called Great Orc.'

Numen approaches the fireplace again and looks at the flames.

'The time is ripe for a new depopulation of their planet. The souls, caught in humans here on Earth, have weakened and need new information. Xenu is the source of our information and intelligence, Bely. Without him we'd be nothing but ordinary animals. But despite all this intelligence and knowledge we can't answer even the simplest of questions. You say that you believe that people are more than just the carriers of Xenu's souls. Or, at the very least, that there are certain forces among these souls that concur with your beliefs about what's good. You think that life itself brings new life, without retribution. You believe in absolution, Bely. But what is absolution? And if you believe in the absolution of others, please tell me, how do we absolve ourselves? Who is he who will judge our own actions? Who will absolve us from within? A tough question to answer, isn't it? How do you respond to the paradox that you've had to kill in order to do good? Aren't you, who has murdered consciously, worse than those who murder in a fit of passion? Your cold-blooded justification of murder with a higher purpose makes you no different from Xenu, does it? Aren't you, Adam Bely, just a lesser reproduction of Xenu? Can't you see that your efforts to change the existing order will only solidify it? This order was established by the same act with which you try to start a new order: murder. What kind of information is absolution? None at all! Let me show you something.'

Numen steps closer to Bely and removes the compact from the pocket of his jacket.

'You see, in this constellation I could eat all of your oyster crackers, and nothing would happen to me, nothing at all. Next to my crystal ball they're just oyster crackers, soiled and soaked in abdominal juices. I prefer something else.'

Numen, placing her crystal ball on the glass table before Bely, opens a drawer and pours a small amount of white powder out of a little bag on to the table top, chops it, shapes it into lines and snorts it up.

'Ah, nothing better than tarot cards and cocaine, Bely. Want some? Oh, I forgot that you no longer have a body with which to enjoy these animal pleasures of life.'

Numen smiles and reaches into the silver bowl, drawing out an ice cube, which she places on her eye. 'What shall I do with you, Bely? Should I change you into a toad? No, that would be too easy. What if I chop off your head? That sounds more like it. I think that I'll wait until the masters come. We could use a little human meat at the building site of the wastewater treatment plant, something to mix into that dull concrete. And it would be in keeping with the common practice of sacrifice at the construction of temples as a deterrent to evil spirits.'

Numen snorts another line of cocaine then puts the accessories back into the drawer and moves over to the aquarium.

'You see, here I have a little octopus to go with my goldfish. Life in the water looks so tranquil. Not like in Maribor, where water means nothing but trouble.'

Beneath the cuff of Bely's jacket the shadow of an octopus leg emerges, then trails meandering across his skin. The shadow slides off Bely and on to the table.

'Not that you're interested in tranquillity. Tranquillity. What a word! Do you really think that you can set people free of their past by cutting off the legs of the octopus? The Great Orc has no concern for time, Bely; the Great Orc is the eye of time. And as much as I can read you, Bely, I can see that you believe that we become *clear* only if we change our own past to the point where it no longer holds us in its grip. At the same time it's clear that your absolution can be understood as total war. What you call absolution is, in fact, spiritual murder.'

Nana Numen picks up a box of fish food and shakes some of it into the water. The fish swim wildly up to the surface of the aquarium while, from under the rocks at the bottom, a long octopus leg extends and then recoils back to the shelter of the hole.

In the meantime, Bely watches as the shadows that have crawled out of his body climb across the table top and start prancing around the blue crystal ball.

'Would you say that absolution, as you call it, is the correction of time? If we can separate ourselves from the past, and all we're left with is the present, then is our present also handicapped by our future? No matter how you put it, Bely, you'll always be a murderer.'

Numen looks at the aquarium and pronounces her last syllables slowly, as if her thoughts were slowly chopped into small pieces, then minced into a fine powder.

'Through absolution we help only ourselves, not others. Absolving others, Bely, is egotism of the highest order. And I've had my fill of selfish men. My father was like that. Voda too.'

The octopus legs wrap themselves around the blue glow. The shadow of the octopus wraps around the crystal ball and holds it tight. The blue glow extinguishes. For a moment Bely can move his limbs. He catapults out of the chair, grabs the crystal ball and flings it at Numen, who is knocked into the aquarium. Clamour, glass, water splattering around the room and into the fireplace, dousing the fire. Squirming fish on the floor. The fortune-teller's body lies in a pool of blood, immobile, impaled on a shard of glass. Around her neck tip-toe the legs of the octopus that has just crawled out of the aquarium.

Bely swiftly searches the apartment, going through books and the displayed photographs. But there is too much of everything for him to find anything significant. After a few minutes he steps from the lift and exits the apartment building. The window of the penthouse still flickers with light, an orientation point for future visitors. Everything else is dark, not a soul to be seen. Bely walks quickly down the street, heading to the theatre. Two crossroads further on, a silhouette steps out of the bushes, mist-like drops obscuring his face. When he draws closer, Bely recognizes that it is Gros. A silent exchange of glances. Bely continues walking; Gros follows. After a long stretch of silent pursuit, Gros finally speaks in a high-pitched voice that surprises Bely – he would never have expected such a corpulent man to have such a high voice. Only then does he realize that he had never before heard him speak.

'Which of Voda's women were you visiting, Bely? The theatre director, Green? She should be at the theatre, but no one has seen her, not even at the première. Or were you visiting with one of the deputy mayors, who both live there? No, they're also at the theatre today. What about the fortune-teller? Although I doubt that she can foresee our destiny, least of all her own, as this is said to be the most difficult to do. What's your opinion, Bely? Can you predict your own future? Do you know what fate awaits you?'

Bely walks on in silence. He tries to walk as quickly as possible, but the faster he moves the more effortlessly the long-legged Gros seems to follow him.

'I assume that you saw what happened to Ms Ornik. She's really in a very poor state,' remarks Gros, smiling sourly. Bely glances at him and further quickens his pace.

'See, Mr Bely, Inspector Maus didn't tell you everything. I think it wouldn't hurt if you knew the whole truth, the last few details of which are far from trivial.'

Bely stops. The impressive façade of the theatre stands before them; they find themselves at the workmen's entrance, with several trucks from the Croatian National Theatre parked outside.

'First, Inspector Maus didn't leave the investigation voluntarily but was forcibly relieved of his duty,' says Gros in his high, whiny voice – more a chirp than speech. 'The police chief takes his theory very seriously, but there are doubts as to his impartiality, or at least his tendency to cast suspicion on the mayor in his desire to have him charged. No one believes that the mayor is innocent. His guilt is obvious, and it's just a matter of time before he will pay for what he has done. But there's a large gap between suspicion and concrete evidence, and criminals should no longer be able to evade prison only because the incriminating evidence against them was not obtained lawfully, because it was modified or might not hold up in court. As for the other thing that Inspector Maus withheld from you …' Gros pauses here, as if to increase dramatic tension, but his odd voice and cumbersome way of speaking do just the opposite. 'We've discovered another case this morning, aside from Pavel Don Kovač and Magda Ornik. It's Samo Gram, the owner of the New World restaurant. You know the man, I believe?'

Bely observes Gros, who serves his sentences slowly, as if he were trying to learn correct grammar.

'He has been missing for several days, but today his staff found him in the pantry – naked, in a barrel of cabbage. They had to lure him out with a big pork leg. His employee last saw him in the restaurant a week ago after he had closed up. There were two people with him, you and Ms Portero, isn't that right?'

Bely nods. 'He was one of our interviewees, yes,' he says.

'The interviews, of course. Wouldn't you say it's a bit strange that three of the four victims went crazy immediately after speaking to you?'

Bely is silent. At that moment a flutter is heard above Gros's head. Two grey blobs of bird dung fall on his black coat.

'Disgusting,' Gros squeals and carefully wipes most of the excrement off with a handkerchief. 'I wouldn't object if these flying rats were exterminated, regardless of Maus's theory,' says Gros. 'Tell me, Bely, did you also know Kovač?'

Bely nods.

'Have you seen him at all in the past few days?'

'I saw him in passing at the opening of the Marx Centre,' says Bely.

'Did you talk?'

'Like I said, very briefly.'

'Hm, Mr Bely, who else do you and Ms Portero intend to interview?'

'We're slowly wrapping up the interviews. We've already been here a week, and we have to start production.'

'I could arrest you based on all my leads, but I won't. I suggest you come by the police station tomorrow morning at 8 a.m. We'll take a brief statement, and we'll let you walk, for now. But I warn you, Bely, if my investigation is headed in the right direction ...' Assistant Gros suddenly falls silent. He looks around, as if in search of something. Finally, he adds, 'Going back to the theatre? The performance is probably over by now.'

Bely nods, then turns to leave Gros behind in the darkness.

# Complete Archive

People are outside smoking, in front of the theatre and on the balcony above the main entrance. On the first floor the reception area is crowded with people milling around an enormous cake made of Kranj sausage, capped by a miniature Napoleonic cannon. Chewing mouths, clinking glasses, laughter and clamour. Gubec in his tracksuit and trainers, flash, lighting up the famous faces of Maribor with his camera. Rosa Portero stands at the other end of the hall.

'How did the play end?' asks Bely. 'War or peace?'

'I'd rather you tell me about the fortune-teller,' she replies.

'Her souls were absolved, that's the end of her career,' says Bely, glancing around. 'Anything new on Voda? Have they found him yet?'

'Not yet,' Rosa whispers. 'Do you really think we'd have a reception going on here if they'd found him? Don't forget that he's the mayor.'

Bely shrugs. 'It's obvious you still don't know this city. For most people here, this evening won't be memorable because of what took place on-stage but because of an off-stage event which they'll happily chew over for the next few days.'

'Did you find out who the other two members of the Great Orc are?'

Bely shakes his head. 'Unfortunately Numen didn't say anything useful.'

'Then Father Kirilov's box is our only chance. If we can't decipher the glass lens and the empty manger, then it's all over.'

'That's exactly what worries me. If that happens nothing will be over,' says Bely.

'Whatever,' says Rosa reluctantly.

'Bely, Ms Portero, give us a smile, please,' Gubec interrupts them.

Flash. Gubec checks the quality of the photo on the display screen.

'You seem tense, Adam. Relax. Didn't you like the performance?'

'The performance was OK, especially the first act,' says Bely. 'Did Andreas show up in the end?'

'Of course not, but it was clear from the start that he wasn't coming. I wouldn't be surprised if this feast here is his message to the Maribor public, a cake made of Kranj sausages. I mean, really!'

'I hear what you're saying, but people clearly love sausages, look at this feeding frenzy,' says Bely.

'Of course. It's free. When wasn't there a feeding frenzy when something was free? But we know, Adam, that nothing is really free, right?' says Gubec, snapping another photo before he moves on.

'How does he know my name?' Rosa asks.

'You were already introduced,' Bely said.

'Yeah, but you never told him my name. I only noticed it because that's what you usually do. One more thing, I think I've solved the mystery of the lens that Father Kirilov had put in his Nativity scene. It's not a magnifying glass as we've thought all along. It's a camera lens.'

Bely looks at her. Suddenly the theatre fills with screaming. Adam and Rosa rush down the stairs. A group of people stand around Mayor Voda, who is down on all fours licking the floor. Soon the paramedics arrive, but Voda escapes from their clutches. People begin to back off. The mayor climbs up one of the decorative metal reliefs in the foyer, above the crowd that carefully studies his every movement. Before he reaches the ceiling, he starts swinging and crying out like some animal. The paramedics are embarrassed. No one can reach him, but finally someone lures him down the wall with a handful of sausages, which prove enough of a distraction for the paramedics to be able to grab him, wrestle him to the ground and take him away.

'Go after them,' Bely tells Rosa. 'See if Maus and Gros will escort him to the hospital.'

Rosa nods and follows the paramedics.

People are talking, up in arms about the incident. Someone explains excitedly that he heard strange noises coming out of the men's toilet, and when there was no response he sought out the caretaker. When they unlocked the bathroom stall, they found Voda licking the inside of the toilet bowl. His head was wet from the toilet water and scraps of wet toilet paper clung to his face. The man explains that Voda lunged at the crowd like a rabid monkey. People scattered in revulsion. When they dared to come close again they saw him licking the urinals. Only then did the paramedics arrive.

The mayor's tragic fate has shocked the city, especially the élite who attended the première. Speculation runs rampant as to the connection between the madness of the mayor and the director of the city cemetery. Most believe that they had been drugged, but with what? Had they taken the drugs themselves and simply gone too far, or were they victims of sabotage? What if Voda never recovers? This may very well mean a new constellation of political power in the city. Various scenarios run wild behind the gloomy faces of all those who worked closely with the mayor.

'It looks like we're going to have a preliminary election for the mayor of Maribor again,' Bely hears Gubec says behind his back.

When Bely turns around, he is blinded by a flash.

'Smile,' says Gubec. 'Attaboy.'

Gubec checks the photo on the camera's display.

'No, these won't work. Too grim, Adam. The first batch was much better, but I see that you're wearing a different outfit. I don't know any other person who would change in the middle of the show. Very interesting. You and the performers. Go figure. The world is one big stage anyway, right, Adam?'

'You have a photographic memory, Gubec,' says Bely.

'Not really. Much better than memory, I have film. You know, an archive like this is a very valuable thing if you know how to interpret the photos. What are photos without the stories behind them? Imagine, in a few centuries our descendants will be able to travel back by looking at all these shots. In the past the past was erased, but today everything is forever saved, nothing can be erased, Adam, nothing.'

'Even the photos of the mayor licking the urinal?'

'They're already online, Adam. You'll see. In the coming hours the number of visitors to my website will increase a thousand-fold. Information is power today, not money.'

'Whoever's got pictures is in control of the world?'

'Whoever's got the pictures and knows how to interpret them controls the world,' says Gubec, raising his camera to snap a photo of the minister of culture heading out of the theatre.

'Today the minister and Voda were chatting about putting up a national memorial to the victims of post-war massacres in the square in front of the theatre. I've heard they were quite serious about it, but who knows what will happen now, in light of all this, with Voda going mad? But even if he returns to the land of the sane, this was his political burial. Preliminary local elections, I'm telling you, Bely. Three months, tops, before we'll vote again.'

'Do you have photos of all the members of the Great Orc, Gubec?'

Gubec raises the camera again and photographs the deputy mayor, who wrings her hands with concern and desperation while giving a statement to the local newspaper.

'Very strange questions you're asking today, Adam. Who is this Orc? A new band?'

'I thought you knew about the Great Orc.'

'How should I, Adam? I'm no know-it-all.'

'You have photos of just about anyone who means anything in this town, don't you? Who knows what you've seen and documented?'

'Do you know the wet dream of every reporter, Bely? Not only to shoot the mayor in a licking frenzy in the gents, but to capture everything he sees or anyone else for that matter. A complete archive. Can you imagine? Our eyes like cameras, running from conception through to death. And all of this documented and publicly available.'

'An archive of everything?' asks Bely. 'Even our dreams?'

'Even our dreams,' says Gubec, adjusting his sweatshirt.

'Even our fears and nightmares?'

'Even those.'

'Not bad,' says Bely. 'But I've got a better idea.'

'And that would be?'

'An archive of all the dead souls. An archive of everything that's happened to them and that's still happening to them in various constellations, even after death.'

Gubec smiles. 'Photography doesn't know death, only the problem of the material carrier but not the problem of death as such. When films deteriorate or when photographs fade, it's not photography, it's time that's accountable for that. When the format of a photo becomes out-of-date then that's a software issue. You don't seem to understand, Bely, that we're immortal. Everything that surrounds us is and will be forever. Photography is living proof of this. Memories fade, but photographs remain.'

'That may be true, but with one caveat.'

'Tell me.'

'That death is recycled, time and again, which disables the sequence of memory. Gubec, tell me who the thirteenth member of the Great Orc is.'

Gubec sneezes violently and wipes his nose on his sleeve.

'This air conditioning will be the death of me, Adam. I really don't know what you're talking about. I don't know this rock band of yours. But it's interesting what you say about death. In a sense, you celebrate it.'

'Not really. I think death is a driving force for someone who's bigger than the system, someone who controls it. And this someone has his own guardians. Most of them don't even know what they were chosen to do, but others, the chosen ones, they're better informed. I assume that you photojournalists are the best-informed of all. You've got photos of everyone.'

'Not everyone, I'm afraid, Adam, but I do have photos of almost everyone. Even our new mayoral candidates. I'm telling you, if you know how to read images you can go a long way to predicting the future. And when you can see into the future, then you can also change its course. Even better, if you know how to read images then you can sort of create what will become of all those people in the photos. I can tell you quite accurately who will win the preliminary mayoral elections.'

'Then surely you can tell me who, by tomorrow, will have replaced the missing members of the thirteen-strong Great Orc,' says Bely dryly.

Just then, Rosa appears. Bely looks at her, Rosa shakes her head.

'Ms Portero, so nice to see you again,' says Gubec. 'You know, you're very photogenic. I'd love to photograph you more. Your face tells me your ancestors come from Latin America?'

'Cuba,' says Rosa.

'Oh, that's where you do Santería, isn't it? I've never been, but I dream of going. They say that Havana is magical.'

Rosa remains silent, looking at Bely.

'Although you'll find some magic here, too. Last week I worked with a journalist who did a report for an English newspaper on secret cults and sects in central Europe. We were at Lake Balaton. Who would've thought that the Hungarians are open to sects? Nevertheless, there're quite a few. But there wasn't much to photograph. A few shots of the lake, the reeds and deserted ritual sites. Pretty boring, really. But I managed to take some wonderful shots of tourists, people taking a stroll, of children playing in the sand. I ended up with great shots of identical twins, completely blond, just beautiful. They sat in the sand, playing with toy cars. They were so cute I wanted to slip them into my pocket and take them home. Ms Portero, are you all right? You're gone completely pale.'

'That's enough, Gubec. Father Kirilov told us everything. You can stop playing dumb,' says Bely, grabbing him by the collar.

'Let go of my jacket, Bely, or people will think that you've gone mad, too,' says Gubec calmly, removing Bely's hand. 'In this country there's a thing called freedom of the press. We journalists are a protected breed, or didn't you know that? You don't have that in Austria? What do you think, Ms Portero? In Austria do journalists get a better deal than we do here? Because you're a journalist, right? Even if I couldn't find your name on any list of Austrian national radio and television journalists. Honestly, you don't give the impression of being a journalist either. For a journalist, your spectrum of interests is too narrow, covering only very specific subjects. For instance –'

'For instance what?' Bely asks in an angry whisper.

'For instance, underwater fishing. Particularly catching cephalopods. A horrible word, don't you agree, Bely? Cephalopod: legs in the head. Disgusting. Although it clearly represents what they do. They think, and they move.'

'There's one other thing they do,' says Bely. 'They kill.'

'Well, that's what people like you do, Bely. Did you come here to kill me, too? A hard nut to crack – too many victims in too short a time in a small town like Maribor. The trail will lead to you two, and I for one don't believe that you'll be able to wriggle your way out of this. Especially after what happened to the mayor. If I may be frank, Adam, I think this is your last taste of freedom. Oh, what a coincidence, look, it's Mr Gros. Quite an ambitious young detective, don't you think? People like him need their victims, their victories, their convictions. He's headed our way. Wait, I'm not missing this historical moment.'

Gubec begins to photograph Gros. An elongated figure approaching with long strides from the other side of the foyer. Bely rushes forward and pushes Gubec, who crashes into Gros. The camera falls and pieces of glass and plastic scatter across the marble floor. Rosa and Bely run.

'This way,' cries Bely and pulls Rosa through the doorway into the auditorium.

'Stop, police!' shouts Gros in his screeching voice. Rosa and Bely dash between the empty seats, jump on to the stage and run past the stagehands dismantling the scenery.

'Where are we going?' asks Rosa when they find themselves breathless in the darkness behind one of the doors.

'There're some exits here. One way or another we'll end up outside. I know this theatre like the back of my hand.'

'We lost Gubec,' Rosa whispers. 'We'll never get another chance.'

'Don't be so sure.'

'We'll be too late, Bely. The Great Orc will recruit new members. Even if we manage to escape and eventually get to Gubec and absolve his soul, it'll all have been in vain. We still don't know the thirteenth member.'

A chirping voice whistles from behind the door. 'They have to be around here somewhere. Send men to all the exits and empty the theatre. Where's the backup? Good, good.'

Bely touches the light switch. He and Rosa are in the props room: wigs, lipsticks, old mirrors, worn furniture.

'This way,' whispers Bely, pulling Rosa behind him.

Dark passage, two doors. The first is locked.

'Damn,' says Bely under his breath.

The second door opens on to more hallway and stairs leading beneath the stage. Gros's voice is now above them. He is talking on the phone. The sound of police sirens grows nearer. Rosa looks around her. Pale light in front of them, around them scenery, angels made of laminated paper and an enormous birdcage in the corner; further in, a stuffed camel, hangers and old costumes.

'Bely, Portero, we know you're in there! Come out. You can't hide forever. There's no getting out of here. The theatre is surrounded!'

Despite his funny, high-pitched voice, Gros sounds determined and authoritative.

'This way,' whispers Bely. In an adjacent room Rosa sees more scenery. For a split second she could swear that she saw the leg of a giant octopus silently slide across the floor.

'Both exits are locked.'

'What now?'

'We have to go back up,' says Bely. 'Out of the storerooms. It's the only way out.'

'What about a fire exit?'

'This one here is the fire exit.'

Bely and Rosa head back. Egyptian masks to their left, Roman pillars and a broken neon sign, large arches with coloured bulbs, rotating wheels.

'This way,' says Bely. He turns in the dim light, but Rosa is gone. He runs back into the shadows of the scenery.

'Rosa, Rosa where are you?'

Groans. Rosa is sitting on the floor. A nail protrudes from her right shoe.

'Damn,' sobs Rosa.

Bely examines Rosa's foot. 'You stepped on a nail. It's stuck in your foot. I'm going to pull it out. Ready?'

Rosa looks at Bely with tears in her eyes and nods. She clenches her teeth. Muffled shouts.

Bely pulls the nail out. 'You're bleeding. We'll have to dress the wound.'

'Just leave me here, Bely.'

'No, Rosa, we got out once before. We'll get out of this again, you'll see. All good things come in pairs.'

Rosa smiles despite the pain. She tries to stand but can't. Bely supports her as she tries to hop along on one foot, then he lifts and carries her. Steps above, more people, closer.

'We have to hide, quickly.'

Bely lowers Rosa behind a model of a sphinx. 'Wait for me here, Rosa. I promise I'll come back. We'll get out of this mess.'

Rosa nods, squeezes Bely's hand and kisses it. Stunned, Bely looks into her eyes as she dives into his. Millions of years, one fleeting moment, what's the difference when and where we will meet again? Bely silently nods and disappears. Just then the lights in the storeroom go out. On the ceiling, Rosa sees the contours of a giant octopus. Or is it only a hallucination? Perhaps the shadow of a wig, hung next to a wall light?

When the door opens, Bely, at the last moment, hides behind a large mirror. Three uniformed policemen enter along with Gros. They split up to search the room. Bely grabs hold of the handle on the mirror, ready to break it over the head of the approaching policeman.

Suddenly a deep, sharp voice sounds from the far end of the room. '*Blanca Tortuga, luna dormida, qué lentamente caminas!*'

It's Rosa's voice. The police rush towards it. Bely seizes his chance and sprints to the exit and down the stairs. One of the men spots him and calls frantically for him to stop. Bely looks back but sees neither policemen nor Rosa, only a staircase leading out of this enormous tomb.

Mirage? Ancient memory? What vanishes beneath the weight of a moment that decides between life and death, somewhere far beyond time?

'Ms Portero,' says Gros, raising her from the ground, 'we'll see how well you'll recite poetry from your cell.'

Rosa tries to comb down her dishevelled hair. The police handcuff her. She tries to put weight on her injured foot, but the pain is unbearable. They uncuff her and support her on their way out.

'And your friend, Bely? Don't you know? You don't want to know?' asks Gros. 'Don't worry, we'll catch him. He can't get away now.'

Rosa silently limps. Above her looms the lift. Long steel cables that raise theatrical scenery. A large empty room above, fully illuminated.

A pair of policemen, scanning the rows of seats as if they were rows of teeth of a giant monster, its jaws agape.

'Wait here,' Gros chirps.

Gros steps away to have a word with one of the policemen. Out of nowhere, a pigeon flutters through the air above the great auditorium. The police are distracted for a moment, looking up at the bird, then resume their search. Rosa is alert, looking for any sign of Bely. Her leg has gone numb from the pain. She lifts her foot. A footprint of bright-red blood on the stage floor. She looks down and sees something in the intersection of its lines. Father Kirilov's Nativity scene? Who is the thirteenth member of the Great Orc? Who is missing from the set? Who has no object that would indicate their origin, nature or character? Who is both present and absent at the same time?

'Ms Portero, so we meet again! Smile, please,' says Gubec. A small compact camera clicks twice, three times.

Gubec looks at the photos, shaking his head.

'Crap. My Canon would've taken better photos, but this will do. You smashed my favourite camera, Ms Portero, just like you wanted to destroy the Great Orc. And you've accomplished nothing. You should've been sacrificed back at Lake Balaton. But never mind. By tomorrow the Great Orc will be stronger than ever. You needn't worry about my camera either. I have another. Mr Gros, our future inspector, please, step this way so I can take a snap that will make the news. Let the world see who captured the runaway killer and poisoner.'

Gros waves him away. 'What are you doing here, Gubec? The police investigation is still under way, and you're not supposed to be here.'

'You know our provincial city, it's pretty obvious that you're a hero. You saved the day, and soon you'll have the second offender in custody. Do you mind coming closer? People deserve to see the hero of the day next to our killer!'

'All right, go ahead, but make sure I'm in the background,' says Gros quietly.

'Understood. Very wise,' grins Gubec, 'very wise.'

'Ms Portero, please don't smile,' grins Gubec as he leans in to catch her up close, with Gros in the background.

Flash. Fire that flashes through Rosa's body. In front of her the staring eyes of her twins, shards of glass following the trajectory of flying metal. The moment that will take her life. Destruction and a new path. Just when you think that you are the master of your own destiny. The old woman circles the chair with the little girl in it, incomprehensible babbling, two of her fingers smothering candles, one by one. Darkness. Bent metal, objects flying across the room, a flash of time. Then and now. Then a pigeon flutters in with the flash of light. Peaceful, wings spread, it sits between Rosa and Gubec, who is waiting for Gros to step back to join the rest of the police force.

Suddenly, like a wounded beast, Rosa rushes at Gubec. The metal fingers of her right hand clamp down on his neck. A wave of surprise mixed with terror flashes across his face. Who is the executioner here? What are the messages, mechanisms and destinies that a split second can trigger? The metal of Rosa's hand clenches like a vice around Gubec's neck. His eyes roll back and extinguish to a blank gaze.

When the policemen drag Rosa of Gubec it is too late. He lies motionless, his tongue slightly protruding, eyes open, head dangling like the pendulum on a clock that no longer swings.

'She broke his neck, she broke his neck!' yells a policeman.

Gros orders that they handcuff her and take her away. 'You'll pay dearly for that, bitch, do you hear me? You'll pay dearly!'

The police cuff Rosa Portero and pull her away. Her foot leaks a trail, a signature in blood.

'Out, out, get her out of here!' Gros screams.

Rosa sees Gros as he furiously kicks the pigeon perching on Gubec's body. The pigeon takes off and then settles again in the same place.

'Dear God, did you see her hand?' says one of the two policemen leading Rosa out.

'Honey, this can't end well for you if that's how you treat people,' says the other.

'Think about her boyfriend. Can you imagine her wanking you off?'

'She'd make mincemeat of you,' grins the first policeman. 'But that's some serious shit to go and kill the most famous journalist in the city. That's something nobody will absolve you of.'

'But as long as you can absolve yourself, lady,' says the other policeman.

In front of the theatre they push Rosa into a police car, deliberately knocking her head against the roof.

Rosa's attention now shifts from the bloody puddle in her shoe to a slow trickle of blood that runs down her face. She feels as the beast within her rises with determination. She touches the scar behind her ear, oozing a bloody, milky mucus.

'Don't worry, time heals everything,' says one of the policemen.

They both burst out laughing. The engine starts.

'And you, sweetheart, you'll have an infinite amount of time to heal all of your wounds,' says the other.

They laugh.

The police car drives down the street in front of the theatre and stops at a traffic light. A cloudy night. Slush and grime everywhere. Police cars with revolving lights. A handful of the curious public beyond the barrier. Rosa looks at the red stain in her shoe, all wet and clumpy, then at the slimy, off-white stain on her left glove, finally stopping at the dark stain that spreads across her right glove. This is Gros's blood. Then it dawns upon her.

'*Bely, du bist der Dreizehnte,*' Rosa whispers to herself.

'What's that?' asks one of the policemen.

'How can you absolve yourself?' Rosa murmurs and closes her eyes.

Then everything begins to shake.

'Earthquake! Earthquake!' cries the policeman.

Falling shingles and plaster. The asphalt before the police car cracks, swaying lamp-posts, cracking windows all around. A great rumbling rises from the police vehicle. The policemen and Rosa turn to see the bricks crumble off the theatre's façade, and the fluorescent blue lights turn on. Smoke and plaster dust is everywhere. In a matter of seconds the Maribor theatre transforms into a spaceship. Shaped like the head of a giant octopus, the spacecraft lifts thunderously into the air with its long legs flailing. The Earth stops to shudder as the spaceship vanishes into the dark skies.

Deathly silence. An enormous chasm gapes where, until so recently, the largest theatre in Slovenia once stood. People flood out of the neighbouring buildings. Police and fire-engine sirens blare in the distance. No one can explain what just happened. An earthquake would leave ruins everywhere. Even a terrorist attack would fail to spare the nearby buildings. But in the central square of Maribor only a single, sturdy building has disappeared. Those who saw the theatre turn into a spaceship and fly into the sky are silent. Probably a case of collective hallucination or hypnosis. The adjacent bell tower of the cathedral tolls midnight. Soon, hundreds gather around the edge of the chasm in the main square of the European Capital of Culture and stare into its depths. The darkness of the enormous abyss before them is like the open mouth of a toothless old hag. The stench of sulphur rises from the hole.

Just then a well-known Maribor character and his pet cross the far side of the square. Despite their striking appearance no one seems to notice them. It's Attorney Maister and his black swine, out for a midnight stroll. The odd pair watches from afar as the crowd stares into the chasm. A few steps further on they pause in front of the marker for the European Capital of Culture, the one in front of the former offices of the archdiocese, now the Blue Night strip club. The balloon is low on gas, so it looks like a giant flabby condom mounted on a long bone. Attorney Maister lights a cigarette. The cooing of dozens of pigeons, excitedly flying over the huge hole where the theatre once stood, drowns out the chirp of the swine. Maister and his black pig turn off Slomšek Square and head towards Gosposka Street. Above them, the New Year's decorations sway like broken cobwebs. It's the end of the carnival. Welcome Ash Wednesday.

# The Author

ALEŠ ŠTEGER is a poet, essayist and novelist writing in Slovenian. His books have been translated into sixteen languages, and his poems have appeared in internationally renowned magazines and newspapers such as *The New Yorker, Die Zeit, Neue Zürcher Zeitung, The Times Literary Supplement* and many others. Among other prizes and honours his English translation of *Knjiga reči* (*The Book of Things*, BOA Editions, 2010) won two major US translation awards (BTBA award and AATSEL). Besides writing and translating from German and Spanish, Šteger is also the programme director of Beletrina Academic Press, and the programme director of the international poetry festival Days of Poetry and Wine, which is held annually in the town of Ptuj, Slovenia.

# The Translators

URŠKA CHARNEY is a Slovene translator, photographer, and graphic designer. Her translations from the Slovenian into English include *The Golden Shower* by Luka Novak, *Instead of Whom Does the Flower Bloom* by Vlado Kreslin and *The Book of Bodies* by Aleš Šteger.

NOAH CHARNEY is is a professor of art history and the best-selling author of *The Art Thief* and *The Art of Forgery*. He has previously translated *Yugoslavia, My Fatherland* by Goran Vojnović for Istros Books.